W A I

MW01487785

THRILLER
VISION

TEXT'D   THE YOMEN   LINE 21

THRILLERVISION
Copyright 2012 by Wade Rivers
All rights reserved.

WadeRivers.com, Inc.
PO BOX 98
Pencil Bluff, AR 71965

ISBN-13: 978-0615742687
ISBN-10: 0615742688
Also available in eBook

Book Cover: Allison Foley, Pure Heart Studios
Interior formatting Print Edition: Ellen C. Maze, The Author's Mentor / www.theauthorsmentor.com

For further information, go to www.waderivers.com or you may contact Wade Rivers at waderivers1984@gmail.com

www.WadeRivers.com

PUBLISHED IN THE UNITED STATES OF AMERICA

DEDICATION

This book is dedicated to my children's generation,
and their children's generation,
for the sake of liberty.

Table of Contents

TEXT'D

Chapter One

The rain always made her feel good. Katherine sat in her car at the far end of the campus parking lot across from Holcombe Hall. It was her first day on campus, and she would have walked to class, but it was raining. She felt a touch of anxiety that morning. Normally she was shy and somewhat introverted in new environments, and this was her first year at the U of A. She only had one more year left and had transferred from UCA to be with Jason her senior year. Three years apart at different colleges had gotten ridiculous commuting, especially if they were actually going to get married.

She sat there watching a group of students trudging by the rain soaked streets. Her wiper blades were worn, and the rain smeared streams of water across the windshield creating a mural of colors. They all collided together like the oils on a painting. She was amused. A convoy of umbrellas and ponchos moved along the designated sidewalks in front of her car. It was like watching the creation of a Monet; the smeared colors came together to make an impressionist painting. She would have much preferred just to sit alone solitarily in the car and watch the rain. Katherine was overwhelmed with apprehension, but she had to go. She couldn't miss the first day.

I'll text Jason. She pulled out her new iPhone. "Luv U."

Jason didn't text back. He seldom did when he was in class. Katherine did though; she texted all the time though she really didn't have that many friends. Her iPhone had become an extension of her hand. The only time she didn't have it was when she was making love or taking a shower. Take that back, she had texted making love, but not often. She never read a text though in that position; that would have been rude. She looked to see if he might by chance texted her just once from class. Nope, not Jason. He went strictly by the rules.

After finishing her coffee, she tossed her books in her satchel. Time to go. It was still a good six minute walk across campus to her first class, and it was one she was definitely dreading, biology. She had put it off for three years, and now it was time to get it over with. Katherine was not big on science. She didn't care for it at all; the only two subjects she hated more were politics and religion. She had grown up a virtual flower child, the product of urban liberalism. Successful liberals, I might add. She had never gone without her entire life. To underscore her sentiments against politics, she had worn a "Vote for Pedro" T-shirt just in case anybody might mistake her for someone who took the subject seriously.

A last minute check in the mirror, and everything was in place. Katherine was the picture of youth and beauty, a tall blue-eyed blonde with polished white ivory teeth. She had a smile that could stop a train dead on its tracts. She slugged down one last sip of coffee and opened her door and then proceeded to drench her Stuart Weitzman sandals in a puddle of rain.

"Uck." Her designer jeans were immersed as well. Katherine opened her umbrella and ran across the street clicking her remote lock in her hand. Fortunately for her, the extra few procrastinating minutes in her car had some benefits. The downpour had diminished to just a slight drizzle, but still the streets roared like a river as the runoff filled the gutters and drains.

She was somewhat pissed at herself though. It wasn't the smartest decision she had ever made wearing $300.00 sandals in the rain. She didn't want to look like a drool either, and her raincoat didn't match her sandals. She was determined to wear the sandals no matter what, figuring it was better to look wealthy and foolish than wise and tasteless. Not everyone would look at it like that, but Katherine was a bit spoiled and often insecure. Her clothes gave her a false sense of confidence. Sometimes.

As usual, she was running late. Up ahead at the intersection, there were perhaps twenty or thirty students waiting patiently in the light rain for the traffic signal to change. In front of the crowd, she heard someone grumbling rather loudly. A few in the group laughed; then the light flashed, and everyone briskly crossed the street.

It was an old lady.

Katherine walked by her too. Creepy she was. Her shopping cart was piled high with what must have been her life's possessions. Pitiful. An old radio, a kerosene lamp, bedroll and dishes were all packed in the cart, and everything was soaking wet because the tarp that had covered them had blown off. The old lady fetched the tarp from a puddle as cars honked at her. "Curses!"

Katherine walked uneasily around her and crossed the street. She watched as a car honked at the homeless woman rudely and then splashed her as it turned the corner. It was awful; the old woman was helpless. Her clothes were drenched, dark dungarees and a sportsman's jacket that smelled like a moldy basement. She figured the old lady had slept many a night outdoors, probably in the park or wherever she could find shelter. She watched from the other side of the street as the woman struggled to pull the front wheel on the cart out of a grate in the gutter where it had become lodged and stuck. Grunting like a goat, she yanked and pulled desperately without success while simultaneously trying to throw the tarp over her belongings with the other hand.

Katherine looked at the time on her phone. She had to go. She was already late. She turned and started walking, and then the old woman yelled. "Please, help me!"

Katherine stopped. She looked back. Cars were splashing back and forth between them on the street. "Wait a sec, I'll be there." When the cars cleared, Katherine ran back across the street. She handed her an umbrella, "Here, let me help."

Just like that, Katherine lifted up the front of the cart, and the wheel popped out. The old woman looked surprised. She wasn't accustomed to kindness. Katherine was taken back. For the first time, she actually saw the woman's face up close. It was a horror story etched in dark wrinkles and circles under her eyes. The wrinkles seemed to converge tightening around her mouth. Then, the woman smiled. Katherine thought that it would split in half when she did. "Thank you, dear child. No one ever helps me."

"Glad I could." Katherine slipped her phone into the side of her coat pocket and lifted the cart's front wheels out of the street back onto the side walk just as another group of students approached the intersection. "Here, let me help you with the tarp too."

Together, they secured the tarp over the cart. Katherine couldn't help but notice a couple of cans of dog food down in the bottom. She knew better than to ask; instead, she pulled out her purse and handed the old woman a twenty she had. Her eyes lit up, "For me? Thank you, darling."

"You're welcome. It is all I have." Katherine then reached in her pocket to check her phone again for the time, and as she pulled it out, the phone slipped from her hands and flew into the street towards the gutter. "Oh, no!"

Like lightning, the old lady's foot stopped it just inches from the drainage grate where it would have surely been swept away, at the very least ruined. Instantly, she snatched it up and handed it back to Katherine, and her face stretched unpleasantly into a smile of tarnished teeth. She took off her hat and bowed, "Yours, I believe."

Katherine was startled. The middle of her head was shaved with a two inch wide strip. A bed of short gray and white hairs were sprouting along the strip like whiskers. It was grotesque and horribly frightening. Her long, dangling and matted hair drooped down the sides of her wet rain soaked face. She stood there with her arm outstretched; the phone lay in her skinny wrinkled hand. "Don't you want it?"

Katherine hesitated, overcome by the shock of the woman's shaved head. Obviously, she was deranged and not just homeless. It was not a sight she was normally accustomed to seeing. There were no homeless in her neighborhood. Her heart fluttered, and then she swallowed. She reached for it with both apprehension and disgust. She was thankful, yet unappreciative. She didn't want to touch the woman. Katherine stood back from her and reached out to take it. Grinning, the woman kissed the phone. Katherine paused. With her withered hand, she reached out and smiled. "You don't want to lose this."

"You're right," she smiled nervously; "it's my life."

The green light walking stick man flashed, and she joined the crowd crossing the street. The rain had all but stopped. The last few drops fell from the sky. She was now a good ten minutes late for class and still had a five minute walk. Just as she was about to enter Kimpel Hall, she felt her phone begin to vibrate. *Maybe it was Jason?*

It wasn't. It was a text. She didn't recognize the number. There was no number. Strange. She looked at the message. *"Hello."*

She text back, "hi." That was weird. Then, just as she was shaking out her umbrella on the steps, it buzzed again. She looked at her phone again, *"r u late?"*

It had to be Jason. No one else knew she was going to class. *Who was this?* She texted, "Who are you?"

"friend."

"Is this a game?" She looked around the building outside to see if anyone was laughing. It might have been Jason. He had pranked her before. There was no one, no one at least who seemed to be laughing or hiding. "Is this Jason?" she typed. Katherine stood there waiting for a response. She was really late now.

"no. friend."

"Who?"

"Go to class. We'll talk later."

Katherine went on. She just knew Jason had put someone up to it, probably a friend of his who might have had the same class she had. She didn't know who it was, but she was determined to find out. It had to be Jason.

Chapter Two

By the time class was over, the sun had begun to break behind the clouds creating a strange mystic effect the way the water radiated off the sidewalks all across campus. She had never seen such an unusual phenomenon. The students appeared to be walking through a long vapor concourse as the fresh rain steamed upwards from the warm concrete. The whole campus dripped from the soaking rain. Lush green trees shimmered in the sun's rays, and the gray morning suddenly was bright with brilliance. The dreary morning magically turned beautiful. She didn't have much time till her next class which was in the art building, a rather old and innocuous looking structure void of any noticeable redemptive charm. It was ugly.

Katherine dreaded art nearly as much as "poli sci" and science. It was not that she didn't like art; she didn't like exposing herself to her obvious lack of talent. Art was something that belonged in museums. Something to go see when you got pathetically bored. It wasn't an activity that she particularly cared to indulge in, especially in front of others. Strangers no less. She walked down the halls looking for her room and quickly took a seat at one of the tables and waited for her professor. Her first thought was, *Can't they afford better tables?*

They looked fifty years old, marred by palette knives and other sculptor tools. Globs of dried paint and various other oils and stains were smeared into the surface. The stools were rickety, and hers didn't fit totally square on the floor. She sat there waiting dispassionately and uncomfortably as several other girls chatted. And then a huge guy came in; they knew him. He looked like a football player. Professor Hensley walked in right behind him and shut the doors to the hall.

Hensley was a rumbled looking soul, a retread hippy with a scraggly looking gray and white ponytail. He looked like the artist stereotype, an image he obviously coveted. Compared to her nearly six foot frame, he looked small. Maybe, it might have been because he was old. Nevertheless, Dr. Hensley had a pleasant aura about him. There was a mischievous smirk on his face as if he just got finishing with a toke before he got to class. He laid a bunch of supplies on his desk and then took a stool and seated himself in front of the class. He told the students that it was "his pleasure" to be their teacher that semester. He loved to see development. He said he was acutely aware that a lot of people dreaded art; that was okay. The purpose was to learn something. He held up a can of paint as if to demonstrate. "We are going to transform things like paint into ideas. We are going to take clay (he held some up demonstrating) and materialize thought. From charcoal, we'll express words. From materials, we create ideas. Inventors take ideas and make materials. Does everyone understand?"

Katherine immediately felt comfortable. She liked her teacher. She wasn't an artist, but she had ideas. The way he conveyed things took the pressure off her to make something beautiful. He walked around the room pushing a cart. He told everyone to choose their tools. They could choose paints, or crayons, clay, charcoal, even pencils. Hensley wanted them to do something that was an impression of themselves. She picked watercolors. He gave her a set and then said, "Begin. You have one hour."

Katherine sat there. Blank. She could think of nothing but her still wet Stuart Weitzman sandals. She looked about the room at all the other students at work. There was nothing that came to mind. She thought about painting a long yellow stick. That was how she saw herself. She remembered fifth grade when she was a head taller than every boy in class. So skinny, they called her the "rail". She thought about how she would draw a rail? She didn't know how. Then, she thought about a rainbow, something with color. How about a peacock? That has color. Too much. She wasn't a peacock. Not at all.

Katherine sat there with a total stare just gazing out the window. She was drawing a complete blank. Dr. Hensley was up at the front of the class talking, perhaps to himself, perhaps to the class. "An impression is the artist view of who he is. It is his view of things. Are you a worm? Are you a building? A bridge? A tree? Are you anything? Are you confused?"

Across the table from her was this meekly little thing with wire rimmed glasses and a bandana, obviously making an artist's statement with her appearance. Her hands were swiftly moving across the paper rapidly painting something. She obviously had ideas, a view of herself. Katherine was jealous; she had none or at least none that she could express. At the very end of the table was the huge jock guy. She almost laughed. He was pounding clay together in a big blob. She thought it was funny. *What in the hell is he thinking?* He noticed her watching him. He twisted his head sideways and then looked at her blank page. A smirk went up the side of his face. The guy had a chin that looked like it was chiseled with a hammer. His face was wide, and his forearms were massive. He nodded at the pad in front of her and teased, "Let me guess, ah, Snow White."

They all laughed, giggled. Yeah, it was kind of funny. All she had was a blank white sheet of paper, a lot of emptiness. She looked out the window searching for something to inspire her when she saw the same old lady pushing her cart across the street. Poor thing. She lugged that cart around all day. The steam was still rising from the concrete creating a transparent vapor waving into the sky. Strange how it looked like a waterfall rising upwards. She thought about it; that's how she was, how she felt. A drift in the opposite direction from everyone else. She had always felt that way, all her life in fact. Katherine picked up her brush, starting with the widest one first. She dipped it in the watercolor and began. Strangely, she felt like someone or something was moving her hand because she was painting things she didn't know how. The blank page was transforming magically into a waterfall that rose from a river up into the sky where it poured into rolling clouds like waves. Dr. Hensley was walking around observing not saying anything. Katherine was not really paying any attention to him, or anyone else. She just kept painting. Finally, he came and stood behind her.

"Amazing."

She turned around. He was smiling. "It's brilliant. How long have you been painting?"

"Never."

He was shocked. "Do you know what you possess?"

Surprised, she shrugged. "I have never painted before. I don't know."

Now, everyone knows about the professor that comes on to a student, especially one as pretty as Katherine, but all the other students came over to see. They were all blown away. In less than forty minutes, she had painted with simple water color an amazing spectacular waterfall. It looked so authentic that it looked like a picture that had been photo shopped.

Professor Hensley asked, "Aren't you going to sign it?"

She thought for a second and then signed "kAt."

The jock came over and looked. Even he was impressed. She couldn't help but laugh though. She looked over at the big pile of clay he made. She quipped, "What's that? A blob?"

"A mountain."

She didn't say anything else. The bell rung, and the students hustled out to their next class. Dr. Hensley was on his lap top, and a graduate assistant came in and pushed the cart around collecting supplies. "Wait up a minute," the professor spoke.

Katherine stood by the locker where she was putting up her painting. "Yes."

"You have an extraordinary talent. I try not to be too complimentary of a student's work if I can help it because I know how some feel about their own work. It can be difficult. But I want you to know that you do possess a wonderful talent. I hope to see the best out of you this semester. I am very intrigued at what you might produce."

"Thank you."

He handed her a towelette to wipe off her hands. "See you Wednesday then."

Katherine was in total awe. Not that she was such a good

painter, but that she never knew she had the talent. She had never so much as had the urge to paint or draw even as a kid. She liked dolls, not paints. As she left the building to her next class, her phone vibrated. It had to be Jason. They were supposed to have lunch together on campus.

Katherine looked at the text. It wasn't Jason. It said simply, *"Good job, Michelangelo."*

She wondered. *Who could this be?*

Chapter Three

Katherine's apartment was just off campus. She had been fortunate to find a basement apartment that summer in a beautiful home which wasn't far off campus. The house itself was not that much different than her home in Lakewood. It sat on a hill surrounded by oaks and overlooked Fayetteville to the west. That she loved; the sun dropping down over the western sky had always been one of her most favorite times of the day. She loved a great sunset.

Jason, on the other hand, probably never would have picked such an apartment. He was not at all reclusive. He had to be where other people were. In that way, they were polar opposites. He had always been "Mr. Popular", president of everything. It wasn't that he was overly ambitious as much as it was the fact that he was just a likeable guy. Some people strive to get themselves promoted or recognized. Jason was the most natural selection. He was in the truest since a natural leader that others galvanized around and for good reason. Jason had tremendously strong qualities: intelligence, compassion, genuineness, reliability and honesty. He treated everyone with respect and dignity. One might think that the attraction between them was based solely on looks, but that would be wrong. They were honestly in love, had been since 11th grade.

Katherine was a beauty no doubt. Stunning. A single child, she was admittedly spoiled, given the best of everything. She was tall, almost six foot with long blonde hair and blue eyes. Some say textbook blonde, maybe so. Her face was the very definition of beauty: perfect nose, perfect eyes, perfect mouth. Despite all that, she was amazingly insecure. It had to do with her height more than anything else. She towered above the other kids all her life. She was taller than every boy in class until seventh grade, and then the only boy that was her same height was acne infested. Everyone tried to match them up, and it was a total disaster. She hated her height, and then as she began to develop it got worse. She was extremely sheltered. Her parents were overprotective so she was shocked to discover that men found her attractive even when she was still a young girl. It was embarrassing. She would be at the mall with her friends, and men would try to pick her up, grown men. It was awkward and scary. They thought she was much older than she was. The typical line was, "I thought you were their big sister."

"No, I'm just thirteen."

It wasn't until Jason came along that she found a guy that she could trust. He was everything, the opposite of her. He was Mr. Outgoing, the co-captain of the football team, and then President of the junior class, and later the senior class. He was handsome too, very. But Jason was also genuine and sweet. They became boyfriend and girlfriend almost immediately, and she finally had her protector. He was that alright, very protective. He was the perfect guy to help her adapt with her insecurities.

When she didn't want to cheer, it didn't bother him in the least bit. She didn't feel comfortable bouncing around in a stadium full of men. He understood. She sat in the stands though and watched his games. That was cool with him. One of the things that seemed to work well for both of them is that while he was in every club there was, she was in none. Not one. That actually suited him because if she was as social as he was, they never would have had time for one another. As it was, it was perfect. Still, it would have never worked if they had not been in love. Jason adored her; he saw himself as her protector and gladly relished the roll. She saw him as her knight in shining armor. There was no one else she would have ever considered, and even when they were young, the two of them discussed marriage.

Both graduated the same year, and Jason had scholarships to the U of A. She had none. She had never been that enthusiastic about studies or school. It wasn't that she wasn't smart; she was. It had to do more with the fact that she didn't have to apply herself. Her parents were upper middle class wealthy, and in the back of her mind, she knew whatever she wanted would be given to her. Nevertheless, they told her she was going to have to pay for college. To keep her expenses down, she chose a nearby school and lived at home while Jason went to the University.

For three years, he had come home at least twice a month to see her and his folks of course. That had put a strain on their relationship, not a lot but some. They still loved each other, but it was a lot of time apart, and so they both had decided that she should move to Fayetteville to be with him. Since she had only her senior year to go for graduation, her parents agreed to pay for her apartment and expenses. The rest she had to get with loans which in three years had already racked up into some considerable debt.

Though she was now in Fayetteville, they still didn't live together. Jason had his apartment, and she had hers. He had a roommate, and she, of course, lived alone. His place was nicknamed the "hub". It was the center of activity. Her place was called the "cave". Both were appropriate names for sure. The house where her apartment was in was a neo-modern design. Dr. Horace Miller, Professor of Music, and his wife Mildred owned the home. They had had it for thirty years or more and rented out the basement to college students, usually graduate students. There were stairs that went down to it from the main floor, and it was sort of a creepy entrance because the stairs were dark and the door which was heavy and thick was tucked in. You couldn't see it from the top of the stairs. The basement itself was constructed with natural stone on three walls. The west wall was primarily glass and rock with curtains which in all honesty needed to be replaced. They had to be at least twenty years old. What was so cool about the apartment was that it had its own hewn in fireplace with a massive mantel. It was a spectacular place to build a fire on a cold winter night. In the summer, the place also remained cool, being built into the earth as it was. There was a dated but attractive kitchenette in a retro style which Katherine adored, and behind the kitchen on the other end of the apartment was the bathroom. It wasn't large but had a great tub and shower with a window that she could look out and watch nature.

The main entrance to her place was sliding glass doors. Typically, she never came through the house, though it was permissible, but rather came around back to her place. That suited her just fine seeing how she loved her privacy. Dr. Miller and his wife told her though that she was welcomed to use the massive deck upstairs anytime she wanted to read or sunbathe. She was allowed to even bring friends over and entertain but just to check with their schedule. It wasn't out of the ordinary for the Millers to entertain, and she had heard that back in the day they use to have some pretty wild parties but not so much now that both had gotten up in years. Dr. Miller was probably in his early sixties and nearing retiring; the hallucinogenic days of his youth were now far in the past. He was just a kindly older man with gentlemanly charm. She was the same.

Jason had helped her move in the week before school began. In all the years they dated, they had never had a place where they could be totally alone. It had always been over at her parent's house or his, or at his apartment with his roommate Calvin. It was great, especially that first week before school. Jason was over there every single afternoon. It was the first real test of how things might be if they got married. They both loved it. Then school started.

That first day after school, she quizzed him if he had someone text her. He said no. She had known him long enough now to know when he was kidding. He wasn't, or at least he was hiding it really good. She lay on her bed and stretched out her legs, "Well, someone texted me." She looked at her phone, and somehow she must have deleted it. It was a brand new iPhone, and she still was hitting wrong keys. "Oh well," she shrugged, and then she told him all about art class.

Jason listened to her talk and then his cell phone rang. He sat up at the edge of the bed, "Yeah, what's up." Then, he started laughing. "No way. No way!" Jason walked over to the window still laughing, "Hey, can I call you tonight? I'm busy.

Okay, cool."

Katherine sat up and fluffed her pillows behind her. "Who's that?"

"Oh, Kris, a guy I met in business school." He acted nonchalant.

"What's so funny?"

"Ah, nothing. Just guy stuff. It's this chick who is after him. No one you know."

"I might."

"Her name is Raven, you don't know her." Jason went to the bathroom and shut the door behind him. He didn't usually shut the door. She thought she heard him talking again on the phone. Then her phone started vibrating. She looked at it. It was the mysterious caller. Katherine was excited. Now, she could show Jason. She looked at the text. It shocked her. *"Liar."*

Liar? What did it mean? Katherine sat on the edge of the bed listening. She knew she could hear him talking. She was sure she did; then she heard the toilet flush, and he came out.

"Who was that?" she asked.

"Who was what?"

"Who were you talking to on the phone?"

"Oh, ah, same dude. He called and asked me about the party this weekend."

"What about it?" She watched his body language.

Shrugging, "Not much. I just gave him the address. He'll Google it."

Jason leaped on the bed beside her and kicked off his shoes and then turned on the T.V. and flipped the channel to ESPN. She got up and went to the fridge where she scrounged around for some chips and salsa. Jason snacked and called some more of his buddies, texted them about the weekend. He said everyone was going to have to pitch in; he couldn't afford to float the whole thing himself. After catching some highlights, he went to the bathroom again. His phone lay on the bed next to him. She looked at the bathroom door. It was shut. She picked up the phone and scrolled through his texts. He had just texted Ryan and D.J., and then there was a text to

Kris. *Kris who?* She scrolled through more of his texts. *Geez, he was worse than a girl. Kris again, and then again.* She looked at the day before, *Kris, Kris, Kris.*

Katherine put the phone back down and waited. Jason came out wiping his hands. She heard the toilet flush. She asked, "So what have you got going tonight, big plans?"

"Research. Going to the library with the guys. What about you?"

"Guess I'll just read." She wagged her leg teasingly, "Since I don't have anything else to do."

He changed subjects, "Hey, do me a favor."

"What?"

"I need somebody to get some ice for Saturday night. Will you do it? I'll give you the money. Gonna need at least ten bags, maybe twelve."

"Sure, is that it?"

"I'm getting the food; some other guys are catching the brew. It would help."

"No problemo."

He kissed her, just a peck, and was out the door. He had no sooner closed her sliding door and bounced up the steps when her phone rang again. She rolled over and looked at the text. It said, *"Kris, huh?"*

Who was it? Katherine was speechless. Who was this friend? *How could they know everything?* It was bizarre. That was just the beginning. From the day it started, it never stopped. She would be sitting in the library or student union, and it buzzed. "He likes you." She would look up, and a guy across the room would be staring at her. Another time, she got a message, and it was about a girl next to her in class. "Slut." It was about the girl sitting in front of her. Somehow it knew. Then, another time she was in class, and she got a text. They weren't supposed to text in class, but nearly everyone did. She looked down in her purse and could see the message on her phone. "He's wrong." That's all it said. A second or two later a student challenged the professor. The professor stopped and flipped back through his notes. "My mistake, the correct date is…."

Her friend was right. *How did it know?* In another class, her least favorite, her professor asked the class if anyone knew who wrote the Federalist Papers? As soon as he asked the question, she heard her phone vibrating. Katherine pried open her handbag with her foot and looked. It knew the answer, *"Jefferson, Hamilton, and Madison."* No sooner than she was texted, the answer flashed on the screen behind the professor. It was right again. Amazing. Katherine started to chuckle. She was being pranked. Had to be. She looked around at all the faces in the class. *Okay, who was it?* Whoever it was, it was one good prank. Katherine then pulled out her compact from her purse and opened it to see if she could spot someone in the tiny mirror behind her smirking. There was no one, just glib faces enduring the boring subject of governments. They all looked like they were falling asleep. Katherine put up the case and glanced back over her shoulder. *Okay, where are you, Ashton Kutcher? Give it up; I know this is a joke.*

Nothing. No one was there. How bizarre. Whoever was doing this was brilliant. Kudos to them, it was magnificently orchestrated. Then, she heard the humming of her phone vibrate in her purse again. She didn't want to look. She didn't want to answer it. It kept vibrating. Buzzzzz. Buzzzzzzz. Buzzzzzzz. *Stop!*

Finally, she slipped her hand down to her bag and pulled it out. Now she was frightened. The message was a question, *"Convinced?"*

Katherine was terrified. She didn't know what to think. It was too much for her to handle. Her phone buzzed again. She held it under her desk and took a peek. *"No, Ashton Kutcher."*

Katherine texted, "Unbelievable, you are reading my mind."

"I am your mind. I'm u."

"You can't be. U r scaring the hell out of me."

"Don't be afraid. I'm ur friend".

"How can you be me?"

"I'm part of U. I'm in U. I am u, and u are me, and we are all together."

She was petrified, sat perfectly still but ready to freak. Her eyes looked down at her phone in utter disbelief. This couldn't be real. It was. She texted, "What if I want u to go away?"

"I can. Do u want me 2?"

Just as she was asked the question, the professor asked if anyone knew the difference between confederalism and federalism. Her phone instantly vibrated. Her hands now trembled. She was afraid to look at the answer. She did. Several seconds later the answer appeared on the screen behind the professor. Confederalism is where the central government remains relatively small as opposed to federalism where the central government has broader powers. *How did it know...so quickly?*

Buzzzz. Buzzzz. Buzzzz. *"Do you want me to leave?"*

Katherine was trembling. She was on the verge of crying. She wasn't sure. Finally her fingers texted back, "No, stay."

"Good. Don't be scared. I am here to help. I like u. I am friend."

"I like u 2."

"ttyl. Study."

"Where will u b?"

"Everywhere. Bye."

Chapter Four

By 7:30, there must have been fifty cars there. Ten bags of ice would not be enough; she had figured that out. The crowd was all over the balcony and a huge crowd had gathered around the pool. Some Maroon 5 was playing; a few minutes later, it was Sons of Silvia. Everyone was having a great time. There were so many people Katherine would have felt better if everyone had name tags. She hardly knew anyone there. Jason of course knew everyone. Everyone she met she introduced herself as "Hi, I'm Katie, Jason's girlfriend."

Katie is what he always called her. Everyone had heard of her. She was all he talked about for the last three years. Katie this and Katie that. Everyone knew about Katie, and now that she was there, they saw why. Katherine was beautiful, a for sure head turner. You couldn't help but notice her, and the fact that she was so tall, a head taller than the average girl there. And with her long legs and that snug red dress, no doubt about it, she was an attention getter. All eyes turned. But for Katherine, Katie, somewhere after the first thirty to thirty-five introductions, it began to get old, especially meeting all of Jason's girl friends; albeit, they were all with dates, but still. It was stressing. It was Jennifer, then Samantha, Diane, Cameron, Haley, Kelly, Becky, Tiffany, Brittany...oh my god, there were so many of them. They never stopped coming. Enough already. Introductions were painful.

"Hi, how are you?"

"Do you like Fayetteville?"

"Jason is so cool. You are so lucky."

"What's your major?"

"Now, where are you from?"

"What was your name again? Cathy?"

She corrected a few, "No, it's Katie. Katie with a K."

By 8:30, she felt like her hand was going to fall off or her head would explode. She didn't know which would happen first. She shook so many hands she felt like she would retire that evening in a nice anti-bacterial solution. Jason of course never gave it another thought. He shook hands and fist bumped all his buds. The one person she was looking for was Kris. *Where was she?* She had to be there somewhere, hiding. The meekly little mouse didn't have the guts to come up and introduce herself.

The difference between her personality and Jason's became magnified though Jason never seemed to be cognitive of it. She was. People literally crowded around him. He drew them to him like a magnet. He was always the center of attention, and it was understandable; every person he met was like a friend. He had thousands of them; she had one. She watched him as he man hugged his buddies with a pat on the back. He wasn't aware though that she felt isolated, alone. Even as she stood by his side, she felt like she was somehow left out. It was strange, and then finally, she couldn't take it anymore. It was getting just too hard to prop up her smile.

"I'll be back." She excused herself from the group and walked out to the parking lot. She had told herself she wouldn't call her friend. She had even left her phone in her car so that it wouldn't be a distraction. This was going to be their night, their big party. Her friend was not going to be part of it. That's what she had said. Katherine leaned against her Dodge Charger and thought about it. It wasn't fair. He had all those friends, and she had none, well one. She didn't want to call, but she was alone. She wanted at least one person to talk to. Finally, she clicked her remote, and her car unlocked. Katherine picked up her phone. She needed a little assistance to help her cope. To her disappointment, no one had called. That was a sure sign she should just turn her phone off and go back to the party. It was stupid for her to be out in the parking lot alone. It was a great party, enjoy it. She tossed the phone back in the seat and locked the door. Time to go back.

Buzzzz. Buzzzz. Buzzz. She could hear it. Katherine immediately opened back up the car and looked at the message. *"Overwhelming, isn't it?"*

Katherine smiled. Her friend understood. "How did you know?"

"I know u. I am your friend, or have u forgotten?"

"No, I haven't forgotten."

"Liar, but that's ok."

Katherine laughed. It was the first real laugh she had had all night. She and friend texted back and forth chatting. Finally she felt relaxed. Her loneliness instantly vanished, just went away.

"Wanna have some fun?"

"Yeah. Sure."

"Let's go back to the party."

"R u sure? It was boring."

"Trust me."

As she walked back, she could hear Edens Edge playing "Too Good to be True." It made her want to dance, and she wasn't really much of a dancer. Katherine loved the song though; she loved the group. The first couple she ran into was a couple she had met earlier. The guy's name was Jim something; she couldn't remember. And the girl, well, it didn't matter. Her pal buzzed. *"bty. He's gay. ;)"*

"He is."

"He should be leading the parade."

"what about her?"

"clueless."

"That's too bad. That's gonna hurt."

"Got that right."

It was like that the rest of the night; she (they) milled around. Suddenly, it was interesting; hilarious would be a better word. Her friend had a line about everybody. Nobody was excluded. One girl was wearing a very low cut blouse. It was really too much, should have been very embarrassing. Her boobs were practically falling out. Even the guys were snickering. *"They're fake"*.

"r u sure?"

"in 12th grade they called her pancake."

"How do u know?"

"All her dates brought syrup =)"

Katherine couldn't help but laugh. She was clairvoyant, or at least her friend was. Then she saw Jason waving his arm by the pool. He called her name. She could barely see him with all the guys standing around.

"Katie. Come here. Meet some friends!"

The crowd between them sort of parted. The lyrics to "Too Good to be True" was still playing in her head. Standing next to Jason was a bunch of guys, obviously football players. They were huge. "Say, I want you to meet some friends. This is Coby, Ryan, Travaris, and this dude is Max." She had heard of all of them.

They all were impressed with Katherine as well. "Say Jason, you didn't say she was *this* fine."

"Yeah, I was just thinkin' of some skinny homebody." They all laughed again. "Now we know, he has been hiding you all this time. He's 'fraid you'll run off."

"Sorry fellas, she's taken." He turned around and pointed to a big guy behind them with his back turned. "Here's another guy I want you to meet. "Hey, KJ." A huge guy with a plate full of sandwiches turned around. Katherine couldn't believe it; it was the only person at the party she recognized. It was "blob" from art, the jock.

"Hey hon," Jason grinned, "I want you to meet Kris Jones. He scored the winning touchdown today."

Katherine's mouth dropped wide open. "You're Kris Jones?" She had heard of him; everybody had. Kris was Razorback all American tight end and expected to go in the first round of the draft.

He looked equally as shocked. "So, *you* are Katie?"

"Y'all know each other?" Now Jason was shocked.

They explained they had the same class together. Sat at the same table and joked around in class together. "He's the guy I was telling you about," she laughed, "I swear (she demonstrated) it looked like he was making a big blob."

"Mountain."

"No, that was no mountain. That was a blob." They all laughed especially Jason. He was glad to see his girlfriend having a good time. That's the way Jason was. It wasn't about him; it was always about his friends. The three of them were laughing when a very well-tanned girl walked up. She looked well done, a bit on the extreme.

"How's that for roasted?"

Katherine texted back, "talk about grilled." She smiled, "Hi, I'm Katherine."

Jason looked almost apologetic, "You two haven't met. This is Raven. She's our head cheerleader."

Raven slipped her arm around Kris. It was hard to even look at her. She had the crispy face thing going on. Hard on the eyes. Katherine stuck out her hand, "So please to meet you." She couldn't help but notice that Kris looked a little uncomfortable; Raven seemed like a bad cold with a drip he couldn't shake.

"SWTS"

She texted back, "What?"

"sleeps with total strangers."

Katherine spewed her drink out laughing. She sprayed it all over her, "I'm so sorry." She even got some of it on Kris. "Really, forgive me…I…I…" She started laughing again.

Jason knew Katie's sense of humor. He didn't even bother to ask what was so funny; he knew. He had been thinking the same thing himself. He told them he had fresh towels upstairs and to go and clean up. Kris didn't seem to mind, but Raven, well, she was a little burnt.

As Kris and raisin face were making their way through the crowd, Jason took Katherine's hand and pulled her to him. "Tell me that was an accident." He was grinning.

"Honest, I didn't mean it. I swwwwear it wasn't on purpose."

Jason laughed and whispered in her ear, "He might try and thank you next week. He's been trying to dump her all night."

"Seriously?"

"She on him like glue." Jason looked over and waved at somebody, a chick. "Hey, there is somebody I want you to meet. She's terrific."

"Who?"

He took her by the hand and walked her all the way around the pool. "This is Joy."

She had heard him mention Joy over the years. They met his first year on campus. She was "one of the guy's", or at least that's how he had been describing her. Katherine had expected a manly looking broad since he said she liked football so much and loved to hunt. Joy was anything but.

Instantly she gave Katherine a big hug. "Oh my god! It's you! I am so pleased to meet you." A big smile radiated on her face. Katherine was stunned. She was much smaller than she was but by no means a doormat. Other than her dark thick framed glasses, she was gorgeous. Striking red hair and a knock down figure. She had cheek bones any woman would die for including her. Her complexion was amazingly smooth, and other than the few freckles on her shoulders, she had not a blemish. Joy was no less than radiant in her white summer dress.

Katherine struggled for words, "So, you're Joy." She tried to make sure her smile was visible and widening; her jealousy concealed.

"And you're the heartthrob." Joy didn't seem to notice Katherine was straining. She punched Jason on the shoulder, "He never shuts up about you. I mean, it can get so annoying. Really. I don't know how many times we told him 'why don't you just go home. We'll pay for the gas. Enough.'" She giggled, "He can be such a dimbo."

"Heyyyy."

"Seriously, we are so glad you moved here." She raised her hands like she was in church, "Thank you God!"

Jason was chuckling, "Come on. I wasn't that bad."

"Worse." She patted Katherine on the arm, "If you ever doubt me, ask Kris. Jason is like so totally wrapped. Nice job, Katie."

Katherine couldn't help but like her too. She knew why

Jason did and the "guys". Some girls know how to hang with the dudes, and Joy was one. She kept trying to figure out who she looked like, and then she realized who it was. Joy had a definite resemblance to that chick that's on the news, the smart one, S.E. Cupp or something like that. Joy definitely had the look thing happening. Guys all over were checking her out, but she didn't seem to notice.

Joy snapped her fingers and pointed to Jason. "Let me show you something. Hey J., gimme your wallet."

He looked embarrassed. She snapped again, "Come on, cough it up. Let's see." Jason reluctantly pulled out his wallet. She acted like it weighed a ton. "It's gotta weigh twenty pounds." Joy was laughing when she opened it up. "You'd think he's trying to stop bullets with this thing." It was thick alright; even Katherine had told him it needed to be slimmed down.

Joy pulled out a sleeve of vinyl picture holders. "Exhibit One." She laughed, "Da boy is punch drunk in love." The pictures unfolded from his wallet and hung down about two feet. There must have been twenty pictures of her. "What did you do to him? I'd love to know the secret."

Katherine squeezed Jason's hand and winked. She was beginning to feel more comfortable with Joy. In fact, she could see herself even being friends with her, although it would probably help if Joy wasn't so pretty. As they were talking her phone buzzed, she felt in vibrating in the little purse she had strapped on her shoulder. At first, she ignored it. She didn't want to look. She was enjoying herself. Buzzz. Buzzz. Buzzzzz. It wouldn't stop.

"Excuse me." Katherine pulled it out and checked her messages.

"She's a slut. Don't trust her."

Joy looked at the expression on her face, "What's wrong?"

"Nothing." Katherine didn't want to hear it. She didn't text back. Friend texted again, then again. Buzzz. Buzzz. Katherine didn't even bother to look. Katherine finally texted back, "Good night. Ttyl." Then she turned off her phone.

"Who was that?" asked Joy.

"Her friend." Jason put his arm on Katie's shoulder. "It's a chick thing. She talks nonstop on that thing."

Katherine was surprised, "Look who's talking. You're twice as bad as me."

Joy snickered, "Oh, I think he's worse. I call him Mr. Tweet."

That was very true. Jason was all over Facebook and Twitter. He lived in social media before there was social media. Twitter was probably invented just for him. Katherine tried to block out what friend was saying and just enjoy the evening. It did turn out great; in fact, it was like the best party she had ever been to. Jason stayed close by her the rest of the evening so she wasn't hanging out there all alone. That made her feel good. A little later they even danced by the pool when some old R & B played. It was about 1:30 when the last of the guests drove off. Jason and Calvin both walked around picking up trash and bagging it. Joy helped too and was one of the last to leave. Finally, after Calvin went back up stairs and Joy went home, they were alone together by the poolside. Katherine soaked her feet in the edge of the pool. The water was cool and therapeutic. The moon was overhead. All was quiet except for some late night revelers down in building C obviously still celebrating the big victory that day.

"Crazy night, huh?"

"Yeah, it was good. You've got some great friends."

"Where did you go earlier? I kinda lost you."

"Just got away. Feeling overwhelmed for a bit. It turned out great though."

"You were stunning, Katie. Everyone said so. I can't believe you knew Kris. That blows me away. What a coincidence."

"What about that Raven chick. What's up with her?"

"She's probably after money. Everyone knows he'll go in the first round. He'll be making three or four mill a year for awhile."

She was surprised, "Serious?"

"Probably. But he's just Kris. He walked on. He had to work his way into it, and it wasn't for the money. Kris is the same ole boy he was down in El Dorado, likes to fish and hunt."

She splashed him with her foot, "Like you."

"Kinda." He stood up and reached his hand down for her. "Hey, let's call it a night. I'm done."

Katherine stood up and grabbed her sandals by the pool. "One more thing, what about Joy. Come on, you want to tell me you never had any interest in her?"

"Who did I drive down to see all the freakin' time?"

"Me."

"Case closed. Let's go upstairs."

Calvin was already knocked out. They could hear him snoring in his room. They went into Jason's room, and it wasn't long and he was out too. He looked like a baby when he slept. It was funny actually the way he curled up his hands under his chin. Katherine lay next to him, thinking. She tried to sleep. She knew he had never lied to her, but still it was hard to believe he had been just friends with someone as pretty as Joy. She had a lot more in common it seemed with Jason than she did. They both were very outgoing; it almost seemed like they would be natural together. Katherine closed her eyes and tried to immerse herself in a dream. She couldn't. *Was Joy a slut? Was she after Jason? Was friend right?*

Her friend had never been wrong about anything. *Was she wrong now?* Katherine laid there awake wondering. *But, what about Kris? Had friend lied? What was the deal with that? Was it Kris, or Chris? Who called Jason that day at her apartment? Why did he go to the bathroom to talk?* That was strange. *Was Jason lying to her?*

The thoughts smothered her mind like a huge haboob across the desert. They grew and grew like a big cloud of sand moving across the landscape, nothing was going to stop it. It was useless. Someone had to be lying. She knew it, and then there was that cheerleader, SWTS. *Had she spread them for Jason? Did he get him some at a bake sale?* She thought about Joy again, if anybody though would be a threat it would be Joy. She was everything Jason would like. She might be legit, but if she was holding back waiting to make her move, that would make her calculating.

No matter how she tried, Katherine couldn't sleep. Nothing was working. Finally, she couldn't stand it anymore and slipped softly out of bed and tiptoed into the living room looking for her purse. Relief.

She sat on the couch and curled up her legs in the dark and texted, "Ok I'm back."

"*Some friend. U leave me just like that.*"

"Srry."

"*4given. U ok?*"

"No."

"*Wats wrong?*"

"Is Jason cheating?"

It didn't answer. Katherine texted again. "Is Jason cheating?" Still no answer.

"Y won't you tell me?"

"*Friends don't want to hurt friends.*"

Katherine was frustrated, "plz."

"*U know the answer.*"

She sat there in the glow of the phone. All alone. Yes, she knew the answer. No one could be that good. No one. All she had to do now was catch him. And, if he was, he would pay.

Chapter Five

September in Arkansas can still be hot. The long muggy summer August days create something like a hangover effect going into fall. September is like a drunk that rolls out of bed sick from the effects of heat and drought. Throw in some humidity, and it can be downright miserable. The green grass has long been withered brown. It is just fuel waiting for a lightning strike, and hay fields have been known to turn into blazing infernos that time of the year especially if the wind picks up.

That's what September is like, but on the plus side, there is football. Everybody is anxious for the first bit of chill to hit the air, Friday night games become more tolerable, and then there is Saturday. In Arkansas, indeed all the south, football is the cultural glue. Black-white, young-old, Democrat-Republican, rich-poor, male-female, even the Baptist and Catholic can come together, doesn't matter, everybody loves football. With that said, there is still another nice feature about September, it is the one last chance to catch some golden rays before the cold rains of autumn blow in.

Katherine never did get dark; she maintained a very nice light Coppertone tan throughout most of the year. So quite naturally, when she came home a little early from school one day, and the sun was blazing, she decided to take advantage of the opportunity while it still existed. The landlord had after all said she could use the deck upstairs, and she didn't want to waste the time driving over to Jason's to lay by the pool, so as soon as she returned home she slipped off her shorts and put on her little white bikini and took the back stairs to the roof.

She knew that Dr. Miller was home because she saw his Volvo out front in the drive, but Mildred's car was gone. The sun was perfect, about 80 degrees, not scorching, but not too cool either. She lay out on a lounge chair on her stomach and turned on her Kindle. There was a good book she had wanted to read but hadn't had time that year.

The deck was truly spectacular. It was massive, the entire length of the back of the house and rose almost twenty-five feet from the ground below. The view could not be beat; it looked out over the western sky, but also it was private. Trees virtually surrounded the property; no one could see her on the deck, except of course from the windows in the house. Katherine laid there with her head propped up on her folded arms and read the Kindle which she had put on the ground. Occasionally, she took sips of water and sprinkled a few down her back. She had her phone with her, but surprising she hadn't hardly talked on it all day. Just as she was getting into the story, her phone buzzed.

Buzzz. Buzzz. She looked at the message. *"Good story huh?"*

"Yeah, you'd like it."

"I know how it ends. Want to know?"

"No, but thx."

"U have to pay rent today. The 15th, remember?"

"U suck. Y did u have to remind me?"

"$700 Wow!"

"U can shut up now." Katherine didn't want to think about it. Even though her folks sent her the money and she had the check, she wasn't use to paying rent. She had lived rent free all her life, reality was slow absorbing.

"U don't have to pay u know."

Katherine leaned up, friend had her attention. "How?"

"Don't look but he's watching."

She knew who he was. She saw the drapes moving when she first sat down. She had heard him playing the piano. "Dr. Miller?"

"He's been watching you for the last five minutes."

"So."

"Don't look back. Unfasten your strap."

"Y"

"Trust me. Then put more oil on your legs. He likes that."
Katherine did. She pulled her hair back to the side and undid her top. He was sitting at the piano working on a sonnet. She was facing away so she couldn't see his face but knew he was there watching her from the great room. She could feel his eyes on her, devouring her body. Dr. Miller was watching her through binoculars he used for bird watching. She pulled her leg up alongside the chair and squirted some oil all the way down the side and then began rubbing it in. She had skater legs; that's what she had always been told, like ice skaters. They were beautifully shaped, long and elegant. She kept them tanned in the summer, and they looked especially spectacular when she wore white.

Dr. Miller started to close the drapes and return to his music, but for some reason he couldn't. He wasn't a perve, but quite frankly he hadn't seen anyone so beautiful in so long. Katherine was breathtaking, literally. He was suddenly spellbound, almost hypnotized as she rubbed the oil into her legs, and then on her back. He could see the tiny microscopic blonde peach fuzz hair on the small of her back. The tiny blonde hairs seemed almost transparent in the light. They illuminated against her brown skin. He followed the tiny hairs all the way down the slope of her back to her butt where tiny beads of sweat were rolling down. Dr. Miller watched as she worked the oil into the flesh of her thighs, and then rubbed it all the way up to the edge of her bikini bottom.

Katherine then leaned up. Her top was completely off, and though she was facing away from him, he could still see her breast from the side. She was something to admire for sure. Her breast were large and no doubt firm. All natural, no plastic. They were all real. She rolled her finger down along the inside of her bikini on her butt like she was adjusting it, then she pulled it up and snapped it. Her butt jiggled when she did it. Katherine turned off the Kindle and turned on some music from her phone. She laid there listening to the boys from Talihina, Oklahoma, Kings of Leon, perhaps her favorite band.

For some strange peculiar reason, she found herself being turned on. The thought of someone watching her excited her. She felt this rush of adrenaline and excitement. She felt high. Exhilarating. She hadn't known why it had bothered her before when men stared at her, but now, for the first time, Katherine liked it.

It was power.

She wanted desperately to watch him watching her. She texted, "Can't I look up just once?"

"take off your sunglasses?"

"Y"

"hold them in front of u. u can see him in the reflection."

She did. She laid there still on her stomach and twirled her glasses in hand like she was playing with them and then held them firm out in front of her. She could see the doctor at the piano looking. He was watching her. She wiggled her butt teasing him. It felt good, almost orgasmic. She wished she had some physical stimulation to go along with the mental stimulation. She was feeling the urge to get off. Katherine wanted more. She decided to turn over so she held her top with her hand and rolled over on her back and let her top just lie across her chest. The sun did indeed feel good. She was glad she had tanned; there wouldn't be many days like that left.

"What are you doing?'

Katherine texted back, "u'll see."

She took the bottle of water and poured a stream down the center of her belly. It rolled into a little pool in her belly button, shimmering like a diamond or a lake of water. It felt refreshing. Then she lifted the top of her bikini bottom and poured some more water on her hot skin. It tingled where she wanted it. The cool beads of water dripped all the way down between her legs. It was all she could do not to smile. Her head was turned away from him, to the side, but she was watching Dr. Miller watching her.

Buzzz. Buzzz. She looked at the message. *'He's ripe. U know what to do now. Go shake your money tree.'*

"Yep, thx."

Katherine sunbathed for just a few more minutes and then

went in. She took a quick shower and put on some jogging shorts and tennis shoes, then slipped on a short sleeve golfing shirt. She wanted to catch Dr. Miller before Mildred got home.

Katherine walked up the dark stairs to the great room. She could hear him playing. It sounded like he was struggling to find the right keys on the piano. No one else was home. The drapes were closed now, and he sat at the bench with his pencil in his hand. He looked surprised to see her.

"Dr. Miller."

"Yes."

"May I have a word with you?"

"Of course." She couldn't help but notice the binoculars sitting on the edge of the ebony Steinway.

Katherine paused. She adjusted the backpack on her back. Her hair was pulled back, and she was wearing a ball cap. Looked like the All-American girl. "I want to tell you first of all, I really love your place here. I feel so comfortable here, just like home. You have been so generous and kind…"

He pulled his glasses down to the end of his nose. "Yes. Go on."

She hesitated, biting the edge of her lip like a little girl. "I would love to stay here forever, but…"

"What's the matter? Something happen?"

"Well, yes, um…no. I feel so embarrassed telling you this, but my parents are in financial trouble. I don't understand it all. They won't tell me everything you see, but my dad is about to lose his job." She shrugged her shoulders up, "We might even lose our home."

He looked worried, "Oh dear. That's awful."

"I know, and so I probably will have no choice but to quit school and have to go back home."

"But you only have one year left."

"But Dr. Miller I…"

"Call me Horace, please."

She couldn't say his name for fear of laughing. Katherine turned away from him, tucking away a smile before it got away from her. She held up her hand in front of her mouth like she was going to cry. She composed herself quickly. "But

Doctor…Horace…see, I can't pay the rent. They told me they don't have the money right now. It may get better; I dunno. I am sure it will, but they don't have it. I have no choice but to quit school and move back home. I hate telling you."

He hadn't expected anything like this. She had only been there one month. It was to say the least an unexpected turn of events. Katherine walked over to him and knelt down, "You have been so kind to open your home up to me like this, but there is no possible way I can stay."

He scratched his head, obviously thinking. The whole thing had caught him off guard. "But Katherine, you have paid for this semester right? You already have your books."

"Yes sir."

"It would be foolish for you to leave now."

"But I can't pay you."

"Look, I am not going to throw you out because of that. I couldn't do that. You have been a good tenant. Why don't we just see if things can work out with your folks? Maybe things will get better."

"You mean it?"

"Let's just play it month by month, okay."

"Oh, how can I thank you?" She gave him a big hug. Her cheek brushed up against the side of his face, and he smelled her perfume. "May I still ask you one small favor?"

"Why sure." He smiled.

"I feel soooo embarrassed about this. My family has never had financial problems. Both my parents are so proud. It is difficult on me too, of course, but I don't want anyone to know. I feel ashamed. I hope you understand, but I will feel better if Mildred didn't know. Could you not tell her?"

"Well, we generally discuss everything, but I can understand."

"Can we keep this just between you and me?"

He rubbed his chin. He looked at the binoculars, and then at her. "I guess. If it makes you feel more comfortable. I won't say anything."

"I wish there was something I could do for you. If you need housecleaning or something, I might be able to do that."

Dr. Miller shook his head and told her not to bother. It was their secret. He wouldn't say anything to his wife. If her parent's financial woes improved, to let him know. Maybe they could "catch up later."

Katherine gave him another sweet hug and headed out the door just as Mrs. Miller came in. As she was backing out the drive, her phone began vibrating. Of course, she knew who it was. She sped up the street checking her messages.

"nice pay day. Way to go."

"thx. $700."

"$700 a month, every month. Let's go shopping, girl."

"I can't, I've got school."

"u don't need school. All u need is me."

"serious?"

"trust me."

Katherine pulled up to the light. She had two classes to make that afternoon; tests were coming up. She sat there with her right blinker on waiting for the light to change. She knew there were big sales at the mall. Summer clothes were being marked down, some 70%. If she bargained, she might get more. The light turned green. She turned her blinker to the left and waited for a few cars to pass. It was a perfect day to go shopping. She had seven hundred bucks to spend, and rent was taken care of. For Katherine, life was looking good, thanks of course to her friend.

Chapter Six

I think all women like to shop. Maybe it had something to do with their genetic makeup or perhaps it developed way back when the first store opened up. It was probably no more than a cave in the side of the mountain where women could barter for hides or some sharp piercing stones. The idea obviously caught on. It had to start somewhere. It was in all likelihood not that much different than; musk ox hides were no doubt big sellers in the winter, grass skirts in the summer. Weaved baskets eventually became handbags. You get the point, not much has changed.

Katherine was a natural born shopper; spender might be a better word. She had grown up in malls. She liked to work the sales clerk. That was part of the fun. As she walked through the mall from store to store, she wondered as she watched the other women talking on their phone or texting, *did they have a friend?* Was there some anonymous person befriending them as well or was she the only one? Katherine wasn't sure, but it seemed rather odd; they were often smiling or laughing like she did. Others seemed glum, indulged in dark thought. Someone was communicating with them all. Right? Everybody was doing it, walking around with their thumbs jittering up and down on their phone. She watched two girls walking together down the center of the mall. Neither looked up; both walked along texting. They walked around benches and then the fountain without raising their eyes like they were on autopilot. Something was controlling their mind.

It was a splendid day that afternoon. She felt especially good having refreshed her tan and then treating herself to a shopping spree. She had no regrets for what she had done. And Jason, well, he never even asked where she got the new clothes. It wasn't until Tuesday the following week when she checked her grades that she felt remorse for her actions. Reality was a cold slap in the face. Katherine went on line to see how she had done on her recent exams. It wasn't good. She had an A in Art; that was expected. Finance was a D; Biology F; Political Science D; Environmental Studies C. She was pissed. Immediately, she texted her friend, "U said don't worry about it. I'm flunking."

"I said trust me."

"Big mistake. I shouldn't listen to you."

"I wouldn't do you wrong."

"Have you seen my grades? You said I'd pass."

"Do u still trust me?"

Katherine thought about it. Friend had been right so many times. After all, she was living rent free. She had new clothes because of friend. She took a deep breath, "Yes I trust you."

"Good, check your grades again."

Katherine had already logged off. "I just did."

"Again."

What was the point? Reluctantly, she got back on her computer and put in her ID number and logged back on. Art A; Biology A; Political Science A; Finance A; Environmental Studies A.

"OMG!!!!! How did u do that?"

"Powers. U have urs I have mine. We're friends."

She couldn't believe it. All her life she had struggled with mediocrity, and suddenly she was brilliant in everything she did. It was due to her friend. She had gone from feeling powerless to feeling powerful. It was an amazing transition. Anything was attainable. She was invincible. She could get any grade she wanted, probably any job. Everything was easy.

Jason had noticed the change too. He recognized that Katherine was different, but didn't seem that impressed. The passive Katherine, sweet and somewhat timid, seemed to have vanished somehow during that first month or so of school. She looked the same of course, but she wasn't the same girl he had dated for five years. She had changed since she came to Fayetteville. At first, he thought the transformation had been an improvement. He saw some growth. She seemed to be coming out of her shell. That was good. He loved her, but she did need to be a little more outgoing. He felt like many times he was carrying the bulk of the emotional load, especially when it came to friends. He saw some positive signs at the party. She seemed more self-assured; that was great, but soon afterwards she developed an air of arrogance. That wasn't like Katherine. And he didn't like the fact that she had told him to call her Kat. She wasn't Kat; she was Katie.

Kat and Katie were not the same. Kat often made snide cutting remarks. They began chipping away at his affections. There were subtle digs; she began referring to Jason as "MC" (Mr. Control). He didn't know where that came from? He had to always take the lead in the relationship, someone usually did. And it sure wouldn't have been her. Now, it was a control thing. It's what she said. Katie was cordial; Kat was anything but. Kat clawed away at all his friends too. One night when she was over at Jason's apartment, Calvin went to the store to go and get some ice cream. She made a remark about his hair cut when he came back in. Being in the Air National Guard, he had a military style cut, shaved on the sides and some on top. "Hey," she smirked lying on the couch with Jason, "it's G.I.Moe with Rocky Road." They both laughed; they thought it was funny, even Calvin did. But after that, the joke became an insult. It was G.I. Moe this and G.I. Moe that. "Where's Curly and Larry?" He got the point; she was calling him a stooge. It got old. Calvin had enough.

One evening they were having dinner over at the apartment and she started in on Calvin. He didn't like it. He slammed the refrigerator and walked to his bedroom. He was angry. He looked at Jason, "Why don't you find a leach and take her for a walk?"

Jason was caught in the middle. The two did not get along, and it really all started with Katherine, Kat.

"You going to let him talk to me like that?" she demanded.

"No, but you started it Katie. You always start it." She was shocked at Jason. He had always come to her defense. He had been her knight in shining armor, and now he was taking his roommate's side. She pushed him off the couch, practically kicking him. "Why don't you grow some balls?"

Jason was shocked. Katherine never talked like this. She never acted this way. She jumped in her car, and he could hear her peeling off. It was like he didn't even know her anymore. But, perhaps she was right. He had always been a peacemaker all his life, maybe to an extreme. Jason wasn't real sure just what to think. Maybe she was right? Maybe he was in the wrong? Should he have stood up for her, even if she was wrong? Is that what a boyfriend is supposed to do? Jason was totally caught off guard and wasn't sure really what to think about it. His buddy was pissed at him, and now she was. Something was going on. Something had changed. Their relationship was nose diving, and he loved her. It was like he was powerless to pull it out of the tail spin. Where was the sweet Katie he had grown up with, the Katie that rescued little kittens? The Katie that helped old ladies with groceries and babysat all the neighbors' kids for free? She was the sweet Good Samaritan. That person was gone. The person she was now had hardly a decent thing to say about anyone, including him. She vanished.

Jason wasn't sure what to do. He took a walk that evening and tried to sort it out. The temperature had dropped; the cool autumn air was just beginning to blow in. Jason walked up the street and turned into a residential district. He was getting hateful texts from Katherine so he just turned it off. She had never been like this. She was sort of like the trees on the street. They had been vibrant and green all year, and then suddenly, in no time at all, they changed. For a very short while, they transformed into brilliant bright colors, yellow and orange. They are spectacular, just like Katie was, and then another change. The leaves withered, quickly turning into something dry and crispy. The colors are gone. Seeing Katherine the last few weeks had been like watching the leaves change. Now she seemed gone, blowing in the wind. There was little left of what used to be.

He was heartbroken.

Jason was searching for a way to get her back but had not a clue of what to do. He was devastated. She meant more to him than anything. It killed him to see the soft tones of her personality develop a hard and brittle edge. She cut down everything and everyone around her. Her jokes were now just stabs. She stuck them in and pulled them out as if her tongue were a stiletto. Two nights before, he had been over at her place, and they almost broke up then. They had words, but she had an amazing ability to turn it on and turn it off. She seemed to know just when to stop and pull him back in emotionally. Jason couldn't let it go on like this. He knew he had to talk to her, to get to the bottom of what was going on. Finally, he stopped under a street light and texted her back.

"We have to talk."

"Come over. I need you Jason. I'm srry."

He went back to the complex and got his keys. Women weren't always the easiest thing to understand. He had heard other guys talk about their girlfriends. Sometimes, it's best to say you're sorry and forget the argument. Make up and go on, that's the only way to win. As he drove over, Jason knew he would do anything for her. She was the only girl he had ever been with. He could never imagine anyone else. He and Katie had discovered love together, that was so very special to Jason. He had not a clue what another woman would be like, but for someone who had been so shy, Katherine was an unbelievable lover. He couldn't imagine a better kisser, how could there be? Her tongue was like a long wet whip. She knew how to use it too. When they first went out, she would kiss him good night, and he literally could not sleep the whole rest of the night when he got home. All he could think about was Katie.

As he drove over to her place that evening, he thought about the old times, how it was. That's the girl he wanted back, the girl that left him panting until the next morning. But here lately, it was like he was happier when she was gone. She had become so cynical and arrogant. Their love making had changed too. It wasn't the same. She had become so

45

dominant; it was weird. If love making were a movie, it was like Katherine, Kat, was the writer, director and actress. Sometimes, he felt like he was no more than a prop. Even worse, it was like she was center stage, and he was the audience. This was not Katherine. Katherine was passionate, not dominant; there was a difference.

Jason parked around back and turned off his lights. He wasn't sure at all what to say or do. He said a quick prayer; not that he was super religious, it was just that he was out of answers. He loved her; he just didn't love this. When he opened her sliding glass door, he saw the fire she had started in the fireplace. He loved the smell of burning wood. The yellow flames were curling up the chimney duct. The logs were radiating red coals. She was in bed. Beautiful.

Katherine smiled. Her blonde hair draped across her shoulders. The sheets were pulled up to her breasts. Her skin glowed in the soft light of the fire. "I love you Jason."

That was all she needed to say. No need for a fight or argument, it wasn't worth it. When she spoke softly like that to him, whatever differences they had, were over, put to rest. Jason walked over to her and stood beside her. He was almost afraid to say anything. She started unbuttoning his shirt, and then his belt. They both just wanted to make love, nothing more. He rarely slept there, but he did that night or at least until early morning, and then something strange happened. As he was about to get up and get dressed for school, she wrapped her long legs around his waist. It was playful, and then she squeezed. "You know I'll never let you go."

He thought it was an odd thing to say. She gripped him hard squeezing. There was power in her long legs. She squeezed harder, "See." He was totally surprised by her strength. She was as strong as any guy he knew. He tried to pry them apart but couldn't. It was like she had the power of a Ukrainian wrestler.

He patted her on the leg for her to stop. He had to get up and get to school. "Katie, stop; I have to go."

There was something about the way she laughed. It was bizarre. It was like she was testing her strength or something against his. Finally after toying with him, she did let go. Jason drove off to class. He was surprised she didn't have to go too; he knew she had classes as well. As he drove away, he realized something else. He was anything but MC. He had no control at all; somehow, someway, she had control of it all. It happened just that fast.

As soon as she heard Jason's truck backing out the drive, her phone buzzed. *"Morning."*

"Wats up?"

"He's such a wus. He's so totally wrapped."

"U told me how, thx."

"Gonna keep him?"

"maybe."

"Someone else u'r thinkin bout?"

"u'll see."

Katherine dressed and headed out for class. There was only one class she had much interest in attending. Art.

Chapter Seven

In Arkansas, hunting is deeply imbedded in the culture of its native citizens. The people here are not that far removed from the day when families were supported by the yearly harvest of squirrel and turkey, and of course deer. Men in Arkansas, women too, get what they call "deer fever" every year as soon as the weather turns cool and the leaves begin to fall. It's no fever of course but more of a primal urge to be in the woods and hunt. There is an exhilarating rush that comes from sitting in a deer stand watching and waiting until finally a huge buck appears in a bevy of brush. The hunter begins to sweat, his hand becomes a little shaky as he waits very still for the right moment to lift his bow or gun and take aim.

Jason and Calvin were both hunters, cross bow hunters. Bow season begins one week before the start of muzzle loading season which is one week before regular (modern) gun season. As much as the two loved football, there was nothing that the two enjoyed more than hunting. For almost a month, it seemed like it was all they would talk about. It wasn't just them either, nearly all their friends were hunters, some girls too, even Joy.

Katherine didn't hunt; she wasn't the outdoor type. She didn't get "deer fever," she got "mall fever," especially since she was getting an extra seven hundred *bucks* a month to spend. The week before bow season opened was eventful if not comical. Ever since her friend had been texting, she started getting these rogue emails and they were if nothing else amusing. She didn't get them daily, but often enough, at least several times a week. Katherine had not a clue who sent them or how they got there. The first one she ever received was from eggman@iamawalrus.com. It made her laugh. Eggman was strange and bizarre, but he cracked her up. It was always stupid stuff and quirky. Then there were other emails. One of her favorites came from a rather startling yet comical source, heresjohnny@deadcomicsclub.com. Katherine read them, and she was always amused. She didn't know if it was really one person or several who might be pulling a ruse, but whoever it was quickly became her friends. She would send emails back, little notes. "How's Johnny today?" He'd email back and then say he had to go, *"commercial break."*

It was like her social club. Jason certainly had his; she had hers though she didn't tell him about *her* friends. Her favorite bud was flirtatious; he was sticks@amishmafia.com. Sticks was different. The Amish Mafia, according to Sticks, beat people with straw brooms if they didn't obey the big boss. Sticks was the enforcer or so he claimed. She had her doubts. He said people paid him off with hens and goats milk. According to Sticks, he drove around the community of Yiddersmackin in his horse and buggy and terrorized the citizens armed with a broom. Sticks was operating an underground cider ring; no one was moving in on his territory. Sticks was also making his move on Katherine. The Harvest festival was coming up, and he wanted her to be his date.

"I'll think about it." She emailed him back. She didn't want to hurt his feelings telling him the truth. He was only 5 foot 6inches, and it would have been a little awkward. Besides, she had googled Yiddersmackin. There was no Yiddersmackin, Pennsylvania. No Yiddersmackin, anywhere. She wondered what he was up to. Sly boy he was. All this was very amusing to Katherine. She looked forward to hearing from her phantom friends, whoever they were. But there was other strange phenomenon happening almost on a daily basis.

One day as she was walking to class, she came to an intersection that had the walk/don't walk pedestrian light. She was standing there with her art work waiting for it to turn green. There was a group with her, not large but still there were five or six other students. It was cold and miserable that morning, and they were all anxious for the light to turn. Katherine was texting Jason when she noticed the flashing pedestrian light. Suddenly, the stick figure started dancing. It was grooving. Katherine laughed. Everyone turned and stared at her peculiarly. She pointed to the light, "Look." They looked back across the street. Apparently, it was no big deal to them.

"No look. Don't you think that's funny?"

They all ignored her. They looked straight ahead and just waited for it to change. She couldn't believe it. She texted friend, "I know U did that. U made me look like a fool. ☹."

"It's just between u and me. Don't u know that?"

"But I wanted them to see."

"They can't. Ur special. Don't u want to be special?"

"Yes."

"Then quit complaining."

Katherine had thought about it then. Friend was right. She had wanted everyone to see the figure dancing, but if they did, it would be just ordinary. She was advanced; her senses acute. She had powers and abilities others didn't. That had to be good. She was privileged.

Katherine walked across campus texting. She stopped briefly by the library to look up some things and logged onto one of the computers. There were some things she needed to look up for one of her classes, but honestly she thought it was just a waste of time since she was making all A's. Why go through the trouble, right? Still, she did make an occasional appearance in class but mainly just to appease Jason. She didn't want him to know she wasn't attending at all. That might draw suspicion. While on the computer, Katherine decided to check on her loan as well. She had heard a lot about the interest rate going up and wanted to check and see what the balance was. She was like everyone else in that regard; a large debt coupled with a crippled job market created anxieties. She had wondered how she was ever going to pay it if she couldn't find work.

"Oh my gosh." Katherine looked at $42,789.00 on her screen. She hadn't realized it had grown that much. Even with her parents paying room and board, the figure seemed excessive.

Her phone buzzed. *"Wats the matter Kat?"*

"My loan. This sucks!"

"Want help?"

"Can u?"

"Maybe."

"How?"

"Do u love me?"

Katherine was startled by the question. Their relationship had just been platonic. It was a strange thing to ask. Friend had been inanimate not intimate. She felt peculiar responding.

"Well?" friend asked.

Katherine hesitantly typed "yes." She looked around the room at the other cubicles to see if anyone was watching.

"r u sure?"

"yes." She didn't realize it, but she did love friend in a way. She was closer to friend than to Jason now, so she must.

"Yes, what?"

"Yes, I love u."

Katherine held her phone in her hand waiting for a response when she noticed something on her monitor. The numbers were moving, calculating. Digitally, the loan amount changed. The number clicked down. "$41,766.89".

"Oh my God".

The number kept scrolling backwards. "$39,553.76.... $33,164.22.....$29,992.83...." Katherine was speechless. Her loan was disappearing before her eyes. It kept going lower and lower. It stopped at "15,646.00."

"Feel better?"

"Yes, thank u."

"do u really love me?"

"yes, of course ☺."

"how much do u love me?"

"more than anything."

"more than Jason?"

"yes. I love u more than anything."

The loan started going down again. "$11,319.66...$9,776.55." Finally it was down to five grand then three. It kept ticking away. *"Feel better Kat?"*

She did; she felt relieved. The pressure was suddenly

relieved. It wasn't orgasmic, but it was certainly satisfying. A tingling sensation went up and down her legs. Then the number flashed "00.00" where it said balance due. It was gone. Loan paid in full. Katherine couldn't believe what had just happened. It had to be love. Her debt was paid in full. She texted friend "luv u, thx." She grabbed up her art and headed out the door racing to her art class so elated her feet hardly touched the ground. The first thing she wanted to do was tell everyone what just happened, but of course she couldn't; they wouldn't understand. Still, they noticed immediately her robust enthusiasm.

"Aren't we perky?" was the curt remark of bandana head.

"Oh, yes we are. Nice wrap." She wanted to say something about the lice trap on top of her head but didn't. Katherine had picked up on the girl's obvious jealousy. After all, it was Katherine's work that had garnered all the attention from Professor Hensley that semester, not hers.

Kris was smiling at the end of the table. He and Katherine began talking, and she decided to move down by him, and he scooted over his things. The other students at the table cast their eyes over at Katherine. She didn't care what they were thinking; she hardly noticed the smirks wiggling on their faces, nor did Kris for that matter. Hensley asked to see their art work, and everyone began pulling it out. Katherine laid hers face down on the table. Kris had his right next to hers. It was always hard for Katherine not to laugh at Kris. The same could be said for the other students. The assignment had been to paint something that demonstrated their view of themselves in the world. It could be anything; they could be an animal, or an eyeball. It could be a painting of a smile or simply a collage.

Kris's painting looked like something you'd find in kindergarten class. It was composed of stick figures with smiley faces in a bowl. And in the middle of the bowl was one large figure bigger than all the rest. The large figure had a frown. She started to laugh until she saw the frown. She asked, "Don't you like football?"

"It's alright."

She was surprised, "I thought you would love it."

There was a gentleness in his eyes. He was massive; muscles rippled through his shirt. No matter what he wore, everything seemed to have been stretched to fit over his frame. He was tough no doubt, but still a gentle giant. She didn't realize how much until that day. Kris shrugged embarrassingly, "I love football; I could just do without the attention."

She was surprised to discover that there was something they had in common after all. She had not liked the attention either, not until recently that is. She had seen herself at various times like the stick figure in the bowl, the center of attention. All that was changing now. Professor Hensley came by to take a look. He had praise for Kris's depiction; he seemed fascinated by the "honesty" of his work.

"Well Kat, you're the last. What have you got for us today?"

Katherine turned her work over. A crowd gathered around her as she revealed her art. It was a self-portrait of her, naked lying in a field. She was two-tone in color like a Jersey cow, black and white. Two calves were nursing off her, and a mother cow stood to the side wearing a bonnet and overalls. People didn't know whether to laugh; a few did. Kris's head jerked back. He hadn't seen anything like this, ever.

The Professor stood there looking at it. He picked up the painting and put it on the easel behind him and then pulled up a chair and flipped it around backwards. He was obviously trying to figure out the meaning, and then asked, "Kat, would you like to share?"

It was obvious by the reaction of some of the students they just thought it was weird. "I think nature would like to nurse from my breasts."

A few in the group giggled. She was equipped for the task that was sure. Katherine noticed Kris's eyes. They were on the canvas. He appeared to be in a trance. She almost laughed. The professor commented that it was an "unusual perspective on the world." He was very well pleased that the whole class was open and liberating about its views. It was what he was after as an instructor, impressions. For the next assignment, it would be fun. They were to do art work that could be silk screened. Their message would go onto T-Shirts. It had to be a statement that they wanted to make to the world because they were going to wear whatever they made for the rest of the day. That was the assignment. The class would be a little longer than usual so he asked them to get their early. It was Wednesday. The assignment had to be ready by Friday. There wouldn't be much time.

Katherine put her art work away and walked out with Kris. The other girls didn't bother to tag along now that all his interest seemed to be on Katherine. "So, are you coming up with any ideas, Kris?"

"Not yet."

"I really liked your last work. I didn't realize you were that thoughtful."

"You didn't realize I could think, you mean."

"No. I didn't realize you were that deep. I could relate is all I am saying. I have felt like I was in the center of a bowl."

"Yeah, it's going to be a big bowl Saturday."

"What's up?"

"We're on national television. Huge game."

"Really, I didn't know, but I'll have to watch."

She felt her phone vibrating in her purse. She told Kris she'd see him Friday in class. As he walked away, she leaned against the wall outside the art building and looked at her text. *"Jason's gone this weekend, don't forget."*

Yes, he would be gone. The last of the autumn leaves were falling. The gorgeous oaks on campus were now bare, stripped naked of their foliage that had been so brilliant just days before. The entire campus was covered with leaves a foot deep that rustled along the ground. She observed the students tromping through them going to and fro classes. She walked back to her car against a cold chilly breeze that was coming in from the north. They were expecting more rain. Katherine liked that, and there was a possibility Jason might come over. When she got back home, she opened up her drapes and stared out at the dark skies coming in. The birds were fluttering about trying to find shelter. A storm was coming. Off in the distance, she could hear the rumbling of thunder. There were flashes of lightning behind the dark clouds. She sat down in front of her easel and began to paint. There was a magnificent oak that stood out from all the rest in the back yard. She observed it. It was speaking to her. The last of its leaves were ripped away by the cold wind. There was none left now of what it had been; it was all gone.

Katherine realized one season was completely over; the next had already begun. She knew it, though no one else seemed to notice all the changes. As acute as she was to what was happening, she wasn't aware that with changing seasons…there always come storms.

Chapter Eight

They say that women are unpredictable; that may be, but I believe with more certainty it can be claimed that men are predictable (me included of course). It is not that we all act the same. We don't. But, men fall into the same predictable snares. A snare by the way is a trap that lies in our path. It is camouflaged to some degree, but the fault of a good many men is that even when they suspect it is a snare, they don't walk around it. Just because it is in the path doesn't mean men have to step in it, but most do.

Katherine, Kat, as she liked being referred to, was on some sort of exhilarating high. After all, her loan was paid off (deleted); she had nothing but A's in school; she had acquired a $700.00 a month stipend courtesy of Dr. Miller, and of course, she was also a gifted artist. Things had changed. She was no longer a sheltered and somewhat socially awkward girl from Little Rock. Kat had power, power over things, power over men. She was dating one of the most dashing young men on campus, certainly one of the most popular. Whatever you might think of Jason, the young man was destined for success. He had the "it" quality, "star" quality, whatever you want to call it. He had all the tools that businesses look for in today's graduates. Personality was the choice club in his bag, but he had something that couldn't be learned or imitated. He was genuine. The thing about power is that it is intoxicating, or can be. Despite Jason's strengths in character, he was no match for Kat. Kat had become dominant, and he had become conciliatory. In her eyes, he had become mousey, and like any other cat, she pawed him around. It was now a game to her.

She pounced on him and then let him go. Jason, because of his natural good nature, hadn't realized what was happening. All he knew was that emotionally he was exhausted. He felt sometimes trapped; other times, he was on the run.

That Wednesday evening, she toyed with him some more. Kat called him to come over. He said he had to study but relented to her demands when she purred how she "needed some." He was going to be gone hunting for the weekend; he didn't want to leave her without. Jason arrived just about the time the storm was rattling the windows of the house. The cave was now always dark, eerie in fact. All about the room were her paintings; on the floor were drops of paint. Kat often laid out a sheet underneath when she painted, but as of late, it didn't seem to matter. Paint was everywhere, on the counters, in the sink, on furniture. It looked like she made no attempt to clean it up.

When he came in, she asked that he close the drapes. Candles were lit all about the room. It was cold, and there was no fire in the fireplace. She sat in a chair she had flipped backwards and was painting on a canvass. Katherine smiled at him and told him to strip. "Leave your wet clothes at the door."

Jason wondered, paint is dripped everywhere, but water is a problem? Nevertheless, he stripped down expecting her to get up and get to bed. But she didn't; Kat kept painting. He walked over to where she was and took a look. He pulled the hair back around her neck and began to massage her shoulders expecting her to put down her brush at any moment. Kat didn't. She was into her painting. It was somewhat unusual, just a fork. On the table before her, she had laid out a fork and knife and was painting just the fork. It was good, very good. Looked like Warhol had done it.

"Hey, can you stop for a bit?"

"Take a look at one I did this afternoon; it's the storm."

It was up on another easel still drying. It was alright, her style was different on it than it had been on her other paintings. It was definitely more of an impressionist painting. The dark colors were blurred; there wasn't the distinct definition that she normally used. The clouds swirled around in the painting, and the lightening was magnified in sharp cutting edges. Jason stood there in the cold chill of the room with bare feet. He felt awkward. "Come on Katie, you can do that later."

"I want to do an impression of you. Can I?"

"I thought you wanted to make love? That's why you called, right?"

"Don't you appreciate what I do?"

"Yes, of course, but…"

She put the painting of the fork to the side and lifted a fresh canvas up on the easel. "Now, think of a position that is you. You want to stand, or sit?" She looked at the bed, "Or, you can lie down. Which is it?"

Jason stood there with his hands on his hips. "What are you doing?" The room was cold and he was standing there in the center of it like an ornament. It was weird. "Katie…"

"Kat."

He refused to call her that. "Katie, what is going on with you? I don't even know who you are anymore. Can't we go see someone and talk, maybe a counselor?" Jason grabbed up his clothes and started putting them back on. She seemed unmoved. She sat there with nothing on but a T-shirt and undies. She had no emotion in her voice. It was flat, like she was reading lines. "Most guys would love to have their girlfriend do a painting of them. You must not care." She put him on the defensive.

"You know I care. Nobody cares for you like I do." Jason zipped up his pants and then slipped on his boots. He was leaving. The night was nothing like he had expected. It was a bust, and he was pissed about it.

Kat then tore into him. She told him that he didn't appreciate her at all. All he wanted was sex that was all she meant to him. He denied it. Then, she said he was jealous. All the years they had been together, it had been about him, what he did. And now she asks him to do "one little thing for her," and he refuses. He didn't love her. He didn't understand the meaning of it. He had talked her into coming to the University and now was just dumping her. All of it, Jason denied. She was twisting everything. It wasn't the way it was at all. Finally she said, "Just go on your hunting trip. A deer means more to you than me."

Jason rolled his eyes. She was being unreasonable now. She was making demands on him. Katherine had never done anything like that. She didn't like to hunt, but she didn't mind if he did. All that had changed. Her attitude was completely different. Jason told her he was going. They'd talk when he got back. Katherine shrugged. It was like she didn't care. "Maybe."

She heard his truck backing out of the drive. The rain was pouring down the gutters outside. It was another torrent, perfect for painting. Kat picked back up the canvas she was working on before, the one with the fork. "Humm, what can I add to this?"

Buzzz. Buzzzz. Buzzz. It was friend.

By Thursday morning, the rain had passed. It was chilly, but the forecast called for temperatures to rise. The highs would reach almost sixty, and the sun would be out. Katherine had recently received another check, and the mall of course had some great sales. She cleaned up and went out, but before she did, she put her trash outside. It was Thursday, and pick up was always on Thursday. A few hours after she left, Dr. Miller went around back to her dumpster, a big green container on wheels, and wheeled it up to the street. It was noticeably light so he opened it and pulled out her trash to put in with his. When he did, two of the lighter bags blew out his hand, and he chased them down before they blew into the street. As he did, he picked up receipts that had blown out too. There were a lot of them. They were all department store receipts. $77.64. $112.96. $203.43. Another $100 was spent at Hobby Lobby. Dr. Miller was stunned. He was fuming. He had been duped. Played like a fool. For someone who couldn't pay rent, she was spending a whole lot of money. Where did it come from?

The doctor rolled her container back down around to her apartment. He went on about his business but was determined to confront her when she got home, and then later he heard her coming into the drive. He walked around to the back of the house and caught her just as she was opening up her door.

Katherine had more bags in her hand. She was wearing skin tight jeans and had a blouse with gold fringe. He knew it was expensive, and his indignation could not be concealed.

"Katherine, I need to talk to you."

She opened her door and tossed her bags on the bed. She quickly pulled the drapes behind her so he couldn't see. Smiling, "Yes, what is it? Some storm last night, huh? I was so scared."

He pulled out the receipts from his coat, "What are these, may I ask?"

The demeanor in Katherine changed. She gave him a glare that he hadn't seen before. "Oh, I see. You're spying on me? Looking through my trash. Got a peephole around here? Maybe I need to check you out."

Immediately, she turned tables and was accusatory of him. "You lied to me, Katherine."

"You are so quick to jump to conclusions. My grandmother sent me a little money for clothes. She knew I needed them and decided to help me out rather than wait till Christmas. But I see, you just want to persecute me. I thought you were my friend."

He obviously hadn't considered that. He had jumped to conclusions. "I think I'll discuss this with Mildred. I don't think she'd appreciate if someone went moseying around in her trash and then accused her."

"No, don't do that."

"Soooo, she still doesn't know."

"I didn't want to tell her. It's what you asked, remember?"

"So she doesn't know I can't pay?"

"No." He looked worried.

"Then I won't tell her about this either. I don't want to get you in trouble. It is our secret." She took the receipts out of his hand, "I might need these in case I need to return them."

Just like that, the tables were turned on Dr. Miller. He still figured she was lying, but he was caught in an awkward predicament. She had gone two months without paying. He messed up in not telling Mildred, but if he told her now, it would look like he was hiding something. He figured that

Katherine was lying about her grandmother, but how would he know? He went back upstairs, knowing that she had him under her thumb for now. All he wanted to do was get her out. He hoped she'd leave by semester's end, go back home. What had begun as a nice sweet courtesy for a tenant was now a manipulating con artist. She was bullying him, and he knew it.

The following day was spectacular. The weather couldn't have been better. Arkansas is like that, the weather can change quickly. Katherine took a bag with her T-Shirt and drove to school early. She made sure she saved a seat for Kris when he came in. She did. He sat down directly across from her. Everyone was in a jovial mood; it was a fun assignment. Lots of students engaged Kris in the talk of the big game, but as was his nature, he shied away from the subject. He wasn't a big rah rah type jock. Katherine liked that. He was just a sweet guy with big muscles.

One by one, the students took their art into the screen room where Dr. Hensley made a print from their work and then laid it over a T-Shirt. Each shirt was then placed in a drying room with fans and in a matter of fifteen to twenty minutes they were dry enough to be worn. One at a time, all the students went to go get their work. They changed in a dressing room and then came out. It was the most fun she had ever had in class. Every student had done something that rendered a message about themselves. They had to wear it for the rest of the day. The bandana chick had a shirt with a gun and a flower sticking out of it. Katherine didn't say anything, but she thought it was not that original. Friend texted and said the same. Another person had the American flag; one dude had a shovel. There were several with slogans for revolution, but sure enough, there were no prints of Chairman Mao. Finally, it was Kris's turn. It was a puppy dog.

Katherine smiled, "Ahhhh. I was thinking more of a bear." She patted him on the shoulder. "You did good."

"Yeah, right."

"No, really." She looked at the crude drawing of a puppy with a shoe. "You just happen to be a big puppy that's all. What I like about it is that you are real. I like real men, real men with heart."

He didn't know if she was joking or what. She had teased him all year, and now she was complementing him. Finally, it was her turn. Everyone in the class had waited with anticipation because she had proven to be without a doubt the best artist in the class. Katherine excused herself from the table and went into the dressing room. When she came out, Kris's back was turned. He heard the response before he saw it himself. There were a few "Wows" and some laughter. The class was stunned. She had managed to do it again.

Katherine walked over to the table and sat down. She was wearing a cream colored long sleeve fleece shirt with a turtle neck. That in itself was different. On the front was a fork about twelve inches long with the words above it "Wanna fork?" It looked like a Salvador Dali print, the way the handle of the fork curved over her breasts practically making a U. It was defiantly shapely. With a glistening smile she looked at him mischievously. "Well, do you?"

He blushed, turning bright red. Several around the table laughed. He was obviously embarrassed. The tips of his ears looked like they were radiating. Kris was speechless and a few girls at another table were whispering some unpleasantries about Kat which she heard but ignored. She nudged him under the table with her foot. "Well, what do ya think?"

The words were stuck to the top of his mouth, like they were lodged. He had to roll his tongue around just to moisten his mouth enough to speak. "Ah, ah, it's good." He appeared almost choking.

"I hope you like it."

Still red and blushing, "Yeah, I do."

"I hope so." She smiled, "I like a good fork."

The class burst out laughing, and then the bell rang. Katherine had a few other shirts to get that were drying. She told him to wait up. He seemed nervous doing so. She could tell he was ready to go. She grabbed the shirts from the drying room and came out. He was waiting in the hall, and a group of girls were around him. Kat came up to him, and the other girls walked off. She nudged him with her elbow as they walked to the door at the end of the hall, "Hey, I just wanted to wish you a good game tomorrow."

"Oh, that."

"What did you think I wanted to talk to you about?"

"Ah, I'm not sure." His eyes were trying not to look at her shirt. She could tell.

"Yeah, I'll be watching you tomorrow, puppy dog. But you play like a pit bull for the team. I want you guys to win."

Kris smiled. Suddenly, he was relaxed. "Will you be at the game?"

"No, I'll be home alone. Jason's hunting. I'll be watching on TV and painting. Maybe I might get out after the game, but I don't really know where to go. I hardly know anybody up here...but you. Where would somebody go to have fun?"

"I like to go out to the arcade."

"I thought there would be a big party or something?"

"There is, but I don't do that much."

"We are both alike…again. I'm not a big partier either."

He started to say something but hesitated. Her phone buzzed.

"Hey, um…guess I'll see you Monday then?"

"Hope so."

They went their different ways. He on to practice and she went home. Friend congratulated her on the job well done. Little did he know, the snare was set. He walked right up to it. It was somewhat camouflaged with words, but it was there. It wasn't open, but it was there covered with words, suggestions, lying in wait under a blanket of leaves. Men have to make choices, steer clear or get caught. Kris was walking right into it. He was walking all around it. He's not alone, lots of men have. Kris was just another one.

Chapter Nine

One didn't have to watch the game Saturday to know that Arkansas won. Cars were honking all over the city. It's probably that way in every college town when the home team wins a big one. Kat did watch; however, just bits and pieces. She went jogging and listened to it on her headphones. Then she watched some more as she cleaned her apartment. Girls typically do that when they expect company.

It was a beautiful Saturday that was for sure. As she cleaned, she thought about Jason and knew he was perfectly content sitting high in a tree stand waiting for his kill. If they were married, it would be like this every year. He'd been gone for deer season, then turkey season. Fishing in the spring. She would spend a lot of time home alone. As Katherine was cleaning house, she assembled all her paintings together. Dr. Hensley had said she might get as much as five grand for some of them. She counted them; she had sixteen in all. *What if I did fifty paintings a year? How about a hundred?*

The prospect of a career as an artist excited her. She was never enthralled about the eight to five routine anyway. She knew she had been spoiled, liked to sleep in. A mundane job behind a desk or counter was something that actually terrified her. She never would admit it to anyone, but Jason was always seen as a *solution*. He would be successful. She could count on him being hard working and industrious. More importantly, he would climb high on that corporate ladder. Pop a few kids for him, and she wouldn't have to make the morning rush through traffic. She could still be in her terrycloth bathrobe pouring out cereal in a bowl and slide it across the table to the youngins'.

Get her a good nanny and go shopping. Deep down inside that had always been the plan, but if she could make it as an artist, she wouldn't need to pop the kids and do the mommy routine. She could skip that all together.

Friend text'd her. *"Don't I get any credit? No thx?"*

"4 what?"

"4 ur art."

"But I did it."

"Who gave u the ideas?"

"You?" She sat down on the edge of the bed and watched the post-game show. They were interviewing the coach and then Kris. Friend was right. Everything in her life was being directed. Until friend came along, it was like she was just bobbling along. She went where Jason wanted, did what Jason did. She was attached to him; it was like she wasn't her own person. Things had changed, and she owed it to her friend.

Kris (K.J.) stood about a foot above the sports reporter who seemed to glow in his presence. It was a little chirpy blonde with a mike. "K.J., sixty-eight yards on seven catches. That's a lot for a tight end. How does it feel going into next week's game against Ole Miss. Will y'all be ready? Will y'all change anything?"

"Ole Miss is a great opponent…(bla, bla, bla)…we'll be ready. It will be a tough game."

"There's talk of you and Ryan going in the first round?"

"There are a lot of great players on this team; a bunch of us might go. Right now, I am just going to focus on Ole Miss. This is the SEC; it is one game at a time. We don't take anybody for granted."

Katherine was impressed. Seeing him in class in person was one thing, but and seeing him on TV aroused her. For such a big name player, he was humble…and gullible. She knew why so many girls were after him. Friend text'd, *"What r u thinking?"*

"Why do you ask? U know."

"Stick to the plan."

"Then it will work?"

"Can't fail."

"Sure?"

"Trust me."

Kat waited till about 8:00. The game had been over about three hours, and the bottleneck of traffic had moved on. A steady stream of cars was heading over the mountains down to Little Rock, but Dickson Street where all the parties are was filling up. The radio shows were abuzz with the high lights. Arkansas had amassed 520 yards against one of the top defenses in the country. There was talk, of course, they might be going all the way and were ranked number six in the country with the possibility of jumping another notch after the great game. First, she drove to the mall where she returned a few items and got some quick cash back. Then she drove up the street a ways to where the arcade was located. The parking lot was full. The sound of go-carts hummed like a swarm of mechanical bees in the cool autumn air. She got out of her car and walked up to the entrance where a group of high school boys were standing. Every eye was on her. They could smell her perfume as she came to the door, and they all turned as she walked in catching all of her that they could.

"Wow!"

"Oh my gosh. Who was she?"

One kid punched the other. "Keep dreaming. That's your only chance."

They all laughed. Katherine paid for some tokens and then went to the games. She played one after another in the arcade. She didn't see Kris and was beginning to think it had been a stupid idea. It was ridiculous to be out there alone. After all, she was decked out in skin tight jeans and a low cut sweater. With high heels, she stood out in the crowd. Finally, she decided she had better go. She had been there about forty minutes and was getting tired of all the stares. As she was leaving, she saw him standing by the doors. He was talking to the kids she saw before. He was signing an autograph on one of the boy's shirts. He looked up, obviously surprised.

"Well hey, puppy."

"Puppy?" The boys were surprised. They looked at Kris, "You know her?"

"Yeah, we're art buds." She smiled, "Hey, you like air hockey?" She didn't give him time to answer. Katherine opened up the door, "I bet I can beat you. I use to be the champ."

She and Kris played air hockey, six games. She won four. Then they raced go-carts together and ended up playing a round of putt putt too. They played games until the place closed. Kris hadn't had that good a time in a long while. Neither had she. She told him that in so many words; in fact, she mentioned that Jason "Never would take her out there."

Kris wasn't totally naive; he picked up on all the vibes. The lights turned off on the track, and they were the last to leave the golf course. It was almost 12:00, and he walked her out to her Dodge Charger in the parking lot where it was all but deserted. Katherine leaned against the outside of her car. The temperature had dropped another ten degrees or so, and the air was brisk. It was cold. She opened up her car and slipped on a jacket. Kris was standing there. He looked at the time. There was an awkward pause. He hit the remote button to his truck, and it blinked and unlocked. It was time to go.

"So, you heading down to the big party on Dickson Street?"

"Probably not."

"Humm. I'm not up for that stuff either."

Another awkward pause. He shuffled his feet, and she looked around. All night, they were laughing and joking, and now both were struggling for words. "In case you are wondering, Jason and I are on the outs. It's been difficult. I know you guys are friends. I haven't said anything because it's hard to talk about."

He seemed surprised. "I didn't know".

"Jason and me are just different. That's all. It was a mistake moving here. Except for you, I really haven't had anybody to talk too much. The best decision I made in retrospect was taking art. You made that class fun."

"Yeah, it's been fun for me too."

"I get a kick out of all the girls around you." She laughed, "I've even told Jason that you have your hands full. All those girls in class and Raven. You're a busy man." She knew he couldn't stand Raven. She was coaxing him into saying it. He did. "Then what's the deal; just haven't found the right one?"

Kris shrugged, "Not really."

"Humm, that shouldn't be a problem. You're a lot of fun. I like being around you." She paused and looked at the time on her phone. "Say, ah," she looked nervous, "Ah, do you want to go someplace and just talk?"

"Sure."

"Want some coffee?"

"Sure." He was thinking a restaurant, Starbucks.

"Good, I'll make you some. Follow me."

A few seconds later, she was driving out of the parking lot, and he was following. Kris wasn't exactly sure what was going to happen, but she did. Once he was back at her place and she started the fire, he was trapped. Katherine looked especially beautiful in the flickering light glowing in the fireplace. Her voice was soft. When she talked about her loneliness and "the awful feelings of abandonment," Kris was pulled into her every word. Then when she laid her head on his shoulder, he was done. He studied plays all week long and drilled for them in practice, but she maneuvered like nobody he had ever prepared for. He couldn't believe how fast it happened. By the morning, he was already wondering at what point he could have turned back? He didn't know; he was baffled, perplexed. It was the oddest feeling. One part of him regretted what he had done, but another part of him was thinking this was the greatest day of his life. Kris left the next morning confused because he wasn't sure what would happen next. All he knew for sure is that he had to see her again. The experience was better than anything he had ever felt in his life.

As he drove back to the Wilson Sharpe Dorm the next morning, the sun had never looked brighter. He couldn't believe what he had just experienced. Normally, he would have a shower and big breakfast, talk about the game with his teammates. Kris was often the one they asked to lead the morning prayer; but not this morning. He decided to skip church; he had other things on his mind. All he wanted to do was to get back over to the cave and see her. It was all he could think about. Kris had found the woman he was looking for. He was absolutely sure; this was his gift from God, and he had never felt better.

Chapter Ten

As soon as Jason got back in town, he called her. Katie rushed over to see the pictures of the big buck. Calvin ignored her and then got some ice cream and went to his room to read the paper about the big game. Katherine spent the night. She texted Kris and told him she had to have "the talk" with Jason and that she'd see him the next morning in class. Jason and she didn't talk much, and Calvin could barely sleep with the bed banging against the wall for half the night.

Kris was the first one to class, and he was all smiles. Occasionally, he felt her foot rub up against him. That seemed to happen every time another girl talked to him. She was letting him know to keep his attention on her. He needed no reminding whatsoever. She was all he could think about. All during class, he couldn't take his eyes off her. It was a bit annoying. She realized that she obviously hadn't told him that she didn't like being stared at. But she would.

After class as they were putting their art away, she whispered to him casually, "Hey, we have to talk."

"About what?"

"Jason. He's such a wuss." They waited till everyone else left. "You should have seen him last night. He was practically crying. Don't worry, I didn't tell him about us. I wanted to talk to you so bad, but he kept going on about us, and I was like trying to tell him I needed space."

"But I thought you were already broken up. You said it was over, right?" He looked confused.

"Yeah, but you know we haven't ever discussed it. It was more implied. He was doing his thing, I did mine. I just don't understand him, Kris. He has been abandoning me. You know how he is; he has always got something going on, and there is so little time with me."

"So what happened?"

"I tell him that this is it. I've had it. No more. Oh, my gosh, it's like you should have seen him. He just can't let go."

Kris was stunned by the development. It wasn't what he was expecting to hear. "I shouldn't have done anything. I…I…"

Kat patted him on the chest. "No, I am so glad you came into my life. I needed somebody. I am so glad it was you; somebody I can trust. If you only knew how trapped I feel right now. It's awful. I want to see you again. I can't tonight. Jason made me agree to go back over." She took a deep breath like she was mustering up courage, "I just have to be firm with him, but this is so hard. I am such a wimp about this. I shouldn't be. You understand, right? You're on my side still?"

"Of course."

She sighed relief, "Good, because I need you Kris. Don't you abandon me, okay?"

"Don't worry. I won't."

"I'll call you as soon as I can, probably be tomorrow. Don't worry about me. Promise." Her phone buzzed, and she pulled it out of her pocket, "Gotta go."

That night, she cooked dinner for Jason. Calvin conveniently went out on a date, and when he came back, they were in Jason's bedroom again. He could hear them groaning and moaning. Sounded like the two of them were being tortured, but he was used to it. He put on his earphones and drifted off to sleep, and somewhere around two, he went to the kitchen. Jason's bedroom door was opened, and he looked in. She was gone. Jason was sprawled across the sheets out cold.

It was pretty late Tuesday night when Kris parked his truck down the street. She told him that Jason had become very "possessive and controlling." He was jealous and insecure. It was best they not take chances. So Kris parked his truck down the hill and walked the half block up to her place. It was the longest two days of his life. He hadn't been able to think about anything but her all week. It was killing him. When he got there and she pulled the sliding glass door back, she was texting her "friend." Immediately, she closed the curtains and began unbuttoning his shirt. He wanted to talk. He had a thousand questions.

"What happened? You talked to Jason, right?"

She just smiled. She was wearing nothing but a long sleeve dress shirt, and her hair was pulled back into a ponytail. The fire was flickering, and she kissed him down the side of his neck. Her fingers scratched at his big chest, "You don't know how I've missed you."

He took it as a sign that she had completely broken it off with Jason. She only commented that she didn't want to talk about it right then and quite frankly as her lips moved across his shoulders, Kris didn't want to talk about it either, not then. Later, she said he had to go; she had some stuff to get done before class Wednesday, so around 3:00 Kris walked down to his truck under the glow of the moon. It was the second best day of his life. Even if he had to wait in the wings a little bit until she "finalized" things with Jason, it would be okay. This was great. The thought of having her all to himself was his one consuming thought. No other woman had come close.

Kris couldn't wait for class. Admittedly, he hadn't put a lot of effort in his recent projects, but it didn't matter. Seeing her was all that concerned him. Life had never been better until that next morning. He was under the impression that Jason had been prepared for the split. He was dealing with it and knowing what Katherine was like; he totally understood Jason's remorse. What man wouldn't go nuts?

He could tell instantly that something was troubling her. She walked into class looking a little frazzled, like she had been up all night. He was naturally worried. "What is it?" he whispered. She was cold all through class, and then afterwards they talked in the hall way. It was bad news. Real bad.

She said Jason had called her after he left. Jason was so depressed he was thinking about quitting school. She was feeling that it was all her fault; she "had no right to ruin his career." What was she going to do? To make matters worse, his mother had called her that morning; she had been like a daughter to them. It was just awful, and it was all her fault. She bit on the side of her lip as she struggled to say the words, "Maybe we just need to chill for a bit until Jason can get it together." She was sorry.

Kris was stunned. It was a blow he never saw coming. It felt like he had just been hammered between two linebackers. He was crushed. His mouth dropped open hanging from his jaw like a loose hinge, "What?" He stammered, "Y…y..ya can't mean it."

She did. A sickening chill rushed through him, the same kind of feeling you get right before you throw up. He almost gagged. Kat put her hand on his chest, "Please Kris, you can't be selfish right now. After all, he's your friend too. You have to be considerate, come on. Please understand, I want you, but I can't leave him right now."

Kris was shaking. The skin in his face was jiggling with a nervous twitch. He was absolutely floored by the news. This was the last thing he was expecting. She pleaded with him, "I need you to be a friend right now."

His shoulders slumped. He was furious. He couldn't believe what was happening. He didn't bother going to his classes the rest of the day. Instead, he went to the weight room and worked out. She texted him repeatedly. He texted her back between his regiments of squats and bench presses. She said that he could never tell Jason about them. He would be "crushed."

Kris was pissed when he read the text. He called her. "What about me? How do you think I feel?"

"Come on, Kris. You're a big guy. You can take it; besides, you and I were only together twice. Jason and I have five years. It takes time."

"You used me."

"You used me. Your best friend's girlfriend. Come on, how does that look? Think about it." She was quiet, waiting on his reaction. "K.J., give me just a little more time with him. Be patient, and he'll move on, alright. You haven't thought once on how hard this is for me. Look at my position. I love being with you but can't. I thought you'd be a little more sensitive. Maybe I was wrong about you. Am I? Did I make a mistake?"

"No."

"Then, don't say anything to Jason. Think about your friendship with him. He doesn't have to know, ever. Understand? We just have to think smart, okay?"

He agreed. She told him she'd talk later. She had things to do. She missed her "big puppy."

Kris put on more weights and did his bench presses. That afternoon, it was a grilling practice. Coaches were making sure everyone had down their assignments. They were playing Ole Miss on Saturday, and they were going to be nationally televised again. It was going to be their "statement game." Arkansas was supposed to win by two touchdowns, a tremendous favorite, and then there was LSU, the last game of the regular season. A blowout of Ole Miss and a win over LSU would put Arkansas in position to fight for the national championship. That hadn't happened since 1964.

Kris was flattening everyone in practice. Hitting some teammates so hard the coaches had to pull him out. They didn't need him hurting their own guys, not before the game. As he walked off the field, one of the line coaches pulled him aside. "You okay K.J.?"

"Yeah. I'm alright."

"Keep your cool in the game. We need you. Got some news this morning; the Patriots and Cowboys scouts are going to be at the game. They aren't coming to see Tyler. They are flying in to see you."

"Serious?"

"Keep it cool. This is the biggest game of your career. A lot is going to be riding on it."

Kris thanked him and then went and showered. He had worked so hard to get to where he was. Later that evening after the meal, he took a walk across campus. It was quiet, and he needed the time alone to think. He walked up to Old Main and sat on a bench, thinking. Coach was right; this was definitely the biggest game of his career. He looked at his phone; Katherine hadn't returned his messages all evening.

She was all that was on his mind.

.

Chapter Eleven

In skydiving, they call it freefalling. In love, it just hurts. Kris was pulling at ripcords; no chutes were opening, and unfortunately for him, it was a long way down. A very, very long ways down.

Friday morning of course was art. Kris had texted her a dozen times Thursday evening. She hadn't returned a one. That sickening feeling of panic was consuming him, consoled only by the fact that he knew he would see her in art. They could talk then. He got there first and reserved a seat for her across the table from him, but when she came in, she stopped and looked around the room, almost as if she was trying to find another seat. She didn't. Katherine sat down across from Kris. She didn't even look at him though; she was texting and pulled out her art work. She never even looked in his direction.

He whispered, "We need to talk."

She pulled out her art work for review. It was a spiral stair case that resembled a DNA chain with a man ascending from an ape to his present form. The girl next to her leaned over, "Wow, that's good." The two of them began talking, and Kris was trying to get her attention.

Katherine turned and looked at him. It was an uncompassionate stare. Everyone knows the look; it's like, don't bother me. She lowered her eyebrow, "Not now." It was obvious she was annoyed.

"Please."

Katherine shook her head and then talked to the girl to her left. She then stood up and took off her coat and laid it over her stool. She was wearing another one of her silk screens that she had made the week before. It too had a fork on it, but the message was entirely different. Above the fork on her shirt, it said in big bold letters. "FORK OFF."

K.J. did a double take. Could that be right? Was it a coincidence? Was the message for him? He nudged her underneath the table with his foot. "Katherine…"

"Can't you see I'm busy?" Everyone at the table was staring at him. A few at the end of the table were chuckling. They were commenting on her shirt. Pride is something that can radiate or wither; Kris was withering right before her eyes. His eyes seemed to melt as they appeared to sink deeper into his face. It was the ultimate blow off.

He stared at the "Fork Off" message on her shirt. So different now than the week before. Her signs could not have been clearer. It was meant for him; he knew it. It was just that he didn't know what he had done wrong. Something happened; he just couldn't figure out what. Professor Hensley was going from table to table grading their work. He sat there like a total oaf. He couldn't wait to get out of there. All he wanted to do is leave and get away. He was trying to regain some composure, trying to think of something to say. His eyes focused on the big fork in front of him. He was struggling for something to say, to act like he was cool. It was no big deal. He pointed to her art work on the table of the spiral staircase. "I like it. Take you a long time."

It was a stupid thing to say. It was like she was thinking, *is that the best you can come up with?* Unfortunately for him, it was. Katherine leaned across the table and whispered. "You know what they do to puppy dogs that misbehave?

"What?"

"They rub their nose in it."

Kris was stunned. What in the world happened? He was just supposed to chill for a day or so until she could talk Jason out of quitting school and now this? Katherine pushed a piece of paper across the table to him. It simply read, "It's over." She looked away and talked to the other girl about her work. That was it. He was done. Finished.

She didn't even acknowledge him as he grabbed his things

and left the class room. She turned back around, and it was like he vanished. A few of the students commented about how he looked. "Yeah, what's with him?"

Katherine shrugged, "Men, go figure."

She did want to make sure she didn't leave class alone. She walked out with a group of girls when the bell rang because she expected him to be waiting outside. He wasn't. He had texted though. Kris said he was going to tell Jason if she didn't call him. He wanted to know just "what in the hell happened?"

Katherine texted him back. "Call me. I can talk now." He called her instantly, and the first thing she did was chew his butt. "Why did you try to embarrass me in class? I told you I couldn't talk." Immediately, she put him on the defense again. It was always like that. Instead of her having to explain her actions, she had him apologizing to her.

Kris was irate. "You! What about me? Why are you giving me the brush off? What did I do? You never returned my messages last night. I was worried sick about you, and then you act like nothing has happened."

"I told you I had to be with Jason. You knew that. You are starting to scare me, Kris. You are so controlling. I mean, I just don't know if I could handle this. Anybody ever tell you that you are controlling?"

"Controlling? What are you talking about? Is controlling just wanting to talk? Come on Kate, get real."

Katherine walked in the Student Union. She didn't want to be walking across campus alone. She was afraid he might be following her so she went into the building and then down the steps and then back out another door trying to lose him in case she was being followed. They argued back and forth. Basically, she just put him down. "What surprises me about you Kris is that I thought you were a better friend."

"What are you talking about?" He was really confused.

"You obviously don't care about Jason. You don't really care about what happens to him. Quite frankly, I'm surprised."

"You aren't serious?"

"Yeah, I am. I am thinking now I made a big mistake. If I have to, I will admit it. If you want to, go ahead and tell him that while he was hunting you slept with his girlfriend. Go ahead. See, you're no friend. You'd do something like that and then hurt him. Way to go Kris, at least if I make a mistake, I don't try to make it worse and tell him."

He was totally baffled now, mystified. She twisted his every thought. Didn't matter what he said, she had a response that just threw him off his feet. He was pulling at cords; nothing was happening. With each second, he was dropping faster. Finally, she said, "Please, can't we just move on?"

"I can't."

"We have to. The whole thing was a mistake. I'll own up to my part."

"I still can't."

"I'm sorry, but I was expecting a little more from you."

"Like what?"

"I thought for a guy who handles the football a lot you'd be better with your hands. You sure fumbled around a lot. Thought you'd take forever with my bra. Geez."

He knew he should have got off the phone. He shouldn't have wasted his time talking to her. She was not who he thought she was. She was someone totally different. "Kris, I hope your hands don't shake like that during a game." She laughed, "Just teasing. I did like your muscles though. I guess that's what attracted me to you in the…."

Click. He was off the phone. It was a hard cruel lesson for Kris, but he had fallen right into it. He was furious at first, almost mad enough to kill. He was heartbroken too. A few days before, and it was like his feet couldn't even touch the ground, and now he couldn't pull himself up off of it. She had smashed him just like those wrestlers you see holding a guy up and then dropping them on their head. He literally was staggering across campus for the rest of the day. Kris took it hard, extremely hard. And the more he thought about it, the worse he felt. He felt sorry for what he had done to his good friend. His gut wrenched with guilt to the point that he was actually nauseous. He kept feeling like he was going to burst into a stall and heave. He never did. It just made him sick.

As always before a big game in Fayetteville, the team

loaded buses to an out of the way motel. They do that to keep the team all together and so that they are concentrating on the game the night before and not the action in town. Friday night, Katherine spent the night at Jason's; they had a romantic dinner at an Italian restaurant in Tonitown. The next morning, she even cooked breakfast, a first. Calvin was surprised; it was like this was the Katie he had heard about. Around 10:30, a group started showing up for the pregame show on TV. Everyone was in good spirits. This was going to be a beat down. That was the expectation. By kickoff at noon, the living room was full, and the beer was flowing. It was going to be one heck of a great game. Jason took his seat next to Katie on the couch and put his arm around her. Nobody was more excited than Jason to see his good friend K.J. on TV.

Players call it their nightmare game. For Kris, it was brutal. Some games are sloppy, but this game turned out downright ugly. The announcers billed this as a showcase game for the Arkansas Razorbacks. A whole lot of the pregame buzz had been about the arsenal of offensive weapons that Arkansas had. The team had superb running backs and was loaded for bear with receivers. The first pass to the heralded All-American Kris Jones was a one yard loss. That happens when the defense swarms the receiver, but K.J. was taken down by a safety. Still, Arkansas managed to score in the first quarter.

In the second quarter, Ole Miss came back. The game was tied seven to seven, and Arkansas's terrific offense was moving again. On third and short, the quarterback found Kris in the open for a dump off. The ball floated over the defense right into his hands. Easy play. He dropped it.

The announcers ripped him. "Looks like he's got gorilla hands."

"Can't drop those in the NFL."

"Well, he's known as Mr. Clutch. He'll come back."

The game was tied 10-10 going into the third quarter, and then it was tied 17-17. Late in the third, Arkansas was marching downfield again. They were deep in the Rebels' territory, but Ole Miss was playing tough. On third and five, the quarterback broke pocket and found Kris at the thirty yard line. He fired a bullet, and Kris caught and turned downfield. He flattened a safety and then another, running over them like a tank. Kris was down to the 17 yard line, and only one more tackler stood in his way when suddenly, a linebacker caught him from behind and stripped the ball out. He never saw it coming. Ole Miss recovered and stopped the drive.

"That was a Bozo play."

"Sure was. All he had to do was tuck the ball in. Just go down. Worst that would happen for Arkansas is that they'd get a field goal."

The tweeters went wild. They were tearing him apart. "Gorilla hands" was his new nickname. The camera even caught a group of fans yelling "Get the hook! Get the hook!" They all wanted Kris pulled from the game. Jason tweeted back to his buds, "Hey, get off his case. Stand with our man, don't turn on him." The whole mood in the apartment was sour. They had come there with high expectations, and Arkansas was struggling in what was becoming a sloppy game. The Rebels had come there to fight, and they were giving Arkansas all they had. In the fourth quarter, Ole Miss went ahead 20-17. The crowd was pissed. This was not the blow out they expected, but still Arkansas wasn't done. Great teams know how to come back, and the Razorbacks did. They drove all the way down field hammering the ball between tackles. Ole Miss couldn't stop them. It was tough brutal football. Finally the ball was down on the five yard line, and there was just five seconds left on the clock. Without question, they could kick a field goal and tie it. The game would go into overtime, and they might win. They might lose. But National Champions are champions because they go for the win; it is why they are champions.

The crowd had been on its feet the entire fourth quarter. People everywhere, all across the state, across the nation, were waiting to see what Arkansas would do. Would they kick to tie, or go for the win? Arkansas called a timeout. During the entire time, Katherine was totally distracted. She hardly looked up; she just texted. Occasionally she smiled. The team gathered in the huddle, and then they ran back out to the line of scrimmage. No kicker. The crowd was roaring; they could be heard from miles away. The ball was snapped, and the seconds ticked off. The quarterback ran to his left and pulled back his arm. His favorite receiver was covered. Tyler fake pumped and then looked right for his secondary receiver who was tripped up at the line of scrimmage. All that stood between him and the end zone was five yards. He started to run, and then the gap closed, but as it did, Kris broke open, wide open in the end zone. Tyler lobbed the ball over two linemen. Every eye in the nation watched as it floated almost in slow motion through the air to Kris's outstretched hands. He was all alone. It came down perfectly. He grabbed it and pulled it down to his gut. The crowd went wild, but the ball kept going. It slipped from his hands and bounced off his knee. Kris reached for it as it tumbled in the air for the ground. He dove for it trying to catch it before it hit the ground. Too late. Incomplete.

The camera caught the dismal faces of the Razorback fans. The whole stadium was stunned. Ole Miss players were jumping all over each other. No flags were thrown. Kris was lying face down in the end zone. His own players walked right by him.

"Pathetic."

"Mr. Clutch is Mr. Klutz."

Everybody's phone was buzzing with tweets. They were ripping Kris apart. "Idiot." "Bozo." "Gorilla."

The announcers were ripping him too. They ripped the whole team. "Looks like Arkansas' hope for a national championship is over."

"Disappointing is all I can say. Let's just say, this was poor coaching. You have to get up for big games like this, and Arkansas was never into it."

"Well, maybe K.J. can redeem himself against LSU. That game is coming up after Thanksgiving."

"Are you serious? After what he did today, I don't know if I'd let him even dress out."

After the game, it was like the whole town was in shock. No car horns were honking that day. It was like a funeral. Celebrations became just another reason to get slammed. One person after another came over to Jason's place, and it was like a wake. Around about 6:00, Joy showed up. She gave Jason and Katherine a big hug when she came in, and she and Jason were about the only two people in the room that didn't dog Kris. Katherine hardly said a word. She just kept her hand around Jason and watched the highlights from the couch. All night long, the sports shows kept showing the dramatic end of the game. They played it over and over. It was most definitely the big story of the day. There must have been twenty different angles they had of the last play. Each time, it showed the ball going right through his hands and bouncing to the turf. He laid there face down. All you could see was his helmet in the turf and players walking by. Over and over again, and then it showed the scoreboard, the big mega tron screen with the final score. Arkansas 17. Ole Miss 20. It made everybody sick in the stomach.

The party got louder through the night. Sometime after eleven o'clock, a neighbor burst in. He looked frantic. "Hey, have y'all heard the news?"

"What?"

"It's about K.J."

Jason yelled for everybody to shut up. To be quiet. "What's going on?"

"Just look." He walked over and grabbed the remote and turned it to the local news. The camera crews were at an accident, a car wreck on a rural highway. "Shhhhh. Listen."

The reporter said that Kris Jones, the All-American tight end from Arkansas, had been involved in a head on collision on Highway 16 West, about 12 miles out of Fayetteville. They showed his truck mangled in a heap being lifted onto the bed of a truck. The crowd was in shock. The guy next door said the reports were that Kris had been drinking. He crossed the line and hit another car with a woman and two children. It was serious. They were all being rushed to the hospital.

Joy asked, "How bad is he hurt?"

"I dunno. He was on a stretcher. He's busted up pretty bad."

"What about the lady and two kids."

"Don't know, but it ain't good. It was on the radio that

he's expected to be charged with DUI as soon as the tests come back."

Jason knew what that meant. "I bet he'll be kicked off the team."

"Probably. He may get charged with DUI 4. That's a felony."

Jason grabbed his keys. Katherine looked at him as he was heading to the door, "What are you doing?"

"Going to the hospital. I need to be there."

Joy grabbed her purse. "I'm going with you."

Katherine wasn't about to let that happen. "Jason, you can't. You won't be able to see him. There will be cops all around. He's being questioned. You can't go there; you'll be in the way."

Jason was resistant. "Katie, he's my friend. I have to show support. I have to be there."

"Why don't we go in the morning? You don't want to interfere with the doctors." She grabbed her coat and went to the door, "Let's go back to my place." She kissed him on his cheek and took the keys from his hand, "I'll drive."

With some cajoling, Kat talked him out of it. He left with her to go to her place. Joy was the only one that went to go see Kris, and it was bad. The woman and the girls were seriously hurt; they were in intensive care but were expected to recover. They all had broken bones and lacerations. Kris's left ankle was crushed. The talus bone was shattered. He was in surgery for two hours that evening. By morning, it was all the talk shows were talking about. The experts said that chances of him playing again were pretty slim. For all intents and purposes, his football career was over. Shattered.

It was so ironic. One week before on a cool Saturday night, he was driving go-carts with Katherine; the next week, he was riding to the hospital in the back of an ambulance. Quite a fall.

Chapter Twelve

The only person that went to see Kris that night was Joy. She reported what she saw the next morning to Jason. The cops were there; she never got to see him personally, but she did manage to get a note passed to him through a nurse. It simply said "We love you."

Katie, Kat, meanwhile tied up Jason long enough the next morning that he didn't make it to the hospital. He thought it unusual that Kris didn't return his texts. It was in fact Joy who informed Jason of the news that Kris had left the hospital at eleven o'clock the next morning. He was rolled in a wheelchair out to a car, and then left. Later, he heard that K.J. went home to El Dorado, Arkansas, to escape the media blitz that had descended on Washington Regional Hospital. His good buddy was gone, and he had no way of reaching him. By Sunday evening, Jason was pissed at himself for listening to Kat. He should have gone immediately to see his friend but didn't.

It was a gloomy week all the way around. No one had the stomach for Thanksgiving coming up. It was awful. The school was in shock from the loss, but even more by the loss of one of its key players. Kris made it official by Tuesday, and the news spread fast; he dropped out. He wouldn't be going back to the U of A. Monday, the team announced that he'd been cut from the team. Speculation ran rampant that the NFL had lost total interest in him as well. When the Talus bone is crushed, a regular athlete might recover, but not for a NFL linemen, especially a tight end. It is hard enough for a 275 pound athlete to sustain such a fracture, but linemen have two or three guys, sometimes four, that weigh 300 pounds apiece pushing against the small ankle bones. In addition to that, the tight end has to make cuts like a receiver. The risk of re-injury is too great. Teams don't want to take the chance, not to mention hiring a player who is facing criminal charges. Kris was. Wednesday, the police department announced that K.J. had class four DUI charges filed against him. The prospect of serving time was almost guaranteed.

It took a day or two for the developments to sink in. Slowly, they did, and Katherine began to feel remorseful. Jason of course did not know. She was relieved that Kris was out of town being harbored by his parents, way down in El Dorado. If they talked, she figured the truth would come out. She even got Jason to sign a get well card she bought, and said she would mail it. She never did. Katherine was beginning to feel like she was coming out of a fog; the whole wreck thing sort of snapped her out of it. She knew that she was the one responsible for what happened, and it got to her. There was a small part of her that wanted to come clean with Jason and tell him, but the more she thought about it, the more she realized that she really didn't have an explanation. There wasn't a legitimate reason for doing what she did. She had mocked a fight between them; there had been no problem. The problem she realized was her friend. Friend was the one that instigated everything. It scared her.

For two days, Katherine decided to just turn off her phone completely. She told Jason to just come by, not to even text. "Don't call, don't text. I won't answer." Jason began seeing a remarkable change in her the week following the big game. The cynical Kat was gone; Katie was back, sweet and caring as she had always been. He even told Joy about it. Joy had become a person in recent weeks that Jason shared confidences with. He had been explaining that his girlfriend, his fiancée, had transformed emotionally in the few months she had been in Fayetteville. Joy mentioned that a counselor might help; sometimes, a sudden change in environments can evoke different reactions in different people. Perhaps, the move was the culprit. A counselor might help.

One afternoon, Katherine backed up the drive, and Dr. Miller was there. He saw her and started to turn and go in. She stopped her car and got out. "Dr. Miller."

She could tell he was uncomfortable. "Yes."

"I have to talk to you for a sec."

Since the last conversation about the receipts, they hadn't talked once. He had completely avoided her. Katherine smiled, "I, um, I think I can pay you this month. I will have the money in about a week and maybe be able to catch up."

He was definitely surprised. A smile came over his face. You would have thought he had won the lottery. "Really." His eyes were gleaming with delight. Then he paused; his eyebrow rose, "What's the catch?"

"Nothing. I promise I will have you the check and thank you for being so kind and understanding. I can't tell you how much I appreciate it."

The doctor decided that he would tell his wife as soon as he got the rent in hand. What a relief. He could explain that he didn't want to bother her before, and that was true. He had felt both victimized and used, but now that was in the past. Katherine had definitely made his day. She got back in her red Charger, and he asked where she was going in such a hurry. She said she had an appointment that she couldn't miss. She smiled and drove off. He walked in thinking *whatever has come over her, please don't change.* He liked the young woman with the perky smile. Perhaps, an improvement in her parent's finances contributed to the sudden change in her personality. He didn't know, but he was glad his cheerful tenant was back.

Katherine had called the school hospital and made an appointment to see a psychologist. She had asked to see a psychiatrist, but that would take three more weeks. She didn't want to wait. During this intermittent moment of clarity, she had wanted to confess to Jason not just her tryst with Kris but the texts. She didn't understand them herself. They had started suddenly, the emails too. She got lost in them, and they began to consume her life. She understood that, but would he believe her? A visit to a psychologist would help her discover what was really happening, to gain a perspective. She didn't know. The whole semester had been a blur. The remorse she felt about Kris had spurred her into taking action. The visit to a professional would be a great start.

The clinic was not that far away. She wanted to make a quick trip to the mail box to drop off the card that Jason had sent to Kris. It bugged her that she hadn't mailed it; so she drove down to the little shopping center where there was a box. Her conscience was clear as soon as she dropped it in. Then, she drove up to the light. It was red. She waited. Across the street was a grocery store with a sign that advertized specials of the day. Katherine looked at it; bottled water was half price. Two cans of green beans for a dollar. "Tyson whole fryers for $3.59." She thought she'd stop back by on the way back and maybe cook Calvin and Jason a chicken that night. Then suddenly, the message changed on the sign. She read the letters as they scrolled across the digital sign. "B…I…T…C…H."

Katherine did a double take. The light had turned green, and a car honked behind her. She drove through the intersection looking up at the sign as she passed. She leaned across the seat to get another look. "Y…O…U…R…M…I…N…E."

Katherine stepped on the gas and raced up the hill to the school, speeding up to the next intersection. She was terrified. She couldn't get to a counselor fast enough. She didn't understand what was happening. How was this possible? Who was it? Why her? She sped into the clinic parking lot and came to a screeching halt. Her heart was racing. Her hands trembled. She blew the hair out of her face and looked at the time. She was already five minutes late. As she got out and was about to slam the door, she saw her phone lying in her seat. She didn't want to touch it. It now scared the hell out of her, but the counselor couldn't possibly believe her unless he saw them himself. She had to show them to him. She just had to. Somebody other than her had to see what was going on. Katherine picked up her phone and put it in her purse. It was still off. She hadn't had it on for two days now. She bounded up the steps to the building, past the other students. She was worried he might be visiting with someone else so she ran down the hall and punched the elevator to go up to third floor.

The elevator opened, and she stepped on. The door closed, and she looked up to see the floor numbers changing. "Hurry." Finally the elevator jarred to a halt. She was there, floor three. The door opened, but not all the way. She thought that was strange. She could see the receptionist station and a few students sitting in the waiting room. Katherine pushed on the doors trying to separate them; perhaps, there was a glitch. They didn't open any wider. She was late, but she went anyway. Slam!

The elevator doors shut. She was trapped! Katherine screamed. Half of her was in the hall, but waist down she was still in the elevator. Her hands reached to the side where it was crushing her rib cage and attempted to pry them apart. A couple of students jumped up from their seats, and the receptionist grabbed the phone and started dialing maintenance. It didn't matter; it wouldn't help. The elevator started shaking; the whole thing shook. Katherine was pushing and grunting, trying to get herself free, and then the elevator started bouncing. It was going up and down. It took her up to nearly the ceiling and then dropped down to the floor. It went back up and shook and then dropped. Katherine screamed out to the receptionist who just stood there in shock, watching helplessly. Finally she pried the door just far enough apart and fell to the floor of the elevator. The doors slammed shut behind her. She laid there for just a second and could hear the people beating on the outside, and then suddenly, it was like the floor fell out. It dropped like a rock. It was freefalling to first floor where she knew it would crash, and then it hissed. The hydraulics caught, and it came to a soft landing and eased to a halt. The doors opened, and a group of students were standing there waiting to get on. Katherine was lying on the floor, crying in hysterics. They looked at her strangely as she sobbed. A girl asked, "Can we help?"

Katherine picked up her purse and stood up. She paused at the door and then jumped off without saying a word and ran for her car sobbing. It was useless. No one would understand. How could they? She sped away in the same fashion she got there and drove straight home, peeling into her drive way. Katherine jumped out and slammed her car door. She reached in her purse and grabbed her phone. She was going to throw it as far as she could when it rang. How could it? She had turned it off.

Buzzzz. Buzzzz. Buzzzz. It vibrated.

She didn't want to answer it. Buzzzz. Buzzzz. Buzzzz.

She read the text. *"I thought u said u loved me?"*

Katherine was trembling. Her hand was shaking so hard she could hardly hold the phone. She yelled at the top of her lungs, "I hate you!"

"Why?"

"Why don't you leave me alone?"

"But we are friends."

Katherine didn't know what to do. She didn't know who to turn to. She was trapped, and she knew it. Friend had all the power. Friend controlled everything. A tear slowly rolled out one of her eyes as she sat on a rock wall in the backyard. She wanted to just crush it, smash it, destroy it, but she knew it would be useless.

Buzzz. Buzzzz. *"We are still friends right?"*

Katherine's deep breaths began to slow. Her hands stopped shaking. She closed her eyes. She knew it was too late.

"Yes."

"I love u Kat."

She totally surrendered. Resistance was over. "Yes, I know."

Chapter Thirteen

Jason couldn't figure her out. How could he? He had not a clue what was happening. She was congenial and sweet one day, and the next day she changed. He never did see Katherine again after her scheduled appointment. He only saw Kat. The expression on her face forever changed. Her demeanor switched from light to dark as quickly as a cloud passes over the face of the moon. He could see it in her eyes that evening; Katie was gone. It was like she never existed.

He came by her place, and it was a mess, looked like someone had torn it up. It was dark, and she was painting. Candles were lit throughout the room, and the fireplace was burning. A sheet was spread out to catch the droppings of paint, and there was just something about the look in her eyes that frightened him. There was a snarl to her attitude the moment he walked through the door. "Soooo, where has Mr. Popular been?" It was Kat.

"Saying good-by to some bro's. Calvin is taking like three dudes home with him for Thanksgiving."

She dipped her hand in some paint and tossed it onto the canvas. He couldn't see what she was painting. Kat turned her head slowly to the side as it began to drip. Her eyes were intense, wide open. A mischievous smile curled from her lip, and she brushed her elbow across the canvas with her sleeve. "There."

She reached over for her phone. Kat picked it up with her left hand and texted. She put it down and then dipped her fingers in the paint and flicked it on the canvas. Jason sat down on her bed and watched. She said nothing for five minutes, maybe longer. It was weird. She was obviously disconnected from him. She was only into her art. He felt like he was being ignored and got up and started to leave.

"Where are you running off to?"

"Well, I can see you're busy."

She slapped some paint on the canvas without ever looking at him. The dark green was rolling through the other oils like a river. "Going to see your little girlfriend?" A snide smirk was tweaking in the edge of her lip. "Gonna get cha' some Joy?"

"What are you talking about, Katie?"

"Don't deny it. I know ya been banging her."

Jason shook his head. He hadn't a clue where she was getting this from. He hadn't seen Joy since the night of the game. Her accusation didn't even deserve a denial. "You know. I think we need some space. Some distance."

Her eyes flashed at him. She was standing there on the other side of the canvas. Candles were lit all around her, and she was wearing one of his white long sleeve dress shirts without anything else on. He could see her body through the shirt, the way she stood in the light by the fireplace. She had paint splashed all across the front. The shirt in the light of the fireplace was almost transparent. It looked more like a sheet, or a robe. The curves of her body were outlined clearly, but the way the paint had dripped down the front of her made her appear ghoulish. She looked like someone that was in a ritual. "Then, you're leaving me?"

"I think it is the other way around. You've left me. I don't even know who in the hell you are anymore?"

Kat took up the shirt tail and wiped her hands on it, making a total mess of the shirt. He could see that she was naked underneath, but it didn't matter to him anymore. "So what are you saying? You want a day or two? Gonna run ta' mamma?" She pouted her mouth mocking a child.

Jason shook his head. He stood up. "We just need time to think about this." He looked around the room and then back at her. "We're at a good point to reconsider some things."

"Reconsider what? You are marrying me right, Jason?"

She then finished wiping her hand on a towel. Her childish smirk was gone. She put her brush on the palette and walked around the canvas toward him. She raised her finger gesturing a threat. Oils were still dripping down her arm. "Cause you're not leaving me. Understand?"

He didn't say anything. Kat shoved her stool out of the way. She walked over to him and raised her hand like she was going to grip his face. Wet paint was still between her fingers. Jason grabbed her by the wrist and pulled her hand down to the side. "We need some distance. Maybe you might want to see someone Katie. Now, would be a good time."

He could feel her shaking. Her mouth drew tight like a fist. She was breathing heavily. "Are you screwing her, Jason? The little tramp. Cause if you are, you are going to pay." She twisted her hand from his grip, and he could see her tighten it into a fist.

"This is not about her. This is about us." He looked around the room at the mess. He expected her to take a swing. She didn't. He stepped back closer to the door. He was ready to leave. "This is not working for me. Do you understand? I'm not into this, and you're not into me. It is obvious things have changed between us."

Her expression suddenly switched from fury into a gentle seductive smile. "I need some Jason. I need some bad. Let's not argue. You know you can never leave me." She started to unbutton her shirt.

He walked to the sliding glass door and slid it open. The curtains blew in the cold gust of wind. "That's not going to work. Not this time. Why don't we talk later?"

"Tomorrow?"

He shook his head. "After the break."

"Thanksgiving?" There was a sharp sting in her voice.

"I'm thinking Christmas."

"What!"

She started for him, and he put out his arm. "Stop! We need some serious time. I am going to think all this over."

Her mouth closed tight into a draw. He thought she was going to come at him wailing her fist, but suddenly she spun around and went back to her canvas. "You'll pay for this Jason." Kat dipped her brush in the paint and started slinging it across the canvas in big broad strokes. She wasn't the same woman he had dated for five years. She was a total stranger to him now. He pulled the drapes back and slipped out the door.

He left the next day and drove back to his hometown. His parents knew he and Katie had split, but he didn't go into a lot of details. He wouldn't know where to start. During the break, he called Kris a few times and left messages. He never heard back. It was official now; he heard on the news charges were filed. K.J. had an attorney. The story was still talked about in the news but mostly on the sports channels. The question that still remained all week in sports circles was whether Arkansas could rebound for the LSU game?

Jason did some duck hunting the first few days of break with his brothers, and though they were close, he didn't talk much about Katie. His parents asked too, and he just shrugged it off. He didn't go into details. Usually Katie would have been over at his house on Thanksgiving Day, and it was odd not having her there. For five years, she had occupied the chair between him and his younger sister, but this year, the chair was noticeably empty. Sometime after the meal he called Joy who lived some twenty miles away on her ranch outside Cabot. He asked if she wanted to watch the game the next day at his house, and she said she'd dropped by. The next day Jason and his siblings gathered in the den to root for the "Hawgs." Even after the defeat against Ole Miss, if Arkansas pulled an upset, they could still get to a major bowl. Joy showed up in a red sweater and a big smile. But no amount of smile could take the sting out of the game. It became unbearable. Sometime during the third quarter, Jason decided he just couldn't watch it anymore. It wasn't the same team anymore. K.J. had been the nucleus all year, and his absence was noticeable to everyone. The season was shot.

He felt badly that she had driven all the way down from Cabot to watch a disaster, so they decided to get out and catch a movie; his little sister came along too. They got there early and grabbed a big bucket of popcorn. Jason sat between Joy and his sister, and they were watching the previews when Jason glanced behind him. He jumped three feet out of his seat. Popcorn was spilling everywhere.

Joy and his sister Karen turned around. Right behind them was a tall blonde with long straight hair. At first glance, she looked just like Katherine, but she wasn't. Her features were remarkably similar especially in the light. Jason apologized to the people in the seat in front of him. They were shaking popcorn out of their hair. The woman leaned forward and teased, "Am I that scary?" She wasn't; she was beautiful.

"No ma'am, I just thought you were someone else."

Joy pulled his arm close to her after he sat down. She could see how startled he was. She whispered in his ear, "Okay, Jason, when are you going to talk to me about what is going on?"

He didn't say anything. Joy tugged on him again. "Jason?"

"After the movie." His eyes glanced over to his sister. Joy could tell he didn't want to say anything around Karen.

"You sure?"

He nodded, and as he did, he looked over Joy's shoulder. Jason did a double take. In the dark of the theater, he saw someone standing in the aisle against the wall watching him. The lights of the movie flickered across the faces of the people. Joy could see the look in Jason's eyes, and she turned around too. There was a tall blonde walking up the aisle. She vanished quickly, ducking out the exit.

Jason looked terrified. "Was that Katie?"

He had been mistaken just minutes before. He felt like an idiot imagining things, but he had to know. Jason handed her the bucket. "I'll be back." He scooted by the people on their row and left. Joy watched him as he walked up the aisle. She kept her head turned. She wanted to go too but didn't want to leave Karen, so she watched and waited. A few minutes later, Jason came back and sat down again.

She whispered, "Was it her?"

"I couldn't find her, but I saw her face. I am sure it was."

Joy took his hand and squeezed. "It will be alright." Jason squeezed back. They held hands the rest of the movie, neither one wanting to let go.

When they left the theater, it was dark. The three walked across the big parking lot, talking about the movie. Jason took Karen's hand and kept her close as cars were quickly backing out and rushing to beat the traffic to McCain Boulevard. It wasn't that great of a movie. Jason never got into it. Joy could see he was on edge, looking back over his shoulder every time he heard a car come. As they approached his truck, Jason suddenly stopped. He could see it even in the poor light. It was very visible. All the way around his truck was a very distinctive cut. Someone keyed his truck. It went from one headlight all the way around the tailgate and all the way back up to the other headlight.

Karen screamed. "Oh my gosh! Look!" She let go of his hand and ran up to the truck. "Who did this?"

Joy looked at Jason. She knew him well enough by now to know he wasn't furious. He was upset, and scared. He walked all the way around the truck, looking at the gouge in the paint. Then his eyes canvassed the parking lot looking. Joy looked too. "Do you think....? Is it...?"

He nodded and told them to get in. They drove away, and all the way back to their house, he kept looking in his rear view mirror. At all the lights they came to, he studied every car that drove up beside them. When they got back, he told his sister not to say anything to his folks. She of course did. It was the first thing she said when they got home. They had lots of questions, but he downplayed the whole thing. Joy wanted to know too. All he would say was, "Not tonight."

"Why?"

Jason was too upset to talk about it. He promised her he'd call her the next day. The only thing he seemed concerned about was getting her home and insisted on following her back to her place in Cabot.

Joy refused. "You don't have to follow me home. That's silly."

Jason was insistent. He followed behind her in his truck all the way back out to her house. It was a beautiful place; he could tell that even in the dark of night. It was the first time he had been there, and her horses came up to the fence along the side of house when she got out of her car. She asked if he wanted to just stay the night since it was so late, but Jason refused. "I have to get back." He stood by his truck and took her by the hand. A car drove down the road in front of her house, and they both watched as it slowly passed. Jason's eyes studied the car carefully. It was late.

"Is that her?"

"I don't think so."

"You'll call me tomorrow?"

He nodded, "Promise."

"There is a lot you have to tell me, isn't there?"

He nodded again, "Yep. There sure is."

She kissed him on the cheek and watched him drive out to the highway. She had never known someone with so much on their mind. She didn't know the details of what had happened to him and Katie. All she knew is that it was serious. Jason was a lot like her father; he was a guy that rarely worried. She had ever known him to be scared.

But he was now. Some things you can hide, but fear is not one of them.

Chapter Fourteen

The weather in Arkansas, especially northern Arkansas where the University of Arkansas is located, can turn bitterly cold in December. A blast of winter sleet and snow blew in from Canada during the first week of December. Students trudged their way to class in a sloppy wet snow and drizzle. The overall mood of campus was dark and dreary just like the weather. The last two games of the season had been a bust, and the Razorbacks were headed to a mediocre bowl game that nobody was interested in.

Jason almost didn't hear from Kat at all. He wondered if keying his truck had satisfied some sort of lust of hers for revenge. He suspected not. He still got a few texts from her, and one time there was a note on his door. He barely recognized the handwriting. It in no way resembled Katie's distinctive expansive cursive style. It said something about love and missing him, but the note was written on a torn white sack. It wasn't even written on a card. It wasn't like Katie at all, so he never bothered to reply. Besides, quite frankly, it was a relief not seeing her. Jason was surprised at how much freer he felt without her. He didn't realize it until after their separation just how much of a drag she had become. Things were different around Joy.

Joy was an optimist. Katie, even when she was Katie, had always been insecure. Emotionally he felt like he always had to take care of her. It was like he was the one always having to lift her up, carry the weight in the relationship. Joy was different; Joy took care of him. It was still in the friendship stage, but Jason was definitely attracted to her and obviously vice versa. It seemed like almost every day after Thanksgiving they were together, but it was usually over at her place. Joy lived on the second floor of an older apartment complex between downtown and campus. He felt secure there, or more secure. The only thing he didn't like about it was the parking lot. It was dark and crowded. He usually had to park his truck on the street, and he was a little paranoid about it. Jason had decided he wouldn't get it repainted until break, and he wondered if he should do it then or just wait until he graduated. He was beginning to believe it might be a waste of time until he and Kat were really separated, living in different towns. Things were happening which scared him.

One evening he came home, and Calvin was gone. He had the strangest feeling as soon as he walked in the door. It was an odd feeling. Jason looked about the living room; then, he opened the door to Calvin's bedroom. Nothing there. Everything appeared the same, but still something was amiss, but he couldn't figure it out. He was tired so he poured himself a glass of water and went to his bedroom. The instant he turned on his light he was startled.

"Hello Jason."

The water spilt all over the front of his shirt. "How did you get in here?"

"I still have a key, remember?" She was naked in his bed with the sheets pulled up to her breasts. He could see her clothes strewn across the comforter and on the floor. She smiled, and her tongue moistened the top of her lip in a slow swath, "Miss me?"

He had no idea she even had a key. He had no warning. He never saw her car in the parking lot. It caught him by total surprise. He wiped the water off the front of his shirt, "What are you..."

She patted the bed beside her. "Come here." He could see her leg wagging underneath the covers. Her long blonde hair was pulled behind her shoulders. She took a long deep exasperating breath. "Jason, I need some."

"No. You have to go."

Her eyebrow arched in defiance. "What?" Her words

were slow, "What… did… you…say?"

Jason had seen the look before. He knew by now when she was angry. The corner of the bed was right by the door, and he picked up her blouse and tossed it to her. "You need to leave. It's over."

He picked up her bra and held it dangling from his fingers. "Not this time." He tossed it to her and reached down for her jeans when something flashed directly over his head. Like light, it blasted out from under the covers. He knew the sound well as it whisked not two inches from where he had stood. Jason leaped to the side and turned around. It was an arrow, completely shot through the door. The tip and blades penetrated to the other side. It was stuck right where he had been standing. It would have hit him directly in the throat had he not bent down. Jason looked back at Kat. She was sitting up with her legs arched and spread, and a hole was clearly visible in the comforter where the arrow shot out. Furiously, he ripped back the covers. There in the sheets was his cross bow. She had another arrow and was trying to reload.

"Get out!"

Katherine acted like it was an accident. "I…I…didn't mean for it to go off. I was just playing."

Jason grabbed her with one hand and yanked her out of bed, and then he grabbed the bow. He threw her clothes at her. He wanted to punch her; he was so pissed. Jason pulled back his fist but stopped. Instead, he walked backwards, carefully, out of the room. He was shaking all over, and his heart was pounding. Jason went to the doorway and pointed outside. His words were firm. "Kate, get out. Don't ever come back. Ever."

"But…but…" She was dressing in a hurry.

"Don't let me see you again."

He looked back at the arrow in the door; just a fraction of a second, and it would have gone right through him. "For God's sake, what are you thinking?" He didn't wait for her to answer. Jason went into the living room and waited for her to dress. He was thinking of calling the police. He pulled out his cell phone and paced back and forth wondering if he should.

Jason still could hardly believe what she had done. Somehow, she had got a key; maybe she always had it. She had got in and took his bow off the wall and waited, just like a hunter. He knew she had been stalking him. Now, she was hunting him.

She finally came out of the bedroom, brushing her hair. It was odd; you would have thought they just made love. She smiled. He grabbed her by the arm. "Where is it?"

"What, you're hurting me?"

He looked at her arm and wrist. There were scratches all the way down to her elbow. "The key."

"I don't know…."

Jason pulled her close and dug his hand down in her pocket and pulled it out. He thought seriously about holding her there until the police came, but all he really wanted was just never to see her again. "If I ever see you back here, I'm filing charges. You hear?"

"I'm coming backwards, and tomorrow I'm gone. I'm with Eggman."

He stepped back and studied her face. She had this strange expression. Totally weird. It freaked him out. She was making peculiar sounds in her throat and talking gibberish.

"What?"

She scrunched her eyebrows together. "You heard me. It's the season." Her expression changed again, instantly. She smiled. "Tis the season to be Molly. Fal a al a la la."

He knew then at that moment she was crazy. Gone. "Katie, you need help. You need help bad."

Just like that, she seemed to snap out of it. She blinked her eyes and stared at him as if waking up. It was like the circuit in her mind was switching back and forth. Positive/negative. Hot/Cold. "Jason, you're so cruel to me. It was an accident, okay? I was just playing. It was stupid I know but…"

He didn't want to hear it. He just wanted her gone. He took her to the front door and shoved her outside. He didn't really expect her to leave, but she did. He waited till he saw her walk across the parking lot and then locked the door. He didn't ever want to talk to her again. He just wanted her out of his life. Gone. He was so totally done with her. This was it.

Jason dialed his phone and waited.

"Hello."

"You'll never believe what just happened. Kat just tried to kill me."

"What!"

"Yeah, stay put, I'm coming over."

"Did you call the police?"

"I haven't decided."

"Jason, you nut. Call them!"

He told her to lock her door, don't answer it for anyone, and that he'd be there. Within fifteen minutes, he was at her apartment. They hugged as soon as he came in, and for the next several hours, she did everything she could to convince him to file charges. She called her dad, and Jason explained to him what happened. He got off the phone.

"What did he say?"

"I don't have witnesses. No one saw her key my truck. I can't say for sure it was her in the theater, so I have no proof of stalking."

"What about the bow? Breaking into your place? Come on."

He shook his head. "I can't honestly remember whether I gave her a key or not. I dunno. He said it would be hard to prove she tried to kill me. The question he kept asking me was if she threatened me? She never said that. She said it was an accident."

"My dad said that?" She was dismayed.

"Yeah, he told me to take pictures, always have a recorder or a camera. If I saw her following me, I should video her and take it to the police."

Joy still tried to get him to file charges to get a restraining order. He didn't want to. There were only a few more days left at school, and then he thought she'd be gone. "I bet she'll go back home now, graduate at UCA."

Joy disagreed. "I don't think so, Jason." Joy lowered her glasses as to emphasize her point. "She is not going to let you go."

"She has no choice."

"She's not in her right mind."

Jason didn't want to talk about it anymore. He reached down in his backpack and pulled out his books. She took the hint and nestled up next to him on the couch where they both studied for exams the next day. Later, she fixed some popcorn, watched some TV, and then both fell asleep on the couch. It was the first time he slept over. It felt good. It felt good for both of them. Joy had a hard time concentrating on her test the next day. She didn't know how Jason did. She didn't know if he was able to clear his mind enough to pass his tests or if he struggled like she did? It was a strange mixture of feelings, feelings she had never had in her entire life. Joy knew that she was now in love. Head over heels as they say, but she was also experiencing another emotion, fear. She was scared to death, not for herself, but for Jason.

Joy was a psychology major, and she knew much better than he what he was dealing with. She had read the stories of textbook cases. Katherine was appearing to be all that and more. It scared her. People with her condition go off the edge and never come back. They enter a dark unforeseen world and most never return, but even Joy had no idea just how far she was gone. No one would until it was too late. Joy was determined that she would not leave Jason alone. He was way too naive, way too trusting. He could easily be lured into a trap. There were but a few more days of tests, and they would be heading home for Christmas break. Then she thought they might breathe easier, and all this might be behind them.

Wrong.

Chapter Fifteen

Calvin finished his last test the next day and told his good buddy that he'd see him "next year." He suggested he call the apartment manager and have the locks changed. Jason promised him he would and then watched as Calvin drove off with his Jeep packed to the brim with camping gear. The weather had turned miserable and cold. Jason wondered if he was really going camping; he knew he sure wasn't. Not in that kind of weather. The bright spot in his day was thinking about Joy.

He locked the door to their apartment and started doing the laundry, and cleaning up. He was going back over to her place to do some more study. He turned on the news and caught the weather; a cold wintery blast was expected for the next two days and then clear with rising temperatures. Great, maybe he and Joy could ride her horses when they got home. After doing dishes and tossing a load in the dryer, Jason jumped in his truck and headed over to Joy's place. They had talked briefly on the phone earlier, and she suggested (hinted) he might stay the night. Jason wanted to, but he had reservations, major ones. He really didn't want to enrage Kat any more than she already was. His plans were to simply study and then leave.

She had a great meal cooked for him when he got there that evening. They both tried to talk about things other than Kat, but the conversation kept making circles back to the one subject that neither could avoid. Joy wasn't stupid; she knew that Jason was struggling emotionally with the breakup. He still had feelings for "Katie" and was trying to rationalize in his mind that this was the girl he fell in love with back in high school. The reality that she wasn't the same person was obviously painful. His pain was evident; it was like he was soaked in it. She could see the hurt in his eyes, and his whole expression appeared to be dipped in denial. He thought the entire ordeal would blow over. Katherine would go back home and then move on with her life. Joy believed differently, but there was no point in pushing the subject. Instead, she tried as much as possible to divert their conversation away from Katherine, but Jason seemed somewhat lost in thought. He was a bit aloof, not like himself at all. After the meal, they washed dishes together and then sat down to go over preparations for tests the next day. He had a test in statistics, and she had one in juvenile behavior disorders. After about five minutes of quizzing Jason, Joy closed the book.

"You know what I think? I think you need to give your mind a rest. You just have too much going on."

Jason couldn't think at all. He missed every question she asked, every equation. Normally, Jason would have breezed through them. But not that night. If he didn't clear his mind, there was a good chance he would flunk the final. She picked up the remote; she flicked through a dozen channels. The Office was on. "Why don't we just relax? You'll nail it tomorrow."

They watched several reruns, and she thought he would fall asleep on the couch again, but he didn't. He was uncomfortably restless. All evening, he was on edge, and finally about 11:00, he said he had to go.

"Why? It's raining. Why don't you just get a good night sleep on the couch, and I'll fix you breakfast in the morning?" After several minutes of pleading, she saw that it was no use. He grabbed his coat and went to the door. Jason pulled back the curtains to her upstairs apartment and looked out. He didn't see anything. The coast looked clear.

She walked over to him by the door, and he pulled her close. He didn't say anything. He bent his head down to her with his nose resting on her forehead. His voice was soft. It was deep. "Just give me one more day, and I'll be fine. Let me just get this behind me."

"I understand. I do, but you don't have to go through this alone."

Jason looked at the old lock on the door. It wasn't the best, but she did have a chain. "If anybody comes to this door that you don't know real well, don't open it, okay? I'll see you tomorrow night after I finish my test."

"You think she might come here?"

"Maybe. Let's not take chances."

Joy watched as he went downstairs and splashed across the parking lot to his truck and drove off. She latched the door securely and then waited for his text. About fifteen minutes later, she got it. It simply said "Home safe. All clear. Night." Though she was uncomfortable about the whole situation, she managed to nod off somewhere after midnight, and the next day, she was done with her test about noon and texted him afterwards to come over when he finished. He texted her back when he finished his test. "Gotta pack some more. I'll see you about six, will that work?"

"Yes."

Joy cleaned up her place as well. She paid her bills on line and then started cooking. She was torn. There was a part of her that warned her to be cautious, just keep it all at arm's length. Don't go any further, but her heart said otherwise. She realized she had been in love with Jason for a long time. There were lots of guys but only one Jason. Joy knew that she wasn't the only one that believed that way. Katherine felt the same. She wouldn't let him go easily.

Sometime after six, there was a knock on the door. She went to the door and peeped through the peephole. It was Jason. Joy quickly unlocked the door. His coat was dripping from the rain, and he hung it on the coat rack as soon as he came in. She stared in his eyes. He looked in hers. Jason didn't say anything, and then he took her by the arm and pulled her to him close. He flicked off her hallway light and then kissed her. Joy was somewhat surprised. Her hands clutched his arms. They kissed for a long time, and his hand fumbled with the lock behind them on the door until he locked it.

Finally, she took him into the kitchen where a warm pot of homemade chili simmered on the stove. It hit the spot, and for the first time in a while, Jason actually seemed relaxed. He said he didn't ace the test, but he "pulled it out." He was relieved. It hadn't been the easiest semester for him. The entire semester had turned into a disaster, but it was over. The two of them talked and joked. "I know you're a city boy, but maybe I can still teach you to ride."

Jason rebuffed the notion of being "city", but then he smiled and leaned her back against the armrest of the couch, "But I will let you teach me all you want."

"Really?"

"Yeah, I'm ready."

She sighed. Joy was a bit tentative. "I hope this is not a rebound Jason."

"No. I probably should have been with you all along." He paused and looked at his phone. Something was still bothering him, but Joy was absolutely sure he was going to spend the night. She had even washed the sheets and had them folded down, but sometime after ten o'clock, he surprised her. Jason leaned up and took a sip from his water. "Hey, I have to go."

Joy couldn't believe it. It had been their first really relaxing evening together, and suddenly he was going. "What? Why? You can stay."

"I know, but I think I better be cautious. It is just one more night. I'll see you tomorrow, and we can drive down together. I'll follow you."

Joy wasn't happy with the idea of him leaving. She obviously wanted him to stay; nevertheless, she relented, though reluctantly. He went to do the door and unlocked it.

"Wait." She pulled the curtains to the side and looked out. It was a rainy drizzling mess. The bitter cold swept into the apartment when he opened the door, and she heard the sound of the rain splashing out the gutters downstairs. "Geez", she said, "Sure you want to go? Can't I at least make you a cup of coffee before you leave?"

She was trying one last time to coax him into staying, but

Jason wasn't hearing it. He shrugged off the suggestion with a smile, "Nah, I'm fine."

"Okay then, lemme grab my coat."

"Hey, it's cool." He opened the door wider and stared down at the parking lot, "I'm okay. You stay dry. It's a mess tonight."

Joy wouldn't hear it. She grabbed her coat and rushed out the door behind him taking his hand. They trotted down the stairs together and started across the parking lot to his truck. Joy heard the sound of an engine rev and turned around to see a car roaring from the shadows of the big sycamores. It was heading straight for them with its headlights on full beam blinding both of them in the glare of its lights. Instantly, she was shoved out of its path. Joy fell stumbling, trying to regain her balance landing on her hands and knees as the car raced for them.

She turned around and caught just a glimpse as the red Charger shot by. It happened so quickly. Jason didn't make it.

The force literally knocked him in the air, and he came crashing down on the hood. The car roared across the lot and skidded to a halt. She watched it idling in the rain. She struggled to her feet watching as the steam lifted from the car. She could hear the sound of its windshield wipers swishing. Joy could see a driver but not the face; it was too dark. Jason was lying face down on the hood looking through the glass. The engine revved again, and then again. Jason could see her face in the glow of the lights. It was Kat. She heard him call her name. Joy stumbled across the lot toward them with her hands and knees bleeding. She could hear him groaning and squirming on the hood. His legs were shattered, and his head was bleeding.

Joy let out a long scream. "Jason!" He looked through the windshield at Kat. He could see something dripping from her hands clutched to the steering wheel. It was hard to see through the glare that was cast from the lights of the building, but he saw something bright and shiny dripping from her fingers. It looked like paint. Red and black paint.

Jason grabbed the edge of the hood and tried to pull himself closer. He looked into her cold eyes, trance like, and gazing at him. Joy hobbled closer to the car still screaming. Just then the car revved again, and Kat shifted it in reverse. The wheels started spinning in the wet pavement as she roared all the way backwards across the lot. Jason fell off the hood and hit the ground, and when he did, the car screeched to another stop. The engine revved again, and they could hear her grinding the gears, shifting back into drive. Jason was lying on his back, and he turned over to his stomach and tried to crawl away, but it was too late. Joy screamed as the car roared across the lot grinding him into the pavement. It then dragged him some thirty or forty feet until it came to a jolting halt. Jason was underneath it pinned. She could see his outstretched hands, and then she heard the tenants rushing out of the complex. "She's killing him for God's sake! HELP!"

They saw the red car idling down in the parking lot. It looked like some beastly metallic fire breathing dragon, the way steam rose from the top of the hood. The crowd still could not see him trapped underneath the frame of the car. Several tenants rushed down to help Joy when suddenly Kat shifted into reverse. She began swerving at a high speed backwards across the pavement trying to dislodge him. Finally he rolled out. It was horrible. Jason looked like a mass of crumbled bones lying in the street. His head was already smashed. His body laid there lifeless. They saw his shoe lying in the middle of the lot. It lay in a puddle of water. His foot was still in it. Dozens of people in the complex were frantically calling 911 from their phones. They could do nothing. They all watched in horror as the car continued to rev its engine from the dark shadows below. Its lights shined across the wet pavement. He was her wounded prey. He laid there helpless with his face down on the asphalt, glistening in a pool of shimmering water and blood. Joy tried to run for him but fell. Kat was through waiting. The game was over. She shifted back into drive. The Charger raced across the pavement. Joy could do nothing but scream and watch. The other tenants ran out, but anyone who got in her way would be run over as well, and then finally blue lights came roaring into the entrance to the parking lot. Two cars drove around Jason and came to a stop right in front of her. They blocked her, and the officers jumped out.

Veterans have worked all their life and never seen anything as gruesome as this. In the middle of the lot lay Jason. His chest was crushed; his arms and legs too. His face was unrecognizable, so much that you could hardly tell it was a face. It looked like someone had stuffed his clothes with raw meat and laid him in the street. The officers walked toward the car with guns drawn and gave orders to get out and lie face down on the ground. Kat did not. She just sat in the car.

"Get out, now!"

She still didn't. Then, they heard the engine turn off, and they saw her window coming down. The clink of her keys hit the ground. Joy ran for Jason, and the cops quickly circled her car. To their surprise, they could see a beautiful blonde sitting very still in the front seat. Three officers approached the car with their guns drawn, and one of them reached for the driver's door and flung it open. "Get out!"

She hardly moved. It was like she was in a trance. She sat there naked, completely. Not a stitch of clothing on her, just sandals. Next to her in the seat was a canvas. It was smeared with black and silver oils like a Monet, and paints were dripping down across her arms and legs. Her hands were still clutching the wheel, and they both dripped in red. In the seat next to her was a can of paint and in her lap was her phone. The young officer was completely stunned; he had never seen anything so macabre in his whole life. His hands shook as he held out his gun, and another officer rushed to the other side and opened the passenger door. An eerie smile curled up her lips. Kat turned her head toward the young cop. "You like?"

"Wha..wa.what?"

"My impression…of Jason."

There he lay in the street. The black asphalt glistened in a reflecting pool of rain just like she had painted on her canvas. Red streams of diluted blood mixed with the silver shining lights. The first officer took her by the arm and pulled her out of the car where they put cuffs on her. A stunned crowd came together to watch as the tall naked woman was pressed against the police car. The blue lights flickered, catching rain drops in midair like a strobe. Finally, they put a blanket around her, then escorted her across the lot, and placed her into the back of a patrol car and then quickly drove away.

Joy never got one last look at Kat. She never looked up even as she was taken away. Joy knelt beside Jason and squeezed his hand, knowing he would never make it. Amazingly, she still felt a faint pulse in his wrist. His fingers twitched. Somehow, his heart was still beating. His face, or what remained of it, was shattered. Both his eye sockets were caved in; bones protruded through his cheeks. Joy wept on her knees in the rain and held his hand until the last of life vanished from him. There were no good-byes, no more long kisses. He was gone.

His nightmare was over.

The news of the gruesome murder immediately sent shock waves through the community. Veteran reporters struggled to describe the carnage. Everyone agreed this wasn't the average story; it seemed especially appalling that it happened just before Christmas break. Eventually the story began to fade over the next few months but revived again some nine months later during the trial which was a relatively short time by all accounts considering the delays in today's legal system. Her defense pleaded not guilty by reason of insanity. That was to be expected. She had told the officers that arrested her that evening that her "friend" had told her to do it. They of course checked all her references; there were no texts on her phone, at least not from her mysterious "friend." When they retrieved her lap top, they found no emails either. There was no Eggman, no Johnny. There was no Sticks from Lipsmackin'.

Most schizophrenics say they hear voices. Katherine was quite shocked when they told her there were no texts from "friend" in her inbox. There were plenty though that she had sent, thousands. Same with her emails. No record existed at all in her inbox. Kat, (Katherine) even accused the police of lying, of a cover-up. She claimed that the texts were there; "someone deleted them." The investigators attempted to verify all the things she claimed during her initial interrogation. They even checked on her loan. It was never paid off. In fact, it had increased due to the mounting interest. They checked her grades as well. She had all F's except for art where she did get an A. Nearly all her professors said they hadn't seen her since about the first month of school. Some students you might forget but not her. They all remembered the tall beautiful blonde with an infectious smile that just dropped out, quit coming.

The biggest problem for her defense is that to meet the legal definition of insanity she could not know that she was committing the crime or that it was wrong when in the commission of it. Katherine confessed immediately to it. By all accounts, including her own, she knew exactly what she was doing. They went over this many times to clarify her knowledge of the offense. The transcript taken the night of the murder clearly proved this point.

"So, you knew you were running over him?"

"Yes."

"You intended on killing him, is that correct?"

"Yes." The report noted that her expression was flat.

"Did you know this was wrong? It was a crime?"

"I knew alright, but he cheated on me. That's what is wrong. My friend told me to do it, and so I did."

"What did your friend say?"

"Jason had to die".

"You feel no guilt about that?"

"Should I?"

Three different psychiatrists interviewed her prior to her trial. All three agreed; she was a classic schizophrenic. Nevertheless, she knew she was committing a crime when she did it. That testimony under the definition of the law made her guilty.

In an attempt to sway the jury, dozens of witnesses were called by the defense. K.J. even appeared and gave his shocking testimony which if nothing else answered a lot of questions about him. Now, everyone at the University knew the true story. K.J. was a reluctant witness; he broke down on several occasions as he recalled how he betrayed his best friend. All during his testimony, Katherine never looked up. It was that way all during trial. She was almost completely detached from the proceeding. Most the time, she doodled on paper or just stared off into blank space. Never once did she look at Kris. It was like in her mind he wasn't even there.

Joy was next, to testify after Kris, and her story of the events was most compelling. She was of course the prosecution's main eyewitness to the murder. The courtroom was packed as she solemnly recalled the night in graphic and precise detail. The cops who arrived on the scene also described vividly for the jury the details of violence. The defense did not contest anything she said, and Kat never once looked in her direction. She did on a few occasions slump her head down, especially when Joy described the last few moments of Jason's life. Three cops took the stand after her, and then two tenants gave collaborating statements of their own. The defense sat quietly at the table during all their testimony and simply offered "no questions your honor" as a rebuttal when they were done.

One of the more perplexing and disturbing testimonies during the trial came when the defense called the receptionist at the clinic where Katherine had left in hysterics. Her story was quite different than the one Katherine had described to interrogators after her arrest. Mrs. Peterson said she would never forget the tall beautiful blonde who arrived on the elevator on an otherwise peaceful afternoon. According to her, the staff heard screams even before the elevator doors opened. She and everyone on the third floor were horrified when the elevator stopped on their floor. A scantily dressed girl was screaming at the top of her lungs and beating on the walls of the elevator with her fists. The court sat in stunned silence as she described the episode.

The defense asked, "Did anyone rush to help her?"

"We were all too scared. She was throwing herself up in the air and smashing to the ground. It was like she was a puppet on a string, like she had no control over her body."

"And you didn't try to help?"

"I called security. It is what we are supposed to do when we have a psychotic episode or drug overdose."

"Tell us then what happened."

"The doors finally closed, and we heard her screaming all the way down to the ground floor. By the time security got there, she was gone."

The defense was careful in asking the next question. "How many years have you worked in the clinic, Mrs. Peterson?"

"Going on twelve."

"In all the years you have been there, have you ever seen anything like this in your tenure?"

"Never this dramatic. I've never personally witnessed anyone so traumatized."

"Thank you."

Perhaps, the most dramatic moment in the trial though was when Professor Hensley was called to testify. The prosecution repeatedly objected, but the judge consistently overruled. The prosecution said he was not an authority on mental behavior and should be excluded from giving his opinion on her state of mind. The judge obviously thought different. When asked by her defense what he thought of Katherine, he said that she was "brilliant." The most gifted student he has had in twenty-four years.

"What do her paintings tell you?"

"Objection."

"Overruled."

The professor continued. "She is a superb talent but obviously disturbed. Most of the great ones were, to some degree."

"Objection."

"Overruled."

The defense continued. "What do you mean?"

"Their art is their voice. It is the voice inside they wish to share. Dali, Picasso, Van Gogh used paintings to express not just what they were seeing, but also hearing. Some artists hear voices of darkness; other artists hear voices of light. Michelangelo was a visionary of light, and so you might say was Kincaid. He even called himself that."

The defense continued, "So, there is darkness and light.

What about the middle, what would you call that?"

"Crap." The gallery laughed, even the Judge.

"Would you say from her work that she was insane?"

"Objection!"

"Overruled. He has a right to an opinion."

Professor Hensley looked over at his former student who scribbled quietly on a piece of paper. He didn't know if she was even aware he was there. The jury could tell he didn't want to answer the question. The defense asked him again. The professor sighed, "Yes, in my opinion, based on what her art revealed and knowing the circumstances for why we are here, I would have to say she is insane."

"Thank you. The defense rests."

The jury deliberated for two days. By all accounts, it was a very troubling decision. Later, it was revealed by polling the jurors that they all felt Katherine was insane; yet, she obviously knew what she was doing. What was worse is that she had no regret. She was deemed a threat to society. When they returned to the court room, their faces were glum. Katherine was sentenced to thirty years for first degree murder. Her mother fainted during the reading of the verdict and had to be carried out. The judge then ruled after considerable consultation with both the defense and the prosecution that she would not go directly to prison but would be sent to the State Psychiatric Hospital in Little Rock where she would continue to be evaluated and treated until further notice. He knew that such a woman in her state of mind should not be in the general prison population.

When it was all over, Katherine rose from the table with her defense team. Sitting almost directly behind her was Joy. Katherine stopped. It was probably the oddest moment of the whole trial. Joy was weeping. Her head was down. She was sitting next to her parents and brother. On the other side of the room was Jason's family. Katherine turned her head toward Joy. They made eye contact for the first time, and in a voice as meek and quiet as a mouse, Katherine looked at Joy and said, "I'm sorry."

It was the only words she said during the whole trial. It

was over. Katherine would not be eligible for parole for at least fifteen years. The soonest she could get out unless she was pardoned would be in 2027. She would be thirty-six. If she stayed until her sentenced was complete, she would be fifty-one by the time she would walk free again.

Three weeks after her trial ended, the County conducted its annual police auction and sale. It is not much of a fundraiser, but it helps. All the evidence that had been confiscated in the last year is sold. It usually comprises of some cars, computers, jewelry, even cell phones. Her phone was one of the first items sold. It was a steal at a "buck twenty-five". Ironically, the purchaser was a police officer. He was divorced and lived in a two story home just a block or so off Wilson Park. He bought it for his teenage son who had been after him for two years to get one. Even though he was familiar with the case, he didn't realize who it belonged to. Perhaps, he should have reconsidered.

Later that night, when he was asleep and his son was in the room down the hall, the phone began to buzz. The officer never heard it. It buzzed and then buzzed again. The boy woke up and saw it on his desk. The light was on. He checked it. There was a text.

He rubbed his eyes and looked at the message on the screen.

"Hello."

The boy was confused. He looked at it again, rubbing the sleep out of his eyes. He sat alone in his dark room and stared at the letters glowing on his phone. He texted back, "Who r u?"

He waited for a response; a moment later it came.

"friend."

THE END

The Afterword to Text'd

It has been estimated by various accounts that approximately 2.2 million Americans suffer from schizophrenia or multiple personality disorders. Of the 600,000 homeless in America, roughly one third suffer from schizophrenia. Although there has been an enormous amount of research done on the subject, we still know very little about the illness. What we do know is that in fifty percent of the documented cases of schizophrenia there is a history of drug abuse. Not so with Katherine, she never engaged in any drug use and very little alcohol consumption. As far as we know.

Without a clear understanding of what schizophrenia actually is, I do question whether it is possible to find a cure for an illness when we do not know what causes it? Approximately one in a hundred people are believed to suffer from one form of schizophrenia or another. The medical community claims that 90% of those who suffer can gain back relatively productive lives if treated. That's the good news. For the 10% that are not treatable, it is a living nightmare. One they can't escape.

In writing *Text'd*, I became fascinated by the subject. There are many like Katherine whose lives are robbed, taken from them. Forever lost. They ultimately spend years of their lives in asylums or basically live like vagabonds in the streets. Many become victims of a world that discards them. Even amongst the mentally ill, they are the outcast of outcast.

Since we are obviously still searching for answers, I

wonder if there are perhaps other plausible explanations. What if the voices they hear are not imaginary? Is that possible? What if the voices they hear are real? Is the subject worth considering?

I, for one, believe that it is. We may not be as smart as what we think we are. It is possible we might have rushed to preconceived conclusions. Never a good thing in science. It has happened before, many times in the pursuit of knowledge; ergo I submit that we consider all options until we know for sure. Until science or medicine can claim a "breakthrough," I think it unwise to discount all possible scenarios from the equation.

The question I ask is this, if the voices were real (meaning that the victims do hear them), whose voices are they? The answer, I believe, would have to be demons. You may have other ideas, but schizophrenia, at least the symptoms of it, are nothing new in society. We need not just consult biblical accounts, but there are hundreds if not thousands of cases in modern society of what is considered to be demonic possession. In fact, several famous murderers including the notorious Son of Sam claimed to hear voices. These voices told them to commit crimes, and yet, some of these people live relatively normal lives today. The voices are now gone, and the cure was not the result of psychiatry. The cure has been spiritual.

Many other sufferers we do know were helped immensely by the psychiatric community. We do know that, and I am not discounting some of the great strides that have been made. Nevertheless, there are still hundreds of thousands for which no cure has been found. We owe it to them to consider all options. Or, would you agree?

So, the next time you hear of someone with multiple personality disorders or schizophrenia, don't be so quick to rush to judge what torments them. They really may be no different than you or me. They may have simply, for some unknown reason, been text'd.

Metal Pets

bright eyed metallic beast
  with iron grill front teeth
  roam wild, and roar
  between rows of sedated homes
  and frolic in suburban haze
  through asphalt fields of neon lights.
  I watched the chase of
  swivel painted mannequin heads
  encased in glass, displayed
  like ornaments
  in a mating ritual
  of compact steel
  and groomed metal pets.
But to me
  they are not merely pets, but space machines
  a sojourn ship in which to dream
  atop mountain roads
  that spiral
    on star filled nights.

Aurora?

Is it the land that contains the sea
or the sea which shapes the land?
Is it night that measures the length of day
or does the day determine the length of night?
Is it evil which illustrates to us what is good
or does good describe for us what evil is?
What if there was one without the other?
What would our world look like?
Would we appreciate anything?
Without hot could we know what is cold?
Without our youth would we know what is old?
Without wrong would we know what is right?
Without death could we appreciate life?
So, if your day has turned dark as night
I assure you that there will be light,
For as time is the cruel master of fate
we can take comfort in knowing
that on a cross
love became the master over hate,
And though we may not see it
-in the moment-
and though we are impatient
and seldom wait
all things in the Universe are perfect.

In the Homes of Hidden Manor and Aspiring Heights

Down a long trimmed meandering hedge
White faced columned homes are lined
These are the homes of paradise
Where the quiet streets of Hidden Manor lies
Here suburbia is suited best
With tattered pasts locked neatly away
In attic closets and cedar lined chests.

In Hidden Manor and Aspiring Heights
The Country Club serves graciously
Ice cold members and quests
Refreshing pitchers of vodka lemonade
Pairs of sunglasses polish awkward introductions
While stapled chins and nodding heads
Are clamped together to congregate

Then, after lunch, in the "ladies room"
(ever so politely taking turns)
The anorexic debutantes regurgitate
Their neurotic mothers begin to drink
Every morning after their fathers leave
To his appointments and various affairs
And long line of office flings

But in the homes of hidden manner
Such minor resentments are usually ignored
    Shhhh!
For psychiatrist they are played, until
Defiance knocks abruptly at the door
Young rich white girls (you see) like bad boys

KNOCK! KNOCK! DING DONG! "ANYbody
home?"
Their drunken mothers stagger sideways
Across their marbled foyer floors
"Hello, Mamma… (ain't she sweet) I'M A WHORE!"

  Behind closed drapes the mother peeps
Into mobile phones the father scream
Across dining room tables accusations slam
And blame is passed from hand to hand
Then, indiscretions are finally arranged
Reputations are sometimes saved
In plastic bags "mistakes" are placed

  Ah, so *these* are the homes of paradise
Where quiet streets and hidden manner lies
And where pasts are locked neatly away
In attic closets and cedar lined chests

The Bloodsuckers

In the clutching of madmen
    Past the outer limits of sanity
    Children are torn from limb to limb
    And are clinched between their teeth.
Run! Lock your doors kids!
    Roll your windows up tight
    Keep driving lady!
    Lock down your passenger side.
Do you know who they are?
    Look into their eyes
    They are back from the dead
    They are the living lies
Run, before they get you
    They will feed off you and suck you dry
    They aren't human lady
    They aren't like you or I.
Keep on driving! Get the hell out of town!
    Don't slow up, don't turn back around
    When they try to stop you on the road
    Go ahead and run them down.
They won't feel hurt
    They don't know pain
    Hell, they're just crooked politicians
    They are dead already anyway.

THE YOMEN

Chapter One

Yomen: A backwoods colloquialism meaning any life threatening unforeseen danger, either by nature, man, or an act of God, without premonition or warning.

Nobody ever expects something like this to happen on such a beautiful day. The weather couldn't have been more perfect. On June the 16th, five days after the notorious flood, Tom Johnson kissed his wife Sara good-bye. The trek into town was a short twelve mile trip from their home in Story where they had a few cabins in the hills that backed up to the national forest.

Every Wednesday, for as long as anyone could remember, Tom Johnson took in the checks and cash from the cabin rentals. No one knew why he did it on Wednesday; he just did. He was set in his ways like most men in their seventies are. The girls at the bank knew to expect him around 10:30, that's when he showed up in his coveralls and a mile-wide smile. He was always good for a joke or two and wasn't shy about giving compliments either. He was just a friendly older man that was still in love with his wife of 47 years.

Business had been kinda slow that summer, and the deposits weren't quite as large. People weren't traveling like they once did, and speculation was that the gas prices were going to make ends tight throughout the tourist season. Nevertheless, summer time was just beginning. Schools had let out, and he figured it wouldn't be long before he could take the vacancy sign down at by the road. They'd be full up till Labor Day, or at least that is how it had been in years past. Then,

131

there was always a post summer lull, but that didn't last long, and then it was hunting season and they were booked again.

Sara looked at her watch; it was about ten o'clock when Tom's old Dodge truck bounced down the rocky drive through a thicket of trees onto the highway. She heard him shifting the gears as he turned on to the newly paved blacktop heading into town. She was hoping he wouldn't forget again to bring her back an iron from the Dollar General Store. Her old Hamilton Beach had finally hit the skids after twenty years of daily use, and his flannel shirts were looking a little wrinkled. She had been embarrassed that previous Sunday when a deacon's wife commented that he looked like he "had just rolled out of bed."

Tom was beginning to get a little bit forgetful and at times was a little careless too. He didn't have a cell phone so she knew she couldn't call and remind him, but if he forgot again, she figured he'd just have to go to church wrinkled one more time. Sara would have driven to town herself to get the iron except she didn't drive unless it was absolutely necessary. After he was gone, she went back to her tomato chopping, she was fixing up her famous salsa for the church gathering that night at the Story Church of Christ where they had been members since she was a kid. [But little did she know that when she saw him get in his truck and wave, going down the drive that would be the last time she'd see her husband alive.]

Wednesday, you see, there is just not a lot of traffic on Highway 27 going into Mount Ida. Now, when you get down to where the bridge crosses Lake Ouachita you start seeing folks, but not up by Story. Around the lake, there are ski boats and watercraft galore whipping in and out of coves. The campgrounds there pretty much stay full, and along certain parts, there are fishermen camping by the shore.

But on that Wednesday morning, no one remembered seeing Tom Johnson at all, at least not going into town. It was like he just disappeared. Gone. Vanished. And it didn't take long for the town to know that something was up because 10:30 came and went. 12:00, he still wasn't there, and by sometime after lunch, Debbie at the bank called Sara to see if everything was alright. Of course, it wasn't.

They say some mistakes you only have to make once. Mr. Johnson hadn't a need or worry, his entire life. He was an incredible trusting man even to it being a fault. He would help anyone, anytime just for the asking. He was a trusting soul. Tom was known to give a man a job even when he had to invent things to be done. He had put total strangers up at his cabin whenever there was a need. When a family lost their home in Montgomery County due to a fire, he was generally the first person that was called. He let many families stay at his cabin till they could get their feet back on the ground. One family with five children stayed at a cabin right through the middle of tourist season. Never paid him a dime, and he sure never asked. That's just the type of man Tom Johnson was; so when he saw two men standing on the side of the road by a truck with the hood up, he didn't hesitate to stop.

Now, any other time, on any other day, it would have not been a problem. [But like I said, all it takes is just one time.] Go your entire life and then make one mistake, and you can dearly pay. Tom didn't know what he had stumbled across until it was too late. Seems like their only problem was they had run out of gas, and it was their good fortune that Tom always kept a two gallon jug in his truck. Somewhere in their conversation, he must have mentioned that he owned some cabins and was taking the deposit to the bank. That bit of information cost him his life. They were on the run from Oklahoma and were running short on cash. The four hundred dollars he had in the deposit bag was something they needed, and these weren't the type of men that were prone to negotiations.

By the time Tom suspected trouble, it was too late. They took his gun that he haphazardly kept in a holster that lay on his seat. Before he knew it, he was in the floorboard of his own truck with his hands tied behind his back. Then, they turned off the highway down a forest service road that went for miles deep into the woods. No one saw the actual abduction. It must have happened quick. And for the two men on the run, Tom Johnson happened along at just the right time. They got over four hundred bucks in cash and a thirty-eight; albeit, it did have a partially broken handle grip. It still was a gun.

Now, I am not going to get too graphic here. Graphics will come later. What we do know is this, the younger man drove Tom's truck, and the older one followed in their Chevy. They drove 2.9 miles off the highway until they came to a dead end on an old forest service road. It wasn't much more than a logging trail where they stopped. Tom was beaten profusely by the younger man, and then he was untied and told to run. Tom was in his seventies so he was too weak to go far. Still, he managed somehow to get about two hundred yards away from the truck before he collapsed against an old white oak tree and sat there panting like a coon dog after a long chase. He could see his attackers following after him through the woods, and try as he may, old Tom just could not get up and run anymore.

Both the men slid down a ravine to where Tom was, and the younger one that bore several tattoos and had short cropped hair was laughing. The forensics told part of the story, but the rest was videoed on a cell phone which would eventually end up in the hands of the police. Poor Tom was videotaped begging for his life. He told them repeatedly that they didn't have to kill him. They could take his truck and go.

The young one just laughed. It was a game. He liked to see the old man beg. He smiled, "Sorry, no witnesses' gramps."

Tom pleaded with them to take his truck. He wouldn't even report it.

He laughed again, "That ole piece of crap. You tryin' to insult me?"

The bigger one mumbled in a nearly inaudible gravel, "Come on dude, let's get this over with. Let's just shoot him?"

"How many bullets have we got? Did you find any more shells in his truck?"

"Nope, all we've got are these six."

"Better not waste them." He smashed his fist into his palm, "There is another way to do this."

"No, please," Tom begged his abductors, "You don't have to, I swear. I'm no threat to you."

The young one with cream white skin looked at his partner, "You want some of this?"

"Nah, I got the last one. Gotta keep the score even. Your

turn."

Blood was already pouring down the gashes around Tom's eyes that he had sustained from the initial beating. His famous bright smile was crumpled into a frown that hung down to his chin. His eyes stared petrified into the camera lens. He knew it was useless. The young one grinned and walked over to Tom and pulled him up with one hand and leaned him against the tree. Old Mr. Johnson turned to the older guy, the big one with the beard, and asked if he would just shoot him. He pleaded with them to use the gun and get it over with.

The young one condescendingly patted Tom on the cheek and smiled, "Don't worry ole man. I'll make sure I don't knockout anymore of your teeth." Tom just stared into his face. He looked at the snarl that curled along the edge of his attackers lips. He watched him as he pulled back his fist, and then the video went blank.

In another twenty minutes, they were wiping down the truck, removing all the finger prints. They took branches and raked across the ground to cover up any evidence. Next, they drove his truck off and turned down another logging road, driving it as far as it would go and then ditched it. Then, the two men covered up Tom's truck with broken tree branches and left.

It was a little after 11:30 when they drove back onto the highway and headed to town for some gas. And little did the town know or suspect that there were murderers in the midst, and the terror had just begun.

Chapter Two

(2 Days Later)

It was going to be the perfect vacation. The Roberts' family certainly talked about it long enough. Clint and his daughter Faith were going to spend two weeks at their cabin far away from the city in the Ouachita Mountains. Faith's best friend, Angelina, was flying in from New York, and in a few hours, they were meeting her at the airport.

Clint, the prodigious packer, had already loaded up the truck early that morning. He had taken his customary one mile jog through the neighborhood doing his "howdy" wave to all the dog walkers and was back at the house eating breakfast when Faith, his long legged daughter, came bouncing downstairs.

He didn't say anything.

Clint nibbled on a bagel while skimming over the headlines of the paper where he *used* to work. The BP oil spill was getting worse; economists were claiming the recession was "technically over"; a search was on for a man still missing in Montgomery County; and of course, there was another terrorist attack overseas. Faith raised her eyebrow and studied her father. She walked right by him and went to the frig where she fumbled around for the milk and then checked the date.

"A hum, *good* morning." There was a ring in her voice.

"Morning."

Her mouth squished to the side, "Don't tell me; it's Mr. Grumpy again?"

He stood up and tossed the paper in the trash container. "It's nonsense. Whadda they mean, we're out of a recession? That is just crap."

Faith poured herself a tall glass of milk. "Well, did you look for a job in this morning's paper? See anything?" She knew the answer.

"Didn't bother. They aren't hiring fifty year old ex-journalist."

"Oh well, that's the team spirit. You know like you are always telling *me*. Remember?"

Clint shook his head and turned off the T.V. that he had been watching with one eye. Not so much for the news, mind you, but he liked the array of blondes and tight dresses. He tossed the remote across the room to the couch and grumbled, "I don't want to think about it."

Faith walked over to her father. She was gangly and tall like her mother with long brown hair that came down to her waist. She kissed him on the cheek. "Look at me."

He did, reluctantly.

"We have two weeks together. Angelina has wanted to come down here for years. This is a special vacation. There is nothing to worry about. The mortgage is paid this month, right?"

He shrugged and slid an official looking envelope under a pile of letters, "Right."

"Okay, so let's not worry about it. Promise me you won't even think about it for the next two weeks. You have to believe things will turn out alright. Is that a deal?"

Clint relented stubbornly, "Deal."

She took her fingers and pushed his frown up into a smile. "Now doesn't that feel better?"

He nodded and checked his watch, "Yep, oh yeah, I'm Mr. Happy now. Let's do it." He went over his to do list as Faith finished packing upstairs. The neighbors were going to check on the dogs. Normally, he would have taken them, but there wasn't any room since Angelina was coming. Clint then secured the canoe good in the back of the truck and packed a few more things in the cooler which was already filled with enough food to feed the Russian Army. Then, they locked the house up tight and were off.

A few more hours, and they'd be at their isolated cabin in Montgomery County, tucked away from civilization, just a remote getaway in the hills with a river that hooked around it. It was the only place he had ever found where he was at total peace and serenity. It was an island to itself, removed from the problems that contaminated the world. The cabin was his paradise, unmolested by the vile and devious. It was his fortress of security.

Clint couldn't wait to get there. Two weeks at the cabin, and he knew he would return a new man, rejuvenated, energized, focused, or so he believed that morning as they backed out of the drive. [But as we know, things don't always turn out like we planned. Not in the real world. Our circumstances are often beyond our control.]

At the end of their block, Clint suddenly stopped. Faith could see a twinge of worry on his face. She looked at him and asked, "What is it? Forget something?"

He sat there at the stop sign. "Yeah, you think I need to get the gun. Normally, we take it you know."

"Are you going to be doing any hunting?"

"No."

"Get real. Would you shoot a bear if you saw one?"

"Probably not."

"Case closed. Stop your worrying; we aren't going to need it. We can just beat some pots if we see any bears."

"You're right. We'll be okay. Nothing to worry about."

He put in a Credence Clearwater CD and drove off. "Yeah, babe, we'll be safe."

Faith turned up the volume to one of their favorite songs, Green River. She smiled and tossed her hair back and then snapped her fingers pointing. "Time to go, daddio. It's vacation time." And just like that, they were off to the airport.

Chapter Three

On June 18th, they picked up Angelina at the Little Rock airport at 11:27 a.m., a rarity the flight from New York had actually arrived early. The girls hugged and laughed ridiculously as you would expect two twelve year olds to do who hadn't seen each other in a year. Clint took pictures with his cell phone camera and sent them to Angelina's dad, his childhood friend. The girls, like their fathers had, became best friends from the moment they met, and the bonds of friendship were passed from one generation to the next.

Angelina seemed especially excited. She had heard all the tales of the big adventures the Roberts' family had at the cabin; albeit, she knew from her father that Clint's version was often heavily spiced with hyperbole. The Big Apple, as exciting as it was, just couldn't compare to a Roberts' family outing, to hear Clint tell it. So, after the girls stopped jumping up and down and exchanging multiple versions of the words "awesome" and "cool", Clint retrieved her bags at the luggage terminal, and they were off for two whole weeks of adventure and fun in the Ouachitas.

Within thirty minutes, they were out of metro Little Rock and headed to the hills where they would swim and fish and canoe. Clint hadn't told them yet, but he had a ski boat reserved (borrowed) at Lake Ouachita. Angelina had never skied, and Faith hadn't in several years. Clint had to sell their boat. It seemed like it was always in the shop anyway, ensuring that the local marine mechanic would keep his family well fed. Times had been hard on Clint in the last couple of years, and the boat went not long after his job went. Nevertheless, Clint was determined to put that behind him, at least for now. He had lost a lot, but he still was able to hold on to the cabin even after the divorce. It was the thing that meant the most to him, more than anything, other than his children, especially Faith.

While they drove, Clint attempted to engage the girls in some conversation, but quickly gave it up. They were having way too much fun in the backseat of his truck, giggling and laughing. He watched them in the rear view mirror; it brought back memories of how he and Bert used to act. The conversation was different, but the feelings were the same. Realizing he was being tuned out, he searched the dial on the radio for something interesting to preoccupy his mind while he drove. He listened to sports for a while, but enough of that; he'd grown tired of grown men acting like bimbos. They weren't jocks; they were sports' groupies. He couldn't relate to hundred million dollar contracts, for ball players. Are you kidding? That was insane and downright depressing when you're struggling to pay the mortgage on your home every month.

Clint flipped through the channels some more. He found some seventies music on the dial. It was good stuff, Pink Floyd, but he wasn't really in the mood to trip, at least not now, but who knows? Another year like the last one, and he figured he might move to the desert, grow a beard, get some sandals, and start dropping acid or peyote. He looked at his daughter in the backseat and sighed; he would have already been gone if it wasn't for her. It was getting just too hard, but until then, this was his escape: the cabin in the mountains with the two girls. He changed the station again when he couldn't get in the groove and found the weather on another channel. There was nothing major, just a few storms rolling in from the west, but considering what happened the week before, he and everyone else was being cautious.

After the weather report, he caught the last of the local news. Two men were missing, one from Oklahoma and the other one from Montgomery County. The report said the two disappearances might have been related. The FBI had been called in. Clint didn't want to hear anymore and finally consented to reason and turned the radio off. There wasn't anything on that affected him anyway. He began to daydream about all the things they would do. He thought about the fish he would catch, and the dinners he would cook. He thought about playing Tonk and Spades at night, watching Seinfeld on DVD, Superman (the TV. series), and Dragnet. All their favorites. There was no internet or cable or satellite TV. The world, the busy apparatus of mundane activity spinning incessantly in chaos through space, was far removed from his sacred cabin, and Clint was going to enjoy every minute of it. For at least two weeks. Two weeks of bliss.

The cabin itself wasn't much. It wasn't going to make it to the cover of Country Living or Better Homes or whatever. It wasn't like those majestic structures with towering beams and thirty foot high rock fire places that you see around the Colorado ski slopes. No, this was about as humble as you get. He'd built it himself in the early years of his marriage: a simple two bedroom cedar shank cabin with a screened front porch and deck on the side. No stone fireplace, but it did have a nice cast iron wood burning stove in the living room. It served its purpose well, or so Clint thought. It was a weekend getaway, not to be confused with a vacation home because it was seldom totally a vacation; there was always work to do. Nevertheless, it was where the family unwound and stored up memories. Nights were filled with laughter and games. The floor usually had a trail of popcorn from the kitchen to the couch. Sometimes, there was a line outside the bathroom, and those sticky messy fly traps that hang down had to be replaced every couple of days. It wasn't perfect, but it was theirs. And for Clint, that was all that mattered. To Clint, and to Faith, it was everything.

As they passed through Hot Springs that afternoon, there was an unusual amount of traffic. It seemed like every other rig on the road was hauling a boat or a camper trailer. Clint managed to toss only one finger en route. He made sure the girls couldn't see him. He stuck it out over the cab of his truck and pointed in the direction of the tailgater behind him. The long hair dude with a girlfriend sporting her latest black eye pulled up next to him and chunked Clint his version of the four letter word. Clint waved; it was like 'Oh well, now that that's settled'. Then, the redneck mouthed what appeared to be a profane laced retort through his mustache and slobber, and drove off swigging his beer, and swerving through traffic.

Faith looked at the man barreling down the freeway, "What was that all about?"

"I have no idea honey. No idea." He looked back at the girls exchanging bracelets in the back, "Hey, ya'll want to see downtown?"

"Sure."

"Cool."

Clint knew the girls didn't have that much interest in downtown, but he did. They drove through the spa city with all its historic hotels, passing the thousands of tourists shopping and relaxing. The girls looked out the window while he did sightseeing of another kind. Women were swinging purses and shaking behinds. He couldn't help but give a few honks.

"Daaad," Faith said embarrassingly.

Clint smiled beneath his sunglasses, "Hospitality honey, it's just southern hospitality."

"Geez, I don't see you honk at any homeless people."

"Look, there!" Clint spotted a man with a long beard walking through the crowd toting a couple of plastic sacks. He looked like a panhandler. Clint honked.

"Have you no shame?"

"Alright ladies, tour's over. On to the river." Reluctantly, he turned back onto the highway.

That's what they wanted anyway. It's what everyone did in Arkansas; they did the family thing, headed for water: a river or lake. It was another hour before they arrived at the cabin, and the girls couldn't wait, especially Angelina; she had heard so much about it. The cabin sat on a ridge located on a peninsula surrounded on three sides by the Ouachita River. The backyard was literally the national forest, meaning there were no neighbors behind him. Another land owner owned the rest of the peninsula and used it to raise hay. So, it consisted of fields and large patches of trees with towering oaks, some the width of a car and probably two hundred years old or older.

The peninsula was about half a mile wide and about a mile and a half long. Once you turned off the highway, there was an old one lane bridge that spanned the girth of the river. No one belonged on that peninsula but him and the other land owner. It was all private. What made it really special, the other owner didn't even have a house there, and he just used the fields for hay and cattle, so it was like having the whole place to themselves.

It was as secluded as secluded could be in the modern world. It was paradise.

Friends and guests were always amazed when they went out there. They had never seen anything in all their lives like it. The stars seemed so close that if you stood on a chair on the porch outside you felt like you could snatch them from the sky. Clint used to play a game called "Shoot the Moon"; though it wasn't a game, really, it was an experience. He'd lie flat on his back on the picnic table in the yard and look through the telescopic lens of his rifle at the galaxies. Later, he just took off the lens. Faith would join him, and they would pass the lens back and forth looking at the moon and stars, and talking. They would do it for hours as the bullfrogs croaked in the nearby pond, and the katydids conducted a rhythmic symphony of cadence.

No, they didn't own a lot, just five acres, but they might as well own the world, the universe. It was all theirs. Clint always looked at it like he built a simple ordinary cabin; God built the masterpiece surrounding it. And that's what he went for, the masterpiece, the beauty of it all. Not everyone though saw it the same way. His wife, or more accurately, his ex-wife, never shared the same enthusiasm. She didn't appreciate the cabin the way he and Faith did. In all honesty, it did have its drawbacks. It was too small, and only had one bathroom. There were always bugs in the summer, and the bridge did flood. One time the river went up 27 feet, meaning their bridge was 21 feet underwater. Not good. They were still higher than the river, but the peninsula with miles of fields suddenly became a large moving lake, and only a few acres separated them from the shore line. Clint watched the river from the deck as it became a mile wide swirling snake wrapping its tail around their house. If it got any closer, they were heading up the mountain to higher ground, but then it stopped and slowly began to recede.

Besides the floods that happened yearly, there were other inconveniences. One year they practically had to share the cabin with a family of bears. Not good. The bears not only took a liking to the Roberts' cabin, but they took a liking to the family station wagon as well, particularly the food left in the back. Upholstery is meant for the wear and tear of a family, a human family that is. And it wasn't so much the shredded leather that caused a point of contention in the Roberts' household; it was the smell that was left behind. Now say what you want to about bears, but unless you are up close and personal, you don't realize that they have a rather strong pugnacious odor. It doesn't go away, ever. So, you might understand why the "issue" became a sore spot in the Roberts' marriage when six months later they were still driving around town in the station wagon with the windows down. Such were the memories.

Little did Faith know then, but it was the beginning of the end for the Roberts' family. One year, it was the bears; the next year, it was an ice storm. In the summer, it was the ticks and the snakes; and of course, no vacation was complete without at least one skunk encounter. Holidays it seemed had turned into disasters one too many times for her mother who preferred malls and latté's to porch swings and bug spray. The family became divided, but as much as Faith loved her mother, she was always devoted to her father. It took several more years before the marriage was completely severed, and it was never any one event but all of them. The tears in the relationship just never got patched; they split wider until nothing could hold it together.

Clint tried to put all that behind him as they began to pass all the resorts and marinas along Lake Ouachita. Some memories Clint had a hard time shaking from his head. He hoped *this* vacation would be without incident. The girl's heads were bobbing to some music. He looked in back at the two; they were sharing earphones to Angelina's IPod. He was just glad he didn't have to listen. There was one last stop before they hit the cabin.

"Last chance, girls. Is there anything you need to get?"

Angelina looked around, "Where are we?"

"Mount Ida."

She looked at Faith and raised her eyebrow, "Mount Ida? Is this like supposed to be a town?"

Faith looked at her father, and they both laughed. It was the largest town in the county, population 963. It didn't even have a stop light. To Angie, it looked like they had driven onto the set of Mayberry, or maybe the Twilight Zone.

"Is there a store, here?"

"No Macy's, but we've got Bob's Food City. This is where we do all our Christmas shopping." Clint grinned, "Last chance, if ya need something."

They turned into the crowded parking lot. It was full of a combination of locals and vacationers. It was always easy to distinguish the two. Clint got out and was locking up his truck as the girls started to bolt across the parking lot. A sudden surge of panic went through him looking at the cars pulling in and out.

"Faith!"

Instantly, she stopped and turned around. Clint gave her the eye and lowered his head. She knew what he was thinking. He walked up to them. "Now, you know not to be running in a parking lot."

She raised her shoulders up and dropped them down exasperated, "Sorry, just forgot." She looked left and right, "See, it's okay."

Clint looked at his list of things to get. "You beware of the yomen."

She pointed her finger at him and wagged it, "No, you beware of the yomen, mista." His little brown-eyed beauty with long brown hair put her arm around him and kissed him on the cheek. "Love ya, daddy."

The two girls then went bouncing into the store as Clint checked over his list. Angelina had a peculiar look on her face, "Yomen? What's a yomen?" She knew they had some strange sayings in Arkansas, but she had never heard that one.

They walked past the newspaper stand with stories of the flood on the Little Missouri. Faith pointed to the grim pictures on the first page, "That's a yomen; it's like a, well, it's like an unexpected tragedy. It is something bad that you never expect to happen, but it happens."

"So your dad is always worried about yomens?"

"We use to not be able to buy milk without him mentioning a yomen. He pointed to the missing kids on the back and reminded me to be careful. He said there are good yomens too, as well as the bad ones, but he's never really pointed out a good one. He's just (she paused trying to find the right word) cautious. He's worried about something happening to me."

"Geez, my parents too. My mother is even worse than my dad". She held up her cell phone and showed Faith the text's from her mother. "Every hour", she said mockingly, "R u ok?"

Clint rolled his cart with one bad wheel down the aisles, tossing in the various items on his list: fresh buns, hamburger meat, eggs, mustard, toilet paper, bug spray…" He kept his eye on them by the magazine rack. He knew they were alright; he wasn't afraid some stranger would go, "Hey girls, I've got some candy in my van. Want some?" It's just that it was habit; it was instinct. Twelve years of guarding his child, and in the next couple of years, she'd be on her own. He was letting go, gradually, as parents must which meant shedding the old precautions. She was in that in between stage. In just a few more years, she'd be old enough to drive a car, but right now she still rode a bicycle. Boys who wouldn't even look at her last year were now taking notice, and in another year or two, they wouldn't be able to take their eyes off her. Clint finished loading up the cart and found a place in line at the checkout counter. The girls flipped through a teen magazine. Angelina pointed to the cover of a tabloid with a picture of another celebrity couple breaking up. "Didn't they just break up a couple of months ago?"

"You know what the problem is?"

She could tell when Mr. Roberts had something snide to say. "What?"

He pointed to the other tabloid with a bizarre picture of a space ship and a cartoonish picture of a thing with big ears, "Space aliens. They're here. They are breeding with starlets; they are taking over Hollywood...they've already taken Washington."

She chuckled, "Oh, are they?"

Clint in a perfect deadpan serious look, "Oh, I've got proof. Have you ever noticed how many space alien movies are made? If they weren't real why would they make them? Think about it. They are trying to indoctrinate us, and look at Washington, have you seen Congress lately? They are in all their little space suits, same ties, same hair, trying to act human, but they're not real. They are just taking orders."

The girl at the checkout counter started laughing. She was shaking her head in amusement. She looked at the girls, "He's right." She leaned over across the machine and whispered, "They're here, too." She smacked her gum and pointed with her eyes to a man standing in line, two aisles over, "See."

Clint and the girls looked over trying not to act too suspicious. He was about five feet five, meaning, five feet tall and five wide. If he laid sprawled on a beach in Alaska, he'd probably get speared. Of course, there were signs he was actually human like the yellow sunglasses and purple swim trunks with palm trees. Aliens don't make those kinds of fashion statements, only tourists. His attire also consisted of an attractive muscle shirt that stretched around his torso like cellophane wrap. There was enough hair sticking out of his armpits to make a wig (not that anyone would wear it), but that's not the point. His arms were almost as hairy, but still underneath the mesh of hair, there was a brilliant pink sun burn. He topped off his wardrobe with a quarter inch of white cream on the top of his nose just to add a hint of sophistication.

The girls spun around horrified with a twisted look of disgust wiggling on their faces. The cashier whispered again, "I see a lot of 'em in here."

"See, I told ya. There's your proof."

Angelina wasn't sure what to say; Faith was used to it. Clint smiled and unloaded the cart handing the items to the young lady. She told the girls to be careful. There had been a boating accident yesterday; a drunk ran into a jet ski, "Second time this year. And we've got a missing person."

"Missing person, from the accident?"

"No. Mr. Johnson, he owns some rental cabins out by the lake. He has been missing. He left to go to town and make a deposit. They found his truck between here and Mena in the woods. He was gone. That was a few days ago."

"Do they think he might have run off?"

"He was seventy-three, not likely. Just disappeared. He was the nicest man you could ever meet. He was the type that would have stopped for a stranger or someone broken down." She took a deep breath and shook her head like she was trying to shake the thought from her mind, "Just a great guy."

"Is that the one I heard about on the radio?"

She batted her eyelashes, "Afraid so."

Clint knew she didn't want to talk about it anymore; he picked up the three bags of food and winked at the girl. "Probably, aliens don't cha' think?" She gave a pretentious smile and nodded. Clint and the girls climbed in the truck packed to the brim and headed out to the cabin passing back through Mt. Ida. They drove by the square, the courthouse and the police station. He couldn't help but notice the large number of squad cars surrounding the little jail. There must have been ten or twelve cars in all when normally there might be three, if that many. They weren't all Montgomery County either. There were some from Garland and Polk Counties Sheriff's office, and there were two state police units. He couldn't help but notice there was also one marked "FBI".

Clint looked at the darlings in the back. They were already having the time of their life. "You girls ready for some big adventure?"

"Yeah!"

"Bring it on."

"Get ready girls, it is about to start. The cabin is just a few more miles. A vacation we won't forget."

Chapter Four

"Oh my God!"

Those were the words Angelina used to describe the Ouachita River when she saw it. She and Faith hung out the window of the truck with their hair blowing like ribbons in the wind. They were in awe as they passed over the big bridge crossing from a cliff to the meadows on the far other side. Up the river beneath a mountain was a huge gray stone bluff that looked like an old man's face. Scores of canoes and kayakers meandered through the emerald green waters. Some were diving off boulders into the water. They were in paradise.

Clint hit his blinker and turned onto an unassuming dusty gravel country road. The girls were bouncing up and down in back. "We're here".

The road narrowed to a point, and they came down a small hill to the single one lane low water bridge not but five or six feet above the water. "Take a look Angelina; this is where you're staying for the next two weeks". Clint stopped the truck on the bridge and looked up the river at more folks paddling slowly along the peaceful tree-lined shores.

Angelina couldn't believe it. Its beauty was beyond what they had told her. Their words could not come close to describing how breathtaking it was. The water was the most beautiful emerald green, like thousands, millions of shining round emerald pebbles spinning, rotating in the rapids. The sunlight made the river sparkle like jewels as if the river was a fluid emerald necklace that wrapped around the neck of the hills. No place on earth had Clint found like it. It was both primitive and exotic.

One by one, the people passed underneath the bridge through a series of rapids. Angelina immediately fell in love with the sound of the river running through the shallows. Its peacefulness was strangely seductive, luring.

The people all waved in their canoes. Some yelled "Yippee," or "Yahoo," as they shot through the churning water dodging boulders and raising their paddles triumphantly in the air after they passed. Clint honked and gave them a thumbs up. He turned around to the girls in back and smiled, "Well Angie, so whatcha' think?"

She sat listening to the sound of the water and then turned around and took pictures out the window with her cell phone. "This is so totally awesome! I can't believe it. This is just so cool". She hugged Faith, "I never want to leave. Let's just stay."

Clint and Faith laughed, "Welllll, if y'all lived in Arkansas…" He put the truck back in drive, and they drove on across the river. "The best part is still to come." They passed over the bridge onto a narrow gravel road that crossed through some hay fields and speckling of woods. The massive oaks that arched above the road were so thick it was like going through a circular tunnel in the middle of a forest. Then, after they passed the oaks, they came to another clearing before going up a switchback ridge where at the top she could see the cabin. When they crested the hill, for a second, Angelina's breath was taken from her.

In every direction was sheer beauty. The girls jumped out and ran to the big oak in the yard with the tire swing. Faith was talking excitedly, but Angelina didn't say a word. They jumped on the tire and swung back and forth looking at the scenery. Behind them, beyond the woods at the back of the cabin, there was a mountain. It was rugged and steep and so high you could barely make out the trees at the top. It resembled a camel's back with two huge humps that towered over the valley. In the other direction were the fields of hay and wild flowers that stretched like a carpet that rolled all the way down to the river over a mile away. Way down at the end of the pasture, there were cows grazing; they were no more than tiny black dots on the landscape. An old weather-beaten road followed along a fence that hugged a tree line down the side of the pasture. It reminded Faith of days gone by when the farmer used to trolley the reins of his horses on his hay wagon down through the fields to inspect his cattle. At the very end of the fields were cliffs. They rose above the waters about a hundred to a hundred and fifty feet high with western cedars jutting out from their rocky edges. This was the view they had every day. This was Pencil Bluff. This was home.

Clint got out of the truck with a load of groceries in his arms and walked over to the girls. He breathed in the fresh air, "Babe, why don't you show Ang the cabin?" Faith overturned a rock by the tree where they always left the key, and they ran up to the porch to unlock it. Suddenly, a strange peculiar caution pricked at Clint. He thought of something. "Wait! Let me go in…first."

He took the key from Faith and walked around the cabin just to make sure there weren't any busted windows or screens that had been cut. He didn't want to alarm them either. "We've had bears before."

Faith shook her head and put her hands on her hips, "That was like four years ago…remember?" He ignored her. No one had been there; there weren't any signs of forced entry. Clint then opened the door and set the groceries down on the kitchen table. He walked through the cabin checking out the rooms with the girls following close behind. It was musty, and he opened up the windows and turned on the ceiling fans. "Let me check the bathroom." There was usually a spider in the tub, and sure enough, there was one again. Clint killed it and flushed it much to Faith's appreciation.

"Looks good, but you girls need to help me unload. I'm not going do it alone."

Faith knew the drill. When her father did work around the house or cabin, he always had on dancing music. She popped in a John Lennon CD and put food in the fridge, clothes in drawers, charcoal on the porch with the fishing gear. They all danced around, cleaning tables and wiping down the furniture. The girls looked like two robots from the Jetsons running from room to room with the vacuum, and Clint slid across the floor during "Clean-up Time" with a broom. Finally they were almost done, beads of sweat dripped on all their faces. They were down to just the bathroom, but they had nothing to clean it with. Clint poured some bleach into an empty spray bottle and told Faith to be careful with it and to wash her hands afterwards. "It will burn your skin, and don't get *any* in your eyes. Bleach will blind you." A few minutes more and they were done. Faith came into where her dad was and handed him the bottle, "Okay, now can we like relax? This is a *vacation*, remember?"

"I was ready a long time ago. I was just waiting on you slow pokes."

She threw a towel at him and pointed her finger, "One day, mista."

Clint laughed, "Well, what are ya'll waiting on. I figured you'd have on your bathing suits by now". He looked at his watch, it was 4:05, "We've got about four hours if y'all want to go?" They screamed and ran to the bedroom; he changed into some shorts and sandals and gathered some fishing gear. That afternoon, he took them down to the bluffs where they all swam until evening. Clint didn't catch much, but he didn't fish much either. The girls took turns diving off his shoulders into the water. They had the most pleasant afternoon swimming and talking to the folks that drifted by. Finally towards early evening, nearly all the canoes were off the river; the few fishermen that were left showed Clint their fine stringer of sparkling smallmouth bass. He asked about their technique, and they showed him their lures. That always perplexed Clint; no matter how many he bought he never seemed to have the right ones.

That night, he didn't bother to fry up the two small fish he caught; instead, he popped in a pizza. The girls were barely finished when their eye lids began to droop, and their heads began to sag. There would be no cards tonight. He sent them to bed and went out on the deck where he shot the moon. All he had was the scope; he had forgotten to bring the rifle with him. In all the packing, he kept forgetting to put it back in the truck. Though he didn't expect bears, Clint liked having the gun; it was security.

Clint stretched out on the table and looked up at the moon and the stars. He listened to the frogs and katydids. It was so peaceful, and his body was tired. He felt like sleeping there on that table all night. He put the scope down and just stared out into the sky. He wanted to be there, to be up there in space, but he realized that if he were on the highest mountain or even in a capsule orbiting the earth he couldn't get any closer to the heavens than where he was on that table. And, if he was out there, and looking down on earth, there wasn't a more magnificent place he could be than where he was. It was one of those precious moments when man in search of serenity and peace finds complete and total oneness with the universe. He was alone with God, a place he sometimes felt uncomfortable with, but at that moment, he was in peace.

Clint took some deep breaths and let the air slowly exhale from his lungs. He was imbibing tranquility, refreshing, soothing peace. The stress of life, its toils and cares and burdens leaving him. He had believed at one time very much in God, but for whatever reason, the God who created the magnificent universe no longer listened to him. It is such a lonely feeling, but that's how he had felt. He had felt that way for years. Yet, Clint was still drawn especially at times like this. He laid there with arms outstretched across the table feeling as though his soul was magnetically being lifted from his body and rising through the night air into the heavens. Here, he found total freedom, lying on a table in the middle of the yard staring off into space. It was the only place left in the world where he felt close to God.

After an hour or maybe more, Clint finally pulled himself up from the table and went inside. He shut the screen door and latched it. He thought of locking the front door too, but it was hot, and he wanted the night air to filter through the cabin. He checked on the girls; their window was open, and the drapes were blowing as an oscillating fan quietly hummed in the room stirring cool night air across their bodies. As was his custom, Clint stretched out on the couch, rarely since the divorce had he been able to sleep in a bed. He kicked off his sandals and closed his eyes. Clint was an especially perplexed and troubled man: he knew there was a God; he just didn't know why he didn't seem to listen, or at least listen to him.

Deep down inside, Clint realized he was consumed with fear; fear that God would not protect him. His marriage went bad, then his job. There was a strong chance he might lose their home; payments had been late, and his excuses were wearing thin. There were nights when he woke up in sweats; other nights he paced the floor, and other nights he sat alone in the dark and wondered *why*?

Clint got back up and went to the window. He looked at the tree line. There was nothing there, but he began to see things in his mind, things moving in the shadows, waiting behind the trees, watching. Clint shut the door and locked it. *'This sucks'* he murmured to himself. He didn't know why, but he went to the kitchen and retrieved a steak knife from a drawer and laid it on the coffee table next to the couch. He lay back down and folded his arms across his chest. Slowly, he began to close his eyes. He lay motionless, listening.

Chapter Five

The older we get the harder it is to break old habits. Clint was a journalist, and then became a features editor, and for eleven years, he wrote a column in the state's second largest paper. As far back as he could remember he began his morning by turning on the radio or television to get the news. It was as much a habit as putting on his shoes or turning on the coffee pot, but since being "laid off" nine months ago, he no longer cared. It didn't matter.

It took some major life changes to turn off the news, and for Faith, she saw it as a drastic improvement. Her father wasn't caught up in the crises of the world; instead, he was tuned into the events in their lives. They talked more, and it wasn't about the changing economic climate in Europe, the downward spiral into Socialism, or the global warming hoax. Their conversations were about them and their lives since the divorce.

Their hands were joined over coffee and bagels, French toast and eggs. Short but sincere prayers were said, at least by Faith. She always gave thanks for the day and the meal even if Clint was struggling with gratitude. If he had a paper at all, it was to look at the employment section, and sometimes she'd take the pen out of his hand and lay it down. "Look at me," she'd say, "It is going to get better."

Clint understandably didn't turn on the radio in the kitchen the next morning, and so he wasn't aware of the news. The disappearance of Mr. Johnson was now thought to be linked to the disappearance of another man in eastern Oklahoma. But there were no clues, in both cases their cars had been "wiped clean", and there were no eye witnesses. They just vanished, gone without a trace.

It was for Clint a perfect morning. The girls awoke to the smell of frying bacon on the stove and biscuits in the oven. It was his custom to cook omelets at the cabin with hash browns and biscuits and gravy. After doing their fair share of stretching and yawning, the girls had a hearty breakfast, brushed their teeth, and they were on their way. They were going up river to launch the canoe. There was a place not far from there they called the "Big Cliff", and it was a big cliff, a two hundred foot solid rock bluff that hung out over the river. It looked like an old gray man with a long scraggly beard with the way the bramble brush jutted out of the crevasses.

They put in the canoe and began paddling quietly toward the monument. They must have been the first ones on the river that morning. It was light, probably seven thirtyish, but the sun had not yet come over the mountain. The water was perfectly still, and all three were quiet. Clint was in back of the canoe steering with his paddle, and then he picked up his rod and tossed his lure across the water near the bank. Strike!

He started reeling. The line zigged and zagged in the water. The fish was actually pulling their boat, and then suddenly it broke the surface flipping and flying through the air.

"He's a nice one, daddy!"

Clint chuckled, "He sure is, babe. Get the net ready. He's dinner!"

They hauled in the fish, a sparkling two pound small mouth bass, the first of many they would catch that day. Faith caught two by herself, and Angelina caught three, not bad for her first time out. Clint hauled them in all morning long but threw most of them back except for two that he couldn't resist. That's how fishing is. Some days you have it, and some days you don't. That first day in the canoe was one of the best he'd had in years. They canoed and fished, and when it got a bit warmer, they began to swim. All total, it was a six mile float. They stopped often for snacks, Vienna sausages and crackers, which took Angelina a little getting used to but when you're hungry you realize that everything tastes good.

The best part of the float for the girls is when they came to the section known as the "walking stairs". It was a place where rock ledges crossed the entire length of the river underwater, and it was deep. They were like smooth stone bleachers. You could walk down to the bottom descending like stairs. Here, Clint would sit on the top shelf and lean back; the cool waters cascading around him, his feet hanging off the ledge. He watched as the fish swim about in the deep pool. It was like a natural whirlpool. Clint and the girls sat there in the refreshing waters relaxing. Gradually, other canoers began to come by, and they used it as an opportunity to brag about their catch.

The walking stairs was also one of the best places to snorkel, and the three of them did. It was an unbelievable experience for Angelina as Faith showed her how they did it. With their goggles on, they floated just below the surface. The water was so clear; it was like looking through the glass of an aquarium except that the fish swam below them. They were all sizes and shapes, but the long nose gar was by far the most fascinating. They grew in length up to six feet, a long slender fish with a needle-like snout slowly moving through the waters below them with a tail that swayed back and forth like a long brown feather. At first, Angelina was scared, but the fish amazingly swam right by her. The little ones, sunfish, occasionally pecked at her toes like they might have been worms, but the larger fish primarily ignored her.

Faith and Angelina then trolled the shoals snorkeling where the water was shallow. Clint followed them in the canoe. The girls stayed up ahead of him floating along in about two feet of water. Their hands pulled them through the water reaching underneath and grabbing rocks as they went along. You would think the fish would dart away, but they didn't. The little ones swam in and out of the rocks as they passed. This was nature as Angelina had never seen it before, and Faith was careful not to be too much of a know it all. When Angelina discovered something that Faith knew about, she acted just as surprised. In all likelihood, Angelina had probably done the same thing when Faith was visiting her in New York. That's how close they were as friends.

A steady stream of vacationers began to float through that morning, and none had caught as many fish as they had. That was a first. Then, just as they were nearing the end of their float, Clint heard some guys coming in their direction. They were getting real loose with their tongues, and manners weren't something they seemed particularly interested in. Their whole vocabulary was reduced down to one verb and one adjective starting with the letter "f".

When Clint had heard enough of it, he yelled out to the two of them to put a lid on it. He didn't want to hear that kind of trash around his daughter.

They weren't but probably seventeen or eighteen, and the smaller one of the two seemed to be the mouthiest. He stood up in the canoe, "Who do you think you are? Think you own the whole damn river?"

Clint tossed his rod over to the shore and started wading out to where they were, "What did you say?

Angelina and Faith both kind of ducked behind their canoe. Faith knew how her dad got sometimes, and she wished he would just let things pass, but that was never his way. She watched her dad splashing through the water going for the boys' canoe. "Oh, my God. Oh, my God!" She wanted to yell out for him to stop, but she knew it was too late now. The older boy was saying he was sorry, but Clint kept going straight for them. When he got to the canoe, he knew he was going to thump it over and throw them both in the water. He was pissed. When he got to their canoe, he noticed beer cans lying in the bottom. Clint was fuming; his hands gripped the side of the canoe, and then he stopped. They were both young and not anywhere close to legal drinking age. He realized they weren't doing anything any different than he had done when he was about the same age; in fact, his language wasn't much different either.

Clint looked at the two of them; his hands held the canoe. He looked at the cans, "You boys old enough to drink?" He sounded like a deputy sheriff does. He figured they had heard that before. Neither said anything. They just looked at each other. He knew the answer.

Clint paused and looked at the cans. He looked at the young one who for sure was wishing he had kept his mouth shut. Clint's eyes inspected the young one. Clint could see he was scared. "Y'all be careful." He then shoved their canoe downstream.

"Yes sir."

He watched as they went on down river and didn't hear anymore foul language; a little laughing, but no cussing. As far as he could tell, it was about noon, and the river started getting crowded. Clint was ready for a break. Angelina hadn't realized it, but they were back at the peninsula, and Clint pulled the canoe to shore. They walked up to the cabin with their catch of fish and had lunch (the fish were for dinner). Clint cleaned the fish out on the porch, and the girls changed clothes and put in an old Dragnet. It wasn't until then that Angelina realized she hadn't heard from her mom in a long time. She looked at her phone: no bars. Clint gave her his cell phone; he still had good reception. She called and gave her parents the update. After a while, she looked at Clint, "My dad wants to talk to you."

Clint smiled, "Tell him I'm in the hot tub with my soul mate, Miss January."

She told her father and then chuckled, "He said, you wish."

Clint got on the phone and walked outside to the porch. The girls could hear him laughing. Faith was happy to hear him laugh; again, he hadn't done much of it in the last year. She looked at her father with his legs stretched out relaxed and a big smile across his face. She couldn't hear what he was talking about, but whenever he and Bert got together, they were joking. It was the same with her and Angelina. After a while, he hung up the phone and came in and stuck the phone in the charger and put his hands on his hips. "You girls ready to go get the truck?"

It hadn't dawned on Angelina, but the truck was still about six miles away up river. "I'll be back."

A few minutes later, they heard the roar of an engine. A horn beeped outside. Clint was on a four-wheeler. He revved it and took off across the yard, turned around and roared back to the porch. "Get on, ladies."

The three of them straddled the four-wheeler. He took them down to the low water bridge where they crossed waving to people coming down to the river. They roared up to the highway where they rode the far shoulder all the way up the long winding mountain. Angelina's mother would never let her do something like this. They rode along for several miles crossing over a mountain with the wind in their faces. The view was incredible from the top, and at one point, Clint pulled over and pointed across the valley. "There's the cabin." She could see it across the long narrow peninsula. The river wrapped around it like a silver ribbon shining in the sun. A mile or so further, they turned on the road that leads down to the Big Cliff. Clint pulled out some ramps and drove the four-wheeler up into the bed of the truck, and they drove back to the cabin and picked up the canoe along the way. The rest of the day they relaxed, watched movies, and played cards.

Angelina had never been on a four-wheeler before, and so he let the girls ride around, but he cautioned Faith, "No jumping. We'll do that later." From the porch, Clint watched the girls drive down through the fields. He could hear them almost a mile away laughing as they rode around doing doughnuts in the field. They drove down to where the cows were, and he could hear their distant voices yelling "Yeehaw! Yeehaw!" He grabbed a pen and pad and looked at them across the valley. He was inspired to write, but he wasn't sure what to say. He wanted to describe somehow that this was freedom. The girls were experiencing the sheer joy that is felt in the pursuit of happiness. This is what it was all about, but as he began to write, the words quickly evaporated, like rain drops on the hood of a car after a summer shower. One moment they were there glistening and beautiful; the next moment they were gone. Vanished.

Clint put down his pen and picked up the telescope and observed the girls. They were having the time of their lives. It reminded him of he and Bert when they were young, riding their bicycles down the streets with their hands and feet in the air. They were free, just like the girls were free. It seemed like the rest of the world, especially his life, had somehow become a trap in the years since. Maybe getting fired was freedom. Maybe, he looked at it all wrong. What did it take for a man to actually be happy? Was it the bigger house, the newer car, the promotion with more responsibilities, or was it simply this?

Clint began to think; he searched again for the words to say. For eleven years, he tried to describe what was important in life, but obviously, he failed to get the message across. Perhaps, it was because he didn't understand it himself, and if he didn't understand it, how could other people. All he knew for sure was that our lives evaporate in worry and struggle. We try so hard to gain things, and then we struggle to hold on to them. Before we know it, the time is gone, the years have passed, and we are wheeled to a window in a sterile room, alone, to stare out into a parking lot, wishing we had spent the years of our lives doing more of this.

In the far distance, he could see some dark clouds starting to roll in across the valley. He put the notepad down and walked into the kitchen and turned on the radio to get the weather. It was almost five; the news would be on right after the commercials. He looked at the sky again, and far off in the distance, he could hear the rumble of thunder coming from the west. The news came on: the Dow had had another poor week; Europe was trying to prop up Greece's economy to keep it from collapsing; there were floods in Iowa and locally; there was talk about "the manhunt." *'That's what it was about'* he thought, *'the cars at the police station.'* He turned up the volume and listened. The search had intensified. They had found the body of the man who had been missing in Oklahoma. It was murder; he had been beaten and robbed. There was still no trace of Mr. Johnson from Mt. Ida according to a state police investigator. Authorities from several states were now involved, but they still had no clues, none. Anyone with any information about the disappearances was asked to notify their local law enforcement officials immediately. It was quite a mystery. Finally, the weather came on; a series of storms was blowing across Oklahoma and Texas. That's what he expected. The national weather service said to expect high winds and possibly an inch and a half of rain, which was much needed. Good news was that the storms should clear out by the morning.

Clint breathed a sigh of relief. Storms were fine; he just didn't want to have to deal with a tornado on this trip. A few minutes later, he heard the four-wheeler coming up the road. Angelina was driving.

"You are breaking her in pretty good, sweetheart."

"Man, I've got to get one of these!"

"In New York? Oh yeah, like to see that."

They wanted to drive around some more, but Clint told them to put it up in the shed. He wanted to get the cooking done before the rains blew in. He set the fryer out on the porch and showed the girls how to baste their fish while the fryer heated up the oil. They put rolls in the oven, and the girls chopped up a salad. After about ten minutes when the oil was good and hot, he showed Angie how to put the fish in the fryer. There was the pot with a handle that had the oil, and a separate handle for the strainer in which to put the fish. "If you drop the fish in the strainer while it is in the oil, you'll get burned".

Clint placed the fish in the strainer and then dropped it down into the fryer, quickly putting on the lid. She listened to the sound of the fish popping. "Angelina, prepare for a feast." And it was. She had never tasted fish so good in her entire life. They sat out on the screened porch and watched the edge of the storm begin to blow in. The branches of the leaves began to sway. A cool breeze blew across the porch, and their napkins kept flying away. After dinner when the fryer had cooled down, Clint poured much of the oil back in a jar that he would use again, washed the fryer and put it back inside.

"Why don't you just leave it outside?"

"Bears. If they get a good whiff, they might show up."

"Daaad," Faith looked at her father and rolled her eyes, "We haven't seen any bears in years."

Never being short on questions, Angelina asked, "Then, why don't you cook it inside?"

"Too messy, and believe me, you don't want the cabin to smell like fish, even if it is bass."

Faith held her nose, "We never cook fish inside, or

spinach. Ugh."

"Spinach sounds good, how about tomorrow night? Collard greens?"

"You're pushing it, big guy."

Clint laughed, and they all sat back around the table. He showed Angie a few of his old card tricks before dealing out a hand of Tonk. They showed her how to play the game, and before long, she caught on. The chips started stacking up on her side of the table. She was smart just like her daddy. After a while, the girls were ready for bed; it was barely dark. They took a movie to their room and shut the door; Clint went outside on the screened porch and watched the storm coming in. Thunder pounded the ground from far away, and lightening began clawing its way across the night sky like a cat climbing up a big dark drape. The tree tops swayed, and then the first line of rain suddenly charged across the fields as if running, from something. He sat on an old cushion couch watching. The screen door blew open and then slammed repeatedly against the cabin until Clint latched it. He sat back down and stretched his legs out across the divan as the mist from the rain sprinkled his feet and gusts tossed his hair. That was one of the things Clint loved about the porch; he could feel the storms but still stay dry. He closed his eyes and listened to the sound of the wind and began to drift off.

Later Faith came in from the other room to check on her father. He was asleep. She took a sheet from the closet and laid it over him. He held a pen in his hand; his tablet was blank. He hadn't written a word. She turned off the porch light and looked down the road toward the river. Lightning flashed like a huge spotlight flickering above the fields momentarily. Then, it was dark. It scared her.

She went back to her room where Angelina was out cold. She couldn't sleep so she grabbed her journal and began to write until finally she was tired and turned out the light. For some reason, she too wished her father had brought the gun. For some strange reason, she had an urge to get up and lock the door to her bedroom, but that was silly. She knew she'd be alright. They were at the cabin; they were always safe at the cabin. After all, this was paradise.

Chapter Six

If you've never done it, you should. There is nothing quite like racing in a boat across the water. Clint told them about his surprise the next morning; they had a ski boat reserved at the lake. You would have thought it was Christmas, and he was Santa Claus the way they mauled him. They drove down to Mountain Harbor Marina, and the key was where his buddy told him it would be. They were pumped until the engine fired and a plume of black smoke poured out of the carburetor. It coughed a few times and never came back to life. It just kept dying. Disappointment was something he was accustomed to but not so much with the girls. They picked up a bag with lotion and towels and began walking back down the dock to the car with their expressions sagging nearly as long as their arms drooping from their shoulders.

No one was more disgusted as Clint. As he was wiping off the grease and throwing the scattered tools back in the box, a man who had been watching from a nearby slip came over and offered to help. Clint thanked him but didn't want him to take away time from his family. "Well," he said, "Do you know how to drive a jet ski?"

"Yeah?"

He pointed to a jet ski behind his boat, "You can take mine for a few hours if you'd like. My grandkids won't be down until this afternoon."

He sensed the man had been in his position before. He hopped on the jet and pulled it up to the shore waving at the girls. He wasn't sure about Angelina, but he was positive that he had never seen Faith run that fast in her entire life. They put on their life vests and cruised through the water until they reached the edge of the wake zone, and then Clint gave it full throttle. The stern rose up in front like a knife and ripped across the lake slicing the surface into two big waves parting the lake in half. The girls screamed with excitement. He took them out to a large bay and did figure eights, and then they skied behind a speed boat that was cutting across the lake. They followed it for about two miles slicing back and forth across its wakes. On a good wave, they'd soar about four or five feet in the air. Clint knew how to cut the ski like an Alpine skier on a downhill slope. Finally, after a while, they went over to an out of the way cove. He throttled down the motor and turned around to Angie, "Your turn."

For the next couple of hours, the girls took turns driving the jet ski. Faith hadn't ridden one much herself in the last couple of years, but they sure had fun that day. They didn't do all the things that Clint did; it was just fun jetting across the lake with the spray of water in their face and the power of the ski in their hand. They were cautious of other boats. Clint was wary of a yomen; there was always somebody on the lake that wasn't looking where he was going. And then finally, when they knew it was time to take it back, Clint drove the jet ski over to the marina and filled up the tank and returned it.

"How can I thank you?" Clint asked.

"Ya already have". The man gave Clint his number and told him that if he ever wanted to use it again to just give him a call. He had bought it for others to enjoy anyway. It was unbelievable that there were still people like him in the world, people that were just glad to help other people, not wanting anything in return. It gave him something to think about; he needed to be more like that guy. Be more of a giver and less of a complainer.

They thanked the man, and then Clint looked at Ang, "What do you think?"

"We gotta get one of those!"

He couldn't help but laugh. "I thought you wanted a four-wheeler, now it is a jet ski?"

"Hey, it may not stop there. What else you got?"

"Oh, something you don't have up in New York I guarantee ya."

Faith knew what it was, "The Shangri-La?"

They stopped at their favorite diner for a burger and the best pie ever made. It was a Roberts' family tradition; they couldn't leave the lake without going to the Shangri-La. It wasn't as fancy as Mountain Harbor, but it had a fisherman's ambiance. A family owned establishment since the lake was built, clean but nothing amazing. There were adjoining cabins and docks on the waterfront with a small marina in a lagoon. If you didn't get there early, you could forget about getting a seat. As always, it was packed, but they grabbed themselves three seats at the counter rather than waiting in line for a table.

The waitress recognized Clint but forgot his name, "You're…" She tapped her head with a pencil, "That writer for the ah…"

"Clint Roberts with the Times, but I don't work there anymore. I'm doing some freelancing now."

She rolled her eyes, "I wish I could do a little freelancing. Whatcha' having, Shug?"

Clint smiled teasing the older woman. She wasn't that much older, maybe ten years, maybe fifteen. She had a bouffant hairdo and a figure like the actress Christina Hendricks. Clint teased and smiled, "Shug is what I'd like but considering we're in public…"

She grinned coyly and slapped him on the arm, "Only if it is on the menu, honey."

"Darn. Well in that case better make it burger, burger, burger and peanut butter pie, and don't tell me ya ain't got it.

"Comin' up, *darlin'*."

She spun around and put her ticket in the window and brought them all some drinks. Both he and the girls were starving. They looked across the dining room out the window to the famed Hickory Nut Mountain towering above the lake; boats were zipping in and out of the harbor. The girls chatted, and Clint eavesdropped on conversations throughout the room. He watched their waitress with an inquisitive eye. She had so much hair on top in that bun; she could pack a Luger in there, and you'd never know. He wondered how a woman her age stayed in such great shape. She was quite a specimen. She had curves that kept men up late at night tossing and turning. After so much gandering', Clint started to get a serious headache.

"You got some BC powder?" he asked.

She filled up their glasses, "Coming up. Too much sun?"

"Too much thinking."

She tossed him the BC and leaned on the counter with one arm and the other one on her hip. "Now what could you possibly be thinking?"

Clint poured the powder into his mouth and chased it with water, "Nothing but trouble, always trouble."

She winked at him and walked away, "There's a cure for that you know?"

Clint turned around on his stool as if to get his mind off things, to look at the lake and the magnificent scenery outside, and in the room. A rather spectacular looking woman was sitting at a table in the corner with her son. Faith noticed he had spotted her and hoped he wouldn't do his juggling act with the salt and pepper shakers to catch her attention. Sure enough, his hand reached across the counter and picked up the shakers, she quickly snatched them from his hands.

"I just want to eat. If I wanted to see the circus, I'd buy a ticket."

Clint laughed, "Now, what do you mean?"

"You know exactly what I mean."

He put his arm around her and gave her a hug. "Well yer a little testy. Does that make you feel better?"

"Some."

He kissed her on the head, "That?"

"Keep working it, daddio." She looked over her dad's shoulder. A tall handsome man sat down at the table with the lady in the corner. "Ahem, hubby alert. See."

Nonchalantly, "Oh, I didn't notice."

In her best Chinese accent, "Sorree Charree, outta luck…. again".

He acted bored and tapped on the counter with his fork, eying the pie behind the glass sliding door of the pie rack. He pretended to be uninterested and gazed out the window to the blue water and sailboats in the distance. The girls talked about jet skiing. They were both hooked. Clint was getting impatient for the food. He was starved; three hours riding waves burned a lot of energy. Probably why he had a headache. As he was sitting there eyeing every plate that came out of the kitchen, he overheard Lois, the waitress, talking to one of the cooks in back about "poor Mr. Johnson."

When she came out he inquired, "Are you talking about the man that's missing?"

She refilled his glass, "Yeah, did you know him?"

"Nope, just been hearing bits and pieces."

"They found him this morning, 'bout four hours ago. He was such a nice old man. Why would anyone want to do something like that? Whoever it was is an animal."

The bell rang, and three plates of burgers and chips lay on the window. She sighed and smiled, "Enjoy your meal. Wink when you're ready for dessert."

Before his daughter knew it, Clint was chewing on his second bite by the time she said a prayer which annoyed her to no end. The most he usually did was stop with a mouthful of food and close his eyes. He looked so stupid sometimes, and often reminded her of a big chipmunk. Nevertheless, when she finished her prayer thanking God for the wonderful day and the "great time on the lake", he resumed eating, and in seconds his burger gone, devoured, before she had eaten her first good bite. When it came to appetite, Clint was not one to waste time. As he wiped off his chin with a mouth still full of food chopping away, he listened in on Lois's conversation with the cook. From what he gathered, Mr. Johnson was the type that would have given them his money and more if anyone asked. There was no sense in anybody doing to him what they did. Clint imagined that he was like the gentlemen at the dock, a guy that would loan his jet ski to a total stranger. Tom Johnson was the same kind of fellow. According to people's recollection, he was a saint, and yet from what they were saying from the police report, he had been beaten to the point he was almost unrecognizable even by his wife.

Clint tried not to listen anymore; the thought was beginning to make him sick. He looked at the pie in the pie rack, and as tempting as it was, he decided to take it home and eat it under more pleasant conditions. When they were finished, Clint left a nice tip, and it was around 1:30 or thereabouts when they left. They had mentioned they might go back to the river to catch some more fish. Lois put the tip in her pocket and looked around the counter for a card or a number written on a napkin as she picked up the dishes. She was disappointed there was none. She liked him. As Lois wiped off the counter, she watched them through the windows as his daughter kind of skipped across the parking lot with her arms locked in his. Faith was a beautiful girl, with long legs and brown hair almost down to her waist. It was clearly obvious to anyone who observed them that they were close. She could tell by the way he treated his daughter what kind of man he was like. He was gentle, humorous, and playful. Lois sighed and put down a new set of silverware on the counter as they drove away. She was seeing fewer and fewer men like that.

As Clint drove back to the cabin, he was contemplating a nice nap, but the girls were insistent on more canoeing. Reluctantly, he went along. So, they loaded up the pick-up with the canoe and tubes. Tubes were a little bit more comfortable for the girls, and he could do more angling without them in the boat. They put in somewhere around three o'clock. Clint was tired, and he didn't want to be on the river more than a couple of hours. They passed by the cliffs and went down to an area that they called "clover rock". There were four large flat rocks about ten feet in diameter long just about a foot or so below the surface of the water. It was a perfect place to dive off, and the fishing was pretty good there with larger fish congregating in the depths of the cooler water below the stones.

The girls jumped around from clover to clover. Clint cast and cast without much luck. He changed lures several times, and nothing was biting. Eventually, a couple of fisherman came down and caught a nice stringer of smallmouth. They told him what they were using, and one guy even tossed him an extra lure. Clint thanked them and put it on. He then canoed down about seventy-five yards past the girls and tossed his line in the shallows below some bluffs. Strike!

His line took off downstream. Clint jumped out of the canoe and took off after it, reeling as he tromped knee high through the waters. It was big. The line went down hard, tugging. He was headed for some big rocks where he could break the line. Clint couldn't allow any slack or he'd lose him; so, he stayed right with the fish reeling him in. Then, the fish shot out of the water flapping well above Clint's head, his black and silver body flipping through the air showering Clint's face with water. He smashed back into the river and took off again. The line now zigzagged up river, and then like a torpedo, he turned and shot back towards the bank. Clint could hear the girls shouting with excitement. Out of the corner of his eye, he could see a group of canoers watching. He surely didn't want to lose it with an audience. Clint finally gave him some slack as the fish began tiring, and then he reeled the line steady again and worked him back to the shore. When he got close enough, Clint ran and fetched him from the water. He then held him up, and the girls cheered. He was at least six and a half pounds of sparkling largemouth bass, the biggest he'd ever caught in the river.

Clint put him on the stringer and paddled up to where the girls were. There were several couples that had been watching, and Clint did enjoy bragging about his catch. Faith gave him a big hug and kiss and told her daddy they weren't going to eat his catch, she wanted him to mount it.

"Well if that's the case, I better get to catching us some dinner, huh?"

And, dinner he did catch. Within the next hour, Clint landed five more sizeable fish, enough for several meals. Finally, he went back up to where the girls were. He was ready to go back; they were ready for him to play. They compromised, and he sat on a big clover rock and drank a couple of bottles of water, relaxing, letting the current drift around him. Another fisherman came by in a kayak. He was from Kansas and hadn't been having much luck. Nice guy, about Clint's age, in his forties. They talked about the economy some, the state of affairs in government. He was a knowledgeable man and pleasant; things weren't much different in Kansas. Times were tough, and he just needed to get away. Clint knew the feeling and then remembered something. He went to his rod and clipped off the lure.

"Someone gave it me. Pass it on." He pointed to the spot down the river where he caught his stringer, and told him to try there. A little bit later, Clint saw him reeling in a couple of fish. He looked back at Clint and raised his hat and gave a thankful wave. After a while, he was gone.

Clint was tired. He tried dropping hints to leave, but the girls were having too much fun playing Marco Polo in the clovers, and even convinced him to join them. Clint walked around on the clover rock with his eyes closed.

"Marco?"

"Polo." Giggle.

"Marco?"

"Polo." Snicker. "Polo." Giggle.

Then he heard more laughter, mature laughter, female laughter. Clint peeked through his fingers. There were five girls in inner tubes just upstream heading for him. Girls would not be the right word; they were well endowed young women, in college or in their early twenties. They were laughing, and so were Faith and Angelina.

"Having fun?" one of them asked.

"Polo," another laughed.

"Now, close your eyes, dad, you're cheating."

All the girls had a good laugh. They got out of their tubes at the clover rocks and dove into the waters frolicking in their bikini tops and cutoffs which of course Clint very much enjoyed. As they talked, he discovered they were all from the University, two had graduated, and the others still had another year to go. They said that once a year they take a vacation, and this year they decided to come to the river and skip the beach.

They talked for a long time, and Faith could tell her dad was really enjoying their company, a whole lot. It was amazing how a man who looks so tired can suddenly get these bursts of energy. He started telling them of when he went to college there, stories she had heard many times before, of being banned from the art building, permanently, dancing on cop cars, his fraternity that was closed down. It didn't take him long, and he had them all laughing. She and Angelina went back to playing Marco Polo *without* him, seeing that he was obviously preoccupied. After a while, Faith opened her eyes and looked around; the college girls were half way down the river to the bend. So was her father, swimming along holding on to one of their inner tubes. She could hear them all laughing it up. Faith had had enough. She stood up on the clover rock and shook her head.

Angelina inquired, "Is he always like this?"

"No. He used to not be; he never was like this when my folks were married. But, he came home one day about a year after the divorce and said it was time to start over. Said he was going to get in the 'game', not sit on the bench any longer."

"The 'game'? How long ago was that?"

"Maybe a year ago," she smirked, "but all he does is talk." She rolled her eyes, "His ego needs to get scratched. That's what he says. Says it is good therapy." She giggled

Angelina quipped as he floated further downstream, "Looks like he should be cured by now."

Faith smiled with her hand on her hips, "Oh, don't worry; I know how to get him back. Watch this." She cupped her hands around her mouth and yelled down river, "Oh, grandpa! We're getting hungry now. Will ya take us back to the farm?" She said the word farm with as thick of a country accent as a person can spread on a word.

Angelina giggled. She yelled, "Yeah, *grandpa*, can ya take us back to the truck 'for it gets dark?"

"Yeah, grandpa", Faith pointed to her heart and coughed, "You don't want to forget your medicine. 'Member what the doctor said."

"Grandpa?"

Another girl spun around in her tube, "Grandpa, you're a grandpa?"

Clint displayed his agitation, "No, no, they are just joking…"

"Nice talking to you."

"Yeah", she looked at her watch, "We've got to go."

And just like that, the girls went on downstream. Clint came trudging back up the river through the water with a terse look of irritation poised in his lips. "Now, what did you have to go and do that for? I was just talking".

Faith smiled smugly, "Well, you can just talk with us. Whatcha' want to talk about, daddy?"

Clint shook his head grumbling and grabbed his rod out of the canoe. He looked at the line he'd cut. He didn't really feel like putting on another lure. Instead, he relented and stayed with the girls for a bit until they were ready to go. They were tired too and wanted to ride in the canoe the rest of the way back so he tied their tubes to the back of the boat and was about to launch when a canoe paddled towards them. It was two men in a beat up aluminum canoe. He heard them cussing. Clint stopped. The girls were already in the canoe waiting for him to jump in.

Faith looked at her father and prodded, "Come on."

Clint looked at the two guys in the silver boat that was almost up to the rocks. He didn't move. Faith again called to her father, but this time with urgency, "Let's go, Dad".

Clint could hear them clearly. They might have been far away as a good long cast. They were loud, and he heard them talking about 'screwing whores'. Every other word was "bitch" or a variety of words that you would associate with it. One of them had a rather distasteful laugh; it was peculiar, weird. He knew the girls could hear it. He looked at the girls, and Faith shook her head 'no'. Clint didn't like it one bit, but he reluctantly decided to let them pass and get on down the river. He figured the men would paddle a lot faster than he could with two tired girls lying in his boat, and it wouldn't be long, and they would be out of range. He watched as the men went through the rapids and then steered around the clover rocks, and they were almost even with him. Clint stood on the shore staring at the two.

The one in back was a huge man and looked to be a good fifteen or twenty years older than the one in front. He had thin grayish long hair which was tied in a ponytail in back. He wore a sleeveless denim shirt with jeans and boots which was strange. Nobody wore boots on the river unless they were waders. Everyone wore shorts; it was summer. Along the side of his jeans was a knife in a leather strap. That was not in itself unusual because people carry knives for cleaning fish, but Clint knew the difference between a cleaning knife and a skinning knife. This was a deer knife used for skinning, with a blade at least about 10 inches long. His skin was brown and wrinkled, dried from the sun, and his face looked like a crumpled paper bag. His jaw was amazingly square and stout. He had a slight overbite, and his teeth the way they came together resembled a trap. Clint studied the man, and his lower jaw seemed to move as if from a hinge, like it had been broken and set in place. His face was covered with what was supposed to be a beard. It looked more like thin lifeless gray moss that hung down a couple of inches from his chin.

The other though, the younger one in front, didn't look right from the start. He had this lazy eye, and his head was shaved military style, but he doubted he was ever in the military. His arms were covered in tattoos, and around his throat, he had a tattoo of a rope tied like a noose around his neck. Clint had to do a double take; it looked so real. On one side of his chest, he had a cross and on the other side a pentagram. His complexion was very creamy white, almost like milk. It was obvious he hadn't been in the sun in a long time. He wore cut offs that sagged way down and came to just below his knees. His boxers, red and gold, hung out. He wasn't a typical river person, or tourist, not by a long shot. As he paddled, the muscles rippled across his chest. His ribs resembled a cage cast in ivory tusk, and his shoulders were broad. Clint inspected him as he passed, as did the girls. He was no doubt frightening with his arms bulging with muscles and wrapped in a barbed wire tattoo.

The men looked over at Clint and the girls as they canoed by. The younger one, about twenty five, with the short hair, had a smirk on his face. He turned to the man in back and continued with his conversation, "Yeah, I slapped that bitch and grabbed her by her head and unzipped my…"

"HEY! Why don't you watch what you're saying?"

The young one with the tattoos and the lazy eye stuck his paddle in the water and slowed the canoe down. His lip snarled, "What did you say?" He laughed. Their canoe steered back toward Clint.

"I said to shut... your... mouth." The girls were sitting in the boat looking up at Clint. They were both terrified.

Clint could hear Faith's voice pleading with him, "Daad. Shhhhh." She then closed her eyes and said a prayer.

The guy stood up in the front of the canoe. It had turned around in the water and was coming back toward them on shore. "You said what? You want me to shut my mouth, do ya? Wellll, why don't ya make me, ole man?"

Clint looked at the two men in the canoe. He held a paddle firmly in his hand. The other man slung his paddle out across the water. He motioned with his hand for Clint to come out to him. "Come on, punk. I'm gonna mess you up."

Clint was stunned. The provocation left no room to back off. He knew he was in way too deep; he was going to have to fight. It was a situation impossible to win, and yet there wasn't any other recourse. He wasn't sure what he was going to do at that exact moment. He knew one thing; don't run from growling dogs. You have to stand your ground. Clint clinched his paddle and waited for them to come over. The guy stood up in the front of the canoe and stretched out his arms to the side and then brought them up slowly and flexed his biceps. It was something you'd expect to see in a school yard or prison. The man was not right; he could see it in his eyes. One eye had a steely glare like an alligator, but the other eye that slightly crossed to the outside was dull. It might have even been blind. As the canoe drew closer, the sneer grew wider across his face. "You don't mess with me, punk." He then pounded his chest, "Ya gonna get some, bitch."

Clint, to his own amazement, didn't turn back. In fact, he started wading in the water toward the guy. It was like his body was moving him; strangely, something was taking over. At that moment, it didn't matter to him if he won or lost; he was seething red with anger. The only clear thought in his head was at what moment would he tell the girls to run? That's all he was thinking. Should they go up through the woods or run down the river towards the college girls? He wondered how far away they might be. How far away was that other man whom he had talked to earlier? Clint just wanted them to get out of there as fast as they could. He wanted them out of harm's way. For sure, he didn't want his daughter to see what was about to happen.

Clint waded in the shallow water toward the canoe. He knew he should have kept his mouth shut, but he just couldn't. He tried. It was too late now. His hand tightened into a fist becoming like a piece of stone. He stopped about waist deep and waited for the guy to jump out of the canoe. He was surprised he hadn't already, and it dawned on him, maybe the punk couldn't swim. He was about to find out.

He pointed to Clint as their canoe came closer, "I'm gonna kick your ass!" The veins in his neck spread out across his shoulders like a cobra, that rope stretched wide, and he laughed with this wild, penetrating, cold gaze, "Yer mine, faggot."

Clint didn't say a word. He just waited. The big guy in the back of the canoe put his paddle deep in the water. He suddenly did a back stroke and brought it to a halt. They all looked up river. Canoes were coming. Clint could hear the voices, lots of them. There was laughter.

Looking over his shoulder, Clint could see maybe four or five, possibly six canoes of men, with girlfriends or wives. Clint still hadn't said a word. The big guy in back splashed the menacing one with his paddle. His voice sounded like gravel, like rocks churning inside a cement truck, when he spoke. "Come on. Let's go, Tyrone."

"Won't take but a second. I'm gonna teach this 'n here a lesson."

His voice graveled again, "Hey man, he didn't mean it."

"Yeah, I meant it." He pointed to Clint as the canoe steered around, "I'm gonna get you. You just wait."

The bigger one splashed him again, "He's just drunk; don't pay no attention to him, man." He then nudged him on his backside with his paddle, "Sit down, Tyrone, we gotta long ways to go."

Tyrone sat down in the front of the canoe laughing. He looked over to the girls, and then turned back to the big guy in back, "You know what I'm thinking?"

The older one barked, "Shut up, Ty; get your paddle!"

Finally, and with great relief, they went downstream. Clint watched Tyrone fetch the paddle from a shore of rocks at the neck of the narrows. He stood and raised his arms flexing, looking back at Clint mocking with laughter. He could hear the bearded one growling to get back in the canoe, and then they were finally gone. A minute later the other folks paddled up to the clover rock. Angelina was so scared she was shaking. She looked pale; her face was white. She didn't want to get back in the water. Faith sat with her in the canoe as Clint told the group what had just happened. They knew instantly who he was talking about. Their wives felt uncomfortable, said they had a bad feeling about them. The women said they drank beer and eyed them as they passed, not saying a word. It sent chills up their spines, especially the younger one; he seemed the creepiest.

After a while, they were all ready to leave. They insisted that Clint and the girls stay with them which made the girls feel a whole lot better, Clint too. What Clint didn't like was that the group was in no hurry to get off the water. He was. What should have been maybe an hour, took them two and a half hours and so by the time they got back down to the bridge, it was getting close to dark. There was only about a half hour to go before sunset. Fortunately, Clint and the girls didn't have to get the four-wheeler and cross back over the mountain. The folks kindly offered to give them a lift back to his truck.

They left the canoe and tubes at the bridge and went. Angelina was still very scared, both girls were. They hadn't said much the rest of the afternoon. Of course, it had been a long day, and they were tired. They crossed over the mountain, and the sun was just beginning to set over the far western range. Brilliant orange swirled in the sky and another front of clouds was moving in.

By the time they picked up his truck and left the river, it was dark. He turned on the lights as they cruised up the old dirt road to the highway. It had been a long, long day. The girls huddled in the back seat as he drove back over the mountain. They were all worn out and hungry; and he still had to fix them something to eat and clean fish when he got back. They turned off the highway onto their road, and as Clint approached the crossing, he saw through the trees blue lights flashing from the bridge. He immediately slowed down and approached with caution. There must have been an accident. Somebody's been hurt.

As Clint drove down to the bridge, he realized there were two cop cars on the other bank. The canoe rental guy was there too, and some other people in trucks. He leaned out his window and looked at the men searching the shores with flashlights. "What's going on? Lose some folks? Someone hurt?"

A young deputy walked up the embankment to the bridge and came over to Clint's truck inspecting it with his flash light. His light shined in Clint's eyes and over to the girls in back. "Had some trouble down at Rocky Shoals. A guy was beat up pretty bad. He's at St. Joseph's. Have y'all seen anybody?"

Clint got out of the truck; it looked like Angie had fallen asleep, and Faith had her arm around her. He didn't want them to hear about anything else knowing that they were already shook up enough.

"I'm okay, dad."

"I love you, hon." He shut the door, "I'll be right back."

"I love you too."

Clint walked down to the end of the bridge with the deputy where the officer asked for his driver's license. He was a young well-built patrolman in a neatly pressed brown uniform with perfectly groomed short hair. He appeared very professional which kind of surprised Clint; he expected more of the stereotypical redneck cop. This guy wasn't. Clint studied his eyes; he knew this was serious. "What happened?"

"We're not sure. Two guys were in a fight down by Rocky Shoals. One guy was just fishing. The two men that beat him up were from Oklahoma; we know that. Their truck is still at the canoe rental place. Can't find either one of them."

There must have been five or six men in the woods walking around with flashlights prowling through sycamores and elms. The trees' shadows from the rising moon looked like long fingers stretching across the river, like they were reaching for the rocks on the other side. Clint got a bad feeling. He didn't like what he was seeing; his cabin was just up the road. He was putting it together, and he quickly added it up. "So, there were two? Then, you've got a description?"

The young deputy described them to a tee. They were the same guys alright. He described the rope tattoo and the cross and pentagram on the chest. The officer even mentioned his lazy eye. Then, Clint proceeded to tell him what had happened previously in the day. He recounted everything while the officer scribbled notes. "I've got two girls up there in my truck scared to death right now. I want to know what are you guys going to do about it?"

"Sir, we are doing all we can." The officer explained that they had patrols all up and down the river, and they put out an APB in several counties. "We're letting people know. You ain't the only one scared, sir. We have a camp with a couple a hundred kids just down river from the shoals, and they are on the lookout. There are cabins everywhere in these parts. These guys could be anywhere, and we are stretched thin. We have eight officers and over a hundred square miles to cover."

Clint started to offer an apology, but Officer Hewitt told to him to "forget it". He understood. He said he believed they would have to go back to get their truck sometime that evening so he had it staked out hoping they would show up. "Thing is we suspect there might be receipts in that truck which would be valuable evidence for another crime we're investigating, but we can't get in it till we get a warrant. We are waiting."

"You think they may be responsible for Mr. Johnson?"

"If we could prove they were in the area, it would be our best lead yet, but we have to be wary of probable cause. We do the wrong thing, and it is thrown out of court."

"I've got something you probably don't have yet: a name.

One is named Tyrone, the one with the lazy eye."

The officer wrote the name down on a pad and then handed Clint his card with his cell phone number on it. "You call me first thing if you see anything. My name is Jason. I'll get back with you later about a statement." He looked at his men in the woods, "We are going to have to get off the river or one of my men is going to get snake bit. Tomorrow we'll start early, that is, if they don't show up for their truck. If they don't, I suspect these guys are heading to the lake. There are hundreds of islands down there. We're worried about them stealing a boat and coming up on some campers in the middle of the night. That would be bad. Hate to be short, but we've got a whole lot of area to cover and not that much time."

Clint asked about the truck, "Got anything back on it yet. Know who owns it? Was it stolen?"

"Roy Dale Osborn. No reports on it being stolen. Our Sheriff is talking to the folks in McAlester now. We think the fella with him is his cousin. If it is, he just got out of prison about two weeks ago. He is one bad seed." The deputy turned and yelled out to his men, "Let's wrap it up, fellas! Ain't nothing here."

The men started coming out of the woods swatting mosquitoes on the back of their neck. It was muggy and miserable. Clint and the deputy started walking back to his truck, and he asked about the man that was beat up.

The officer stared at him funny like, "Beat up ain't the word for it. He's in ICU, just holding on."

"Do you know where he's from?"

"Kansas. He's a preacher."

"Oh, Jesus." That got Clint to thinking, "Ah, there were also a bunch of college girls on that river. I hoped they hadn't run into them."

"They're the ones that reported it. They saved the man. He was screaming for his life, and they went back up river. They're the ones that called us. They gave us a really good description of the men."

"Then, the girls are safe?"

"Oh yeah, they are in town for the night; they're alright."

Officer Hewitt then helped Clint load up the canoe into the back of the truck with the tubes.

The deputy looked at the girls in Clint's truck. "Your daughters?"

"One is. The other is our friend from New York".

"It is a shame. Use to not be this way, but in the last ten years, it has just gotten crazy." He looked at Clint, "Do yourself a favor: teach them right now how to shoot." He shook his head, "Guys like this are everywhere now. What do you think it is going to be like in another ten years?" He looked around at the men coming out of the woods. There was still one light down the river flashing through the trees. He yelled for him to hurry up; they had to go.

"Funny thing sir, if they had messed with those girls, we wouldn't be having this conversation."

"Why's that?" Clint inquisitively asked.

"Two of them were packin'. They were criminal justice majors. They had Glocks in their tackle box. They could have blown those dudes apart. That's why they took off; they saw the guns."

Clint was surprised. He never suspected the college girls had guns on them. It never dawned on him.

"You get yourself a gun, and get your girl one. She's gonna need it. You too. That man lying on that table in Hot Springs in that ICU could be you."

Clint was in a state of disbelief. It used to be the most peaceful place in the world, but everything suddenly changed. It wasn't anymore. He shook his head and opened the door to his truck to get in, "What's gone wrong, deputy? Why is all this happening? It is not supposed to happen out here of all places?"

"I almost forgot this." He handed Clint back his license. "It's the law, Mr. Roberts."

"What do you mean?"

"Instead of making us civilized, it has made us the opposite. The law values the rights of criminals more than its citizens. We are paying a big price for being wrong."

Clint looked over at Angie with her eyes closed. She

looked so pale, like a porcelain doll in the moon light. He started up the truck and was about to drive off when the officer stopped him. "Oh, one more thing, I forgot to tell you. That crazy one has got a gun. You see anything suspicious; call." Clint thanked the officer for the advice and drove on up to the cabin. It was dark when he pulled in. He wished he had left on a light, but he never suspected they would be getting back so late. Clint regretted not bringing along the dogs; they would be a big help right about now. He got out and told Faith to wait in the car. As he walked up to the porch, he picked up a hickory stick and clutched it in his hand. Clint paused at the screen door. He should have brought one of the men up there with him. He hesitated for a second as he reached for the door. It wasn't too late to go back. He looked back at the girls in the truck. It was odd, but he didn't want to appear a coward. He opened the door, carefully.

Clint reached his hand inside and felt around for the switch on the cedar plank wall. He found it. When the light came on, it momentarily blinded him. He looked about the room with squinted eyes until everything came into focus. Room by room, he checked to make sure no one was there. He even checked the closets and under the beds; it was fine. Angelina was still asleep, and so he carried her into the cabin with Faith holding open the door and laid her on the bed. The place was stuffy and sweltering so he turned on the fan and opened the window. Faith opened up the other windows, and he unpacked the gear and laid his catch on the counter. They were lifeless. It seemed like years since he caught them.

Faith sat at the kitchen table not saying much. A gloomy look hung on her face, and he wondered if she wanted to go home or if she was just tired.

"You alright, honey?"

"I'm okay. Just worried about Angie."

"If she wants to leave, we'll pack up and go tomorrow. There are things we can do in town."

Clint made a sandwich for the two of them and then sliced his peanut butter pie in half, sliding her plate over in front of her. She started to say a prayer, and he stopped her. "Let me say it". He thanked God for the protection He provided that day, for his daughter and her best friend. He asked God to be with the man from Kansas and to bless the man who loaned them the jet ski. He then kissed her hand and said Amen. They ate quietly together. They could hear the thunder rolling in; the trees began to blow. Neither said much. Clint ate more slowly than usual and looked at his beautiful daughter. Every day now, she was growing older; everyday was more special.

She left half her sandwich on her plate and went to bed. Clint cleaned up and washed the dishes and then cleaned the fish though he was exhausted and as tired as he could ever remember. He needed a good night's sleep and figured tonight he'd probably get it with the rain coming and all. When he was done cleaning, he went out to the porch and sat on the divan watching the storm begin to blow across the fields.

He tried to figure out what he was feeling, and after a while, he realized it was a violation. He had been violated, the girls too. All these years, he had escaped the city for some peace and serenity. The river and the cabin were like his sanctuary. Now, it had been violated. It didn't seem the same anymore; the innocence of all their surroundings had been accosted by filth and vulgarity. Providence destroyed.

After a while, he got up and latched the screen door and went inside and sat on the couch. Just as he was falling asleep, he had the sense that someone was right behind him. He jumped up and turned around.

It was Faith.

"Daddy. I can't sleep."

She lay down beside him and put her head on his shoulder. She hadn't done that in a long while. He held her tightly like he did when she was a little girl. Her cheek was next to his, and she squeezed his broad shoulders. Neither said anything for a long time.

Clint didn't know what she was thinking, but he felt like the trip had turned into another disaster just like the whole year had. He felt responsible that nothing seemed to go right, "Honey, I am sorry for the way things have been this last year. I feel like I've failed you. I've let you down."

"Let me down?" Her voice was still soft against his chest. "Are you serious? I have more respect for you now than I ever have." She sat up beside him, "This is not your fault."

"I feel like I should have done something down on that river. I didn't handle it the best way. I put you girls in jeopardy."

Faith shook his shoulder, "What are you talking about? Dad, you saved us. And you're not to blame for this last year. It wasn't easy for you to take some of the jobs you have. When things got tough you did it for me. You are my hero; don't *ever* forget it."

Clint never knew she felt like that. She never told him. All he ever felt like was a disappointment. He hugged her and thanked her. She was his hero too; she never let anything get her down. She was the one that kept him going. He could always count on her. They sat there in the dark, and she held up her pinky, "Let's make a pinky promise." She grabbed his hand, "You will always look after me, and I will always look after you. We look out for each other, always."

Clint slipped his finger around hers, "But honey, I've always looked after you."

"I know, but when I break up your flirt therapy, don't get mad. I'm looking out for your best interest, just remember that."

"Sweetheart, I'm sorry I do that I'm just..."

"Lonely. I know dad. I know how hard it has been on you."

"Does it show?"

"It does to me, but I know you. I'll let you know when it is the right one; that's a promise too."

"You just remember that when you get older. I've made a promise to you."

She yawned and got up and patted him on the head. "Sure, sure, we'll discuss it later. I'm going to bed."

"You'll be alright?"

"I'll be fine. Goodnight."

Clint went to the front door and locked it, and left only one window slightly open in the living room. As a precaution, he put a steak knife beside him on the table. He placed a baseball bat in the corner and stretched out and relaxed. He was exhausted mentally and physically. The sound of thunder was closing in. Usually, he would stay up and watch the storm, but he was way too tired. He hoped to get a good night's rest and that tomorrow would be better than today. Little did he know as he got comfortable on the couch and closed his eyes, he was not alone.

There were eyes watching from the woods.

Chapter Seven

Perhaps, it was the thunder or howling wind. Most likely, it was the steady rain that drowned out the noise, but he never heard the screen being cut or the window as it was raised. He never heard them creeping cross the floor. Clint had no idea they were there. That's how it usually is when the yomen comes: it's too late. It is just on you. There is no escape.

When Clint awoke, the knife was already a half inch into his throat. He struggled in the dark, but a knee was already crushing in on his chest. Some wake up from a nightmare; Clint Roberts woke into one. He never saw a thing. It was just a dark blur, and a fist pounded against his face, a hand covered his mouth and a knife pushed into his neck. When he tried to shout, blood filled his mouth, and he could only gurgle. But he recognized the voice above him.

It was a laugh he'd never forget, "Remember me, cocksucker?"

Something heavy came down upon his head, again and again. It was at first pain, but then numbness. The voices vanished in the dark. And that's all he could remember.

The next thing he knew it was all black. It was like waking in a cave. It was the first time he felt the pain. He didn't know where he was or how he got there, but he was in a sitting up position; he didn't think he was lying down. He heard voices; he heard Faith. He heard crying. Clint tried to open his mouth to yell. It was like the muscles were ripped out of his throat. He felt air move up and down his tongue, but it was dry and hot like fire. He made barely a sound. He listened. He could hear talking; it must have been Angelina crying. He heard the

191

distinctive rough gravelly voice that he had heard at the river.

Clint still couldn't understand why he was blind. He tried to reach for his eyes, but his arms wouldn't move. They were tied behind his back. His shoulders moved, and his arms pulled, but it was as if his hands had been wrenched off, like they were gone. He couldn't feel his fingers; there was nothing, no circulation. He tried to put his fragmented thoughts together. They were all over the place, like broken pieces, shattered. He wondered if this could possibly be a dream, but he had never felt like this in a dream. *They* were never this horrific. Clint then moved his knee, but his legs went nowhere. He realized he was tied down in a chair. Again, he tried to yell.

"Heyyy." It was not much more than a breath. He then lifted up his chair with his legs and dropped it back down on the floor. They heard him. He heard footsteps, and then the door swung open.

"Looky here; papa is up."

"Daddy." It was Faith's sweet voice. "Daddy," she cried.

"Ah, he's alright."

Clint tried to get out the word, "Hon". It scratched in his throat and dragged like a fingernail drags across an Emory board. Then, the footsteps came closer. His head was jerked back. He felt something pull across his face like a sheet, and then suddenly, a painful rip tore across his face. It was blinding. Clint adjusted his eyes. Tyrone stood in front of him in a convoluted haze. As his vision cleared, he saw that Tyrone had a pillow case and duct tape in his hand and leaned right down into his face and grinned, "Miss me?" He laughed, "Told ya I'd see ya again. Didn't I?"

Faith was standing behind Tyrone at the door. The other guy, the big guy, with the long scraggly gray hair, had her little arm tightly gripped in his huge hand. The only relief he had was that she still had clothes on, the same clothes. He couldn't see Angelina, at least not her face. He just saw her legs and shorts behind the big guy. Her legs looked so small, so frail.

"See, he's alright". Tyrone patted him on the head. He looked around to Faith, "Told ya he'd be okay". Clint tried to say something, but Tyrone put the tape back over his lips and pressed it against his mouth. "Shhhhh."

He turned his head sideways and looked at Tyrone with his dull eye, the one that drifted to the right. A smirk curled up the side of his face, "Don't chu' worry, pops. We are becoming real good friends. Me and Roy Dale gonna take good care of these pretty girls."

Clint tried to yell but to no avail. A low scratchy smothered growl in his throat was the most he could muster. Tyrone put the pillow case back over him and shut the door. Clint pulled on his arms and twisted his wrists, but there was just nothing. The ropes were way too tight. He couldn't do anything. He was absolutely powerless. He sat in darkness and listened; it was all he could do. He listened for anything, for everything. Then, he heard the TV playing. It was Dragnet. He recognized the familiar introduction though it was muffled coming through the wall. Then, he could hear Tyrone. He could hear him laughing; he heard both the men laughing. He didn't hear a word out of the girls, and to Clint that was good. If they screamed or cried, he knew what would be happening, but as much as he hated the sound of Tyrone's laughter, he preferred it to the alternative. It is amazing how the senses adjust. He couldn't see anything, but his hearing became acute. It seemed like his ears could pick up the slightest whisper in the next room. He could even hear Angelina's faint voice asking for something. He listened to her tiny footsteps on the floor and heavier ones behind her. He knew she was in the bathroom, but he also knew the door had not closed. He didn't hear it shut. He listened to the sound of the toilet flushing, and he heard their footsteps on the floor going back into the living room.

Clint was irate. They didn't even let her go to the bathroom alone. They wouldn't even give her that decency. He imagined them standing there at the doorway while she was on the toilet. The thugs! He pulled on his ropes trying to get loose, but it was useless, then realized he needed to stop listening. He didn't know how long he'd live. He needed to start planning, thinking of options. He knew there was no way they were getting out of there alive, unless something happened, some mistake or miracle. He didn't know the time, but he knew it was still dark. Tyrone had turned the light on in the room when he came in. He could see the kitchen light shining off the floor at Faith's feet when she stood at the doorway. He tried to put it all together, figure it out, what they were going to do. They knew the police were after them, and they probably knew their truck had been impounded or was staked out. They were going to take his truck, but when they did, more than likely all three of them would be left behind. They wouldn't be left alive either. It was just a question of how much they'd go through before Tyrone slit their throats. Clint wondered why it hadn't happened already. He figured they knew the Sheriff's office was swarming the area. He suspected they had been down at the bridge deep in the woods watching the activity earlier that evening. They waited until the deputies were gone and then came out. They might have even seen him on the bridge; they might have known he was on that road and just waited till it got good and dark, and followed.

Clint tried to think what was going to happen from here. They had the girls in the next room; he was tied up. Were they going to take the girls in the other bedroom? Would they do it separately? Why hadn't they already killed him? He then wondered about Tom Johnson. These had to be the same guys. They could have just killed him, but the waitress said he was beaten to the point he was unrecognizable. Did they torture him? Did they get pleasure from it? Maybe they would make him watch what they were going to do to the girls? Maybe that's how they planned on torturing him or how they planned on torturing Faith, and Angelina. Maybe they wanted them both to watch?

Clint was going crazy thinking about it. He started hyperventilating in the pillow case; he was getting so worked up. He could feel the linen blowing out and contract across his face. He had to get his mind off of it. The thoughts were driving him insane. He had to think of an escape, of plans. He had to think of things constructively. A surge of energy and relief began to flow through him as he pondered possibilities. The only weapon he had was his mind. He was smarter than them;

he could overcome them. He just had to think. Maybe, he could tell them he had money, get them to take him to the bank. That might work. He could pass a note to the teller. That was a good plan if he could get them to believe it. There was a far greater chance that they would just get his account numbers, kill them all, and go to a bank without him. He wondered if Mr. Johnson had told them the same thing, or the other guy in Oklahoma. Maybe they tried that already, and it didn't work. Clint kept trying to think of ideas, what-ifs, scenarios that might provide an opportunity to escape, or maybe plans just to take him and leave the girls. That might be an option. Perhaps, he could convince them to take him and leave the girls there, but in all likelihood, it would be the other way around. They'd leave him with a steak knife through his chest and haul ass with the girls tied up, maybe pulling into dive motels and rape them until finally they'd get caught. How long could they get away with it? Days? Weeks? He couldn't bear to think about it.

He began to blame himself all over again. None of this would be happening if he had just kept his mouth shut. That's what Clint told himself, but he knew in reality that wasn't true. What did Tom Johnson do? What did that preacher do? What was he doing but just enjoying the river until they came along? Clint hadn't gone out and found trouble. He wasn't looking for it. It found him. He just happened to cross its path. It is like a tornado; they land all around you and never touch you. You can go your entire life without seeing one. They are on TV and the nightly news; fascinating videos taken in another state or the next county, and then one day you look out your window. You hear its roar. You see it coming. Your windows start to shatter. The walls start to shake. The roof over your head explodes. The vortex sucks you into an abyss. It's your turn. It happens just like that. He knew that is really what took place. It wasn't his fault, but still it is a parent's nature to blame themselves regardless of what the circumstances are. With Clint, fault always went full circle, all the around logic and came back to torment him time and time again. His mind was often like a blaze. Worry consumed him racing like fire in the wind. Often, he had no means of stopping it. Guilt and blame raced with complete abandon until some thought would come along and relieve him. It was usually Faith and her sweet sound of comfort. She was always like soothing refreshing water that extinguished the flames. She was his encouragement and strength. But he was without her now, and he needed to find solutions. In desperation, Clint asked for God's help to give him the answers he needed: to help him overcome.

Clint began to focus again on his environment. He didn't know how long they were in the other room, but he knew they listened to three episodes of Dragnet and two of Superman. It had been at least a couple of hours, and he guessed it had to be nearing daybreak. Even through the pillow case over his head, the room was getting lighter. It had to be near dawn. That was good. The two men were laughing in the other room, and occasionally he thought he heard one of the girls. He was getting hungry; his stomach was beginning to growl, and he knew they would be getting hungry too.

About that time, Clint heard heavy footsteps come down the hall. He could feel the breeze as the door swung open. The footsteps came over to him and stopped. The pillow case lifted from his head. It was Roy Dale. "He wants you to cook breakfast."

He untied the ropes around Clint's hands and pulled him up out of the chair. He hadn't realized how big the guy was until he stood up. Roy Dale must have been six foot seven. He was a lot bigger than he looked in the boat. He was huge, and he smelled. His sleeveless denim shirt wreaked and was drenched in sweat rings. Clint exhaled and turned his face away. He rotated his hands and felt the circulation begin to flow back into his wrists. It stung as the blood flowed through the vessels that had been cut off. The sudden rush of blood felt like splinters forced through his hand all the way down to the tips of his fingers.

Roy Dale grabbed him by the shoulder and held him up; then, he untied his feet from the chair but left his feet still bound together at the ankles. He was dragged into the kitchen by the collar like a dog being pulled on leash. Clint had to hop along to keep from falling, and when Roy Dale brought him in, Tyrone started laughing. "Well if it ain't the faggot bunny rabbit."

He was sitting on the couch at the far end of the room with his arm around both girls. It was the first time he saw Faith's face. They both had the same expression. This was their funeral; they both knew it. It is strange in that sort of moment, what you can communicate with your eyes. You are thankful for every day you ever had, every precious minute. You know it is the end so you look back; in every glance, you wring from it the years. Tyrone hurled some more insults at Clint, ordering him around in the process. You would have thought he was at the Beverly Hills Hilton the way he ordered Clint around, mocking.

Tyrone held up his fingers, "I want my omelet this thick and no lumps in my gravy, boy."

The knives had all been removed from the drawer; all sharp objects in the kitchen were gone. He was sure they had them hidden somewhere "safe". He had one butter knife to work with and a rubber spatula. But that was okay. He was just damn glad to get out of the other room, to be able to see his daughter, to see that she was okay. He didn't know how, except for the grace and mercy of God, nothing had been done to her or Angelina…yet!

Every time he hopped from one side of the kitchen to the other, Tyrone laughed or had some smart-assed comment. It wasn't until he was in there that he remembered his throat; he had completely forgotten about it. As he had his back to Tyrone, he reached his hand up to touch it. There was a gauze bandage on it taped with some medical tape they probably found in the bathroom. He didn't know for sure, but he suspected they may have let Faith bandage him. He wondered, because someone did. The cut was below the larynx and above the Adams apple, the same place they put in a tracheal tube. It was a miracle that it hadn't damaged his larynx. It was just sore and swollen. His fingers felt the bandage; he knew to leave it alone. He didn't have to feel his face to know there was a sizeable gash on his forehead, probably several, and his left eye was swollen because his eyebrow covered about half his vision. There wasn't a mirror, but he imagined how he looked, but that didn't bother him. What bothered him is that Faith had to see him that way. It had to frighten her to see her father so beat up. He wondered why they hadn't already killed him. After all, they had Tom Johnson, and that other guy.

Clint knew that they must have some sort of plan, some reason for keeping him alive. In the meantime, he had to look for opportunities, and most importantly do everything right. He shredded cheese and fried bacon. He still had some sliced tomatoes from the day before. Clint put it all together and checked the biscuits in the oven. Roy Dale and Tyrone talked to the girls as Clint caught peeks when he turned around. Angie didn't look too good at all. He wondered if she had already been molested or if she was still just in shock. Her face was completely pale; her eyes dead. It was as if she was in a trance. She stared down at the floor without an expression on her face. It was so odd; they talked to her like she was communicating. She wasn't saying anything. Clint wondered, *'what were they thinking?'* Something would happen on the show and they'd both laugh, and Roy Dale would nudge her teasing like, and she didn't respond. If Clint didn't know better, she was already dead; she was so immobile. Her eyes were open, but it looked like her life was gone.

Faith gave her father piercing glances. From where he was, he could see her lip quiver. She was beyond scared, but somehow she still was maintaining a level of awareness. In fact, she was probably acutely aware. If anyone was thinking of escape plans, it would be Faith. He knew his daughter; he knew she hadn't given up. She would be the last to surrender to anything.

When he finished cooking, Clint told them it was done, and of course, it wasn't good enough for Tyrone to come and get it. He wanted it served to him, and so Clint hopped over to the table and served them both. He put some on the girls' plate too. Angelina never looked up from the table, but Faith did. She fought back tears as her father slid the omelet onto her plate. She wanted so bad to just reach out and touch his arm, but she was too afraid. Her lips quivered and squished up against her nose making a frown. She only did that when she about to cry. Clint shook his head hoping she wouldn't tear up, not now. He wanted her to be brave, but he couldn't say anything. Her eyes met his, and she stiffened her lip and looked away. Tyrone carried on with his non-stop banter making everyone sick.

When they were done, it was back to the couch. The sun was coming over the mountain, and Clint hoped maybe they'd start discussing leaving, but that was not to be the case. Tyrone even tried to make small talk about the cabin, how he "liked it", as if Clint was supposed to be pleased it met with his approval.

Clint didn't know what to expect. He figured they'd take him back to the room again and blindfold him. It was then he noticed for the first time that Tyrone had a gun. He brought it out of his drawers and waved it around in his hand as he talked. He ordered Roy Dale to take Clint in the back. He held a rope in his hand and motioned for him to "get moving", but Faith interrupted. She asked if he could stay there.

Tyrone waved the gun around in his hand. It was directly behind Faith's head on the couch. "I don't see why not. If that's what the pretty lady wants, that's what the pretty lady gets. Tie him up." Roy Dale grabbed Clint by the collar and sat him in the corner of the room and tied him to a chair. They all sat on one couch; the other couch across the room had a towel thrown over the arm rest and was soaked with blood. Clint saw the splatters on the wall and drippings on the floor where he was jumped in his sleep.

Clint didn't know what was going to happen. He tried to study the two men but not look directly at either. He knew not to make eye contact; he just tried to memorize their every feature and record in his head their every word. It came with his training as a reporter, and it wasn't so much for the sake of identification, but their mannerisms that would tell him what was on their mind. What they were really intending, thinking. He could smell them both from the far side of the room. Tyrone picked at his feet pulling off scabs of skin from between his toes. It was mid-June, and his legs were bone white. Yeah, he had been in prison alright, probably a good long while. He figured Roy Dale had probably done some time too but not in a while. He looked cooked; his skin revealed years of doing labor outdoors. By the looks of his face and arms, he figured most of those years he didn't wear shirts, might have been a roofer or maybe a laborer on a farm. The wrinkles on his face attested to more than just the beatings of a brutal sun. Clint figured he'd taken his share of hard winters too; his skin chapped from the freezing winds blowing across a prairie. Good chance he had run cattle for somebody at some time, and there was plenty of that in Oklahoma and Texas.

Clint noticed the hands of Roy Dale; there was evidence of Ichthyosis. Both were used to scrapes; each had lots of scars. The knuckles on Tyrone's right hand were abscessed. Even from the far side of the room, Clint could see pus oozing from the freshly torn skin. That's the hand that beat Tom Johnson to death, and he probably reopened the wounds when he beat that preacher senseless on the banks of the river. That's why his hand was infected and abscessing. It was probably filled with silt from the river. That was something he needed to remember: if it kept getting worse, he might not be able to use his right hand very much; it would begin to swell and stiffen.

Clint tried to think of something to preoccupy their minds. They were still watching shows with the girls sandwiched in between them. He feared what would happen when they got bored. He was thinking of when he might bring up the possibility of money. It was an awkward subject to discuss, and he finally resolved he'd wait. It would be more believable if they brought it up. It would be more believable if he acted like he was trying to hide money. If they went through his wallet and they asked about credit cards, that's when he'd mention it, like he hadn't thought of it before. Until then, he figured he'd just keep his mouth shut.

The morning dragged on and on. He sat tied to that chair like he was their catch of the day, a fish on a stringer. He got the feeling that Tyrone wanted to hold him up by the rope and brag about what a man he was. He did notice that Angie was looking a little better. He caught her giving glances to Faith on occasion; she seemed to be coming out of the initial shock. She appeared to have processed what was going on rather then just pulling into a shell. About mid- morning, Tyrone got up and started going through the rooms. He found a CD player and was looking through the CD's. He came in and turned it on.

"Whatch y'all want to hear?" He looked at a CD of the Beatles and tossed it across the room. Then another, and another. "Ain't you got some Elvis? Cause I can sing just like the King." Tyrone started singing "Love me Tender". He acted like he had a mic in his hand and crooned in front of the girls. Clint was totally shocked; his voice was a perfect rendition of Elvis. He was astonished; Tyrone sang smooth as honey. He stood there in front of the girls with his baggy shorts hanging down and his boxers sticking out. They all watched his act.

"Love me tender, lo've me sweet....never let me go". He sang the first stanza perfectly, and then, as he kept singing, his voice started to choke up, but he managed to finish the song. It was very strange; for a moment, Clint and the girls both thought he was about to cry. He then bowed before them, his audience. And when he was done, he did the strangest thing. He actually walked over to the coffee table and set down his imaginary mic, like it was real. That sent chills rushing up Clint's spin.

After the concert Tyrone went into the kitchen and started going through the cabinets looking for food. He looked back at Clint tied to his chair. "I'm hungry. Fix something."

It hadn't been all that long since breakfast, but Clint didn't argue. Roy Dale untied him, and he fixed another meal, some sandwiches. Tyrone, of course, rambled nonstop with the two girls sitting around him. He stuck the gun down in his pants and scratched himself with it. Roy Dale stood by the big window in front of the porch and kept a look out down the road which is something that Clint wondered about himself. What would he do if the deputy came driving up the switchback? What would they do? He figured it would just be a hostage situation; he didn't figure there could be any other outcome. Clint hobbled around putting the meal together while

Tyrone talked about himself. At one time, he even said to Clint, "See, I'm respectful of the little ladies." Clint nodded his appreciation. "It's the stuck up bitches I don't like." Clint felt ill at the thought. He knew what that meant; anyone who didn't do what he wanted was "stuck up". He understood the implication clearly.

Clint put the sandwiches down on a plate in front of him, and he never stopped talking. Not one moment. "My grandma use to take me to church, my aunt too until she got divorced. They'd be a packed house when I sang. Just a little country church, parking lot was full plum to the street. People came from everywhere." He nudged Faith whenever he made a point, "Came all the way from Arizona one couple did just to hear me sing. Said I was an angel sent from God with a golden voice."

Faith nodded with a placid smile.

"One preacher said he wanted to take me with 'em all across tha' country. Gonna start a revival. Somethun happened to him. He went down to Huntsville and never came back."

Clint wondered if that was the Huntsville prison but dared not ask. He listened to Tyrone bounce from one subject to another. He reminded him of a lizard the way he kept turning his neck around and looked with that steely eye. It seemed especially so when he was eating because he'd swallow and his tongue would stick out as if trying to flick the air for some aftertaste. The more he talked the more the girls got nervous. His thoughts bounced all over the place.

He patted Faith on the shoulder, "I had a daddy too," he said, "a step daddy, for a coupla' years. He and my maw never got along. He took my momma and step brother and sister out to California. I didn't want to go. I stayed back with my grandma and aunt."

Clint read between the lines. That meant his mother remarried and skipped town without him. He already had that picture in mind before Tyrone ever mentioned it. He put together the pieces of this young man's fractured childhood, but Tyrone was filling in the details. The big guy just sat quietly in a chair on the other side of the table with one eye on the road.

He cleaned his nails with a knife, the one he kept strapped to his side. He was a whole lot less talkative than Tyrone which was beginning to worry Clint some. Roy Dale scraped the dirt from his nails and looked at the girls, in particular Angelina. He was literally three times her size; she couldn't have been ninety pounds soaking wet. When he stood up and moved around the room, it was very intimidating. He kept bumping his head into the ceiling fan by the coffee table, and for a moment, Clint thought he was going to lose it and rip it down. But he didn't.

Tyrone finally noticed the ring on Faith's finger. It was a cross. He pointed to it, "So what are ya?"

It was a stupid question, but she refrained from saying something snide, "Christian."

"I know dat, but what are ya? Baptist, Missionary Baptist, Pentecostal? Gotta be somethun."

"Just Christian."

"That don't belong to nothing. That ain't a church."

"I belong to Jesus; that's what a Christian is."

Tyrone leaned back in his chair, "That don't make no sense. Where I come from, you hafta' belong to a church. We had a church; there was another one down the road and another one a few miles away. Some of 'em had really strange beliefs. We didn't have nothing to do with them others."

"I see."

"Some of 'em worshipped on Saturday; some didn't believe in dancin'. Them Catholics worship da Pope. So we stayed away from 'em. In our church, weez all waiting like it says in the Bible on the rapture. One of us will be workin' in the fields, and he goes up to heaven, and another over here goes some other place. My grandma sat out on that porch just a rockin' and waitin' for glory day. So you gotta find a church and belong to one." He kind of nudged her with the gun, "If everybody believed like you, there wouldn't be no church, see."

"Or there would be only one church: His church."

He put his arm around her and called out to Clint, "You know she needs a momma. Somebody to take care of her."

"She's got a mother. A good mother." Clint suddenly realized he could talk; his voice was back. It didn't hurt that much. He didn't know how that was possible, but it was.

Tyrone gave him a glassy stare. It was also the first time he made eye contact with him. Tyrone got up and put the gun back in his pants. He had no idea what this maniac would do. "Y'all want to hear some music? How 'bout some ghetto boys? Tupac? Eminem?"

He started walking around in the living room acting like he had a mic in his hand. He was strutting like the hoods, grabbing his crotch and giving hand signs. He yelled out, "Whassup? Thank y'all for coming tonight!"

Then he yelled, "Eat ME!"

Tyrone grabbed hold of himself and started doing a bass sound. "Boom, boom, boom…boom-baa, boom-baa, boom-baa, boom!"

The girls looked at each other in disgust, and then he started rapping, 'I'm a gangsta', I'm a playa', a love makea' and a gang banga'."

Faith turned her face away in utter repulsion and thought, 'You're an idiot.'

The next fifteen minutes was a superfluous tirade of insane lyrics that no one in the room understood but him, if he understood it at all. He was back to cussing; there were lots of lines about "niggaz" and "bitches" and "hoes", and all the while, Roy Dale looked on with his knife eyeing the girls. Then Tyrone jumped on the divan with the blood and started singing "Let's party…Let'party…Let's party." He was holding his forked fingers up in the air, "Come on, let's party uh huh, let's party." He motioned for the girls to join him, and Angie suddenly turned pale as a ghost, and her lips turned fuchsia. She felt sick, and got up holding her hand over her mouth and ran to the bathroom.

Roy Dale followed her. Faith looked at Tyrone, "She hasn't felt good since yesterday." That was true, yesterday since about the time she first saw him.

Just then the phone rang. Clint had wondered where his cell phone was; now he knew. Tyrone pulled it out of his pants and looked at the number, "Who is in the 212 area code?"

"That's Angelina's mom."

Tyrone let it ring, and when it stopped, she left a message. And he made Clint play it back. He untied his arms and handed him the phone. "Call her back," he walked over to Faith with the gun in his hand, "And if you say one wrong thing …."

Clint called her back hoping he could just leave a message. He didn't know if he could stay composed enough for Tyrone's satisfaction. Angie came back in the room and sat next to Faith who was as still as a rock. Angie held her hand; they could actually hear her mother on the other end.

Clint told her everything was alright. The girls were fine, and then she asked to speak to Angelina. Clint didn't know what to say. He looked at Tyrone. He cocked the trigger back and stared at his daughter. "She's a, a, ah…"

"Four-wheeling."

Clint breathed a sigh of relief, "She's four-wheeling right now; they both are. They are having a blast."

Her mother expressed all her worries that they'd get hurt, and Clint reassured her they were perfectly safe on it. "Faith is extremely careful." After a few more motherly concerns, Clint was able to get off the phone, and Tyrone uncocked the trigger. Clint knew his fuse was getting short; it would take nothing to set him off. Tyrone paced back and forth like a tiger. He was breathing heavily, and his eyes shifted nervously back and forth. He then, for some reason, went to the table and picked up Clint's wallet. "How much ya got in here?" He emptied it out and sorted through the credit cards. Clint knew this was the time to say something, but before he did, Tyrone pulled out the card the deputy had given him.

"What's this?"

He looked across the room at Clint the way a snake looks at a mouse in a cage. "You been talkin' to the Sheriff? You been talkin' 'bout me?"

Clint's heart sank. It felt like it had just been punctured. His mouth went dry; his throat felt like sand. "They were down at the b..b.. bridge," he stuttered.

Tyrone walked over to him thumping the card against his hand. He was talking to the others in the room, his audience. "You know, I was gonna let bygones be bygones. But you ain't the same kinda man as me. I didn't go and tell 'em about you trying to pick a fight with me. I let it pass. Didn't I?" He looked about the room at the others as if to get some sort of confirmation for his warped mind. "I was the one that turned away. You was the one all huffy up wantin' ta fight." At that moment Tyrone whirled around slapping Clint across the face. "Whack!" The sting was felt by everybody in the room. He looked at Clint with his head sideways, blood trickled down from the side of his mouth. "Here I goes tryin' to be all nice to ya, and this is what you do to me." Tyrone backhanded him again, "Whack!"

"Well, you's wantin' to fight. I guess you gonna get one now." He walked over and picked up a baseball bat that was in the corner of the room. "We gotta a score to settle, boy."

"Stop it! STOP It!" Faith yelled.

"Give it to me." Roy Dale jumped up and growled. He walked over and took the baseball bat out of his hand. "Let's talk."

He and Tyrone went outside to the yard out of ear shot. Faith ran to her dad and laid her head on his lap and began to cry. He watched them both out in the yard. He could see that Roy Dale was upset with him, and for a second, he thought there might be a fight. Roy Dale held out his hand flat and pounded his fist in it. He heard him say "But you promised…" Then they whispered again, and he couldn't make out what they were saying. Clint was trying to discern what he could from their nonverbal interlocution, the way they stood, the pitch of their shoulders, Roy Dale's head bent down. He was pissed.

Clint told Faith to quit crying, "Honey stop. I've got a plan. Okay?" He looked at Angelina, getting her attention, "Now y'all just go along with it, alright? It will work, but I've got to get untied. Listen to me, this is our only chance. When I give you the nod, you say that you're hungry; you want to eat something. Got that?" Tyrone and Roy Dale came back into the cabin. Faith still had her arms around her father.

"We've got a plan. We are gonna be leaving just after dark."

The three of them looked at Tyrone, and they all knew not

to believe a word he had to say. "Don't cha'll wanna know what it is?"

The girls nodded.

"We's going down to Mexico, and before we cross the border, we are all gonna check into a motel. We'll stay the night, and in the morning, we'll tie y'all up. When we get across, we'll call back to the motel and tell 'em you're in the room."

Actually, it didn't sound like that bad a plan except Clint knew he wasn't going. They weren't taking him along. He knew their little plan omitted a few minor details like that. In the meantime, the two of them were going to take turns getting a little "shut eye." Tyrone was the first to go in the other room and lay down. Roy Dale told both the girls to sit down on the couch; they would wait with him.

He stretched his long legs out on the coffee table and put his hand on Angelina's knee. Clint heard him whisper to her, his long scraggly hair down in her face, but he couldn't understand what he said. There were tears that began to well in her eyes, and she feigned a smile. He pulled his hair out of a ponytail and shook it out. He wanted Angelina to comb it for him. Clint knew this wasn't going to end well just by the expression on her face. They needed a miracle, a big one, or in just a matter of hours, it would all be over.

Chapter Eight

You know more about what people don't do sometimes than what they do. Clint on occasion tried to engage Roy Dale in conversation. He had heard one should do that if you were ever a hostage. Not once did Roy Dale look him in the eye. Not once. That was not a good sign. He knew he was a dead man, and he was trying to figure out why it hadn't happened already. He knew then they were going to rape the girls; he had known that from the beginning. Clint concluded they were going to rape them that night, and then they would probably kill all three. For sure, they were going to kill him and maybe take the girls. Whichever plan they had in mind, Roy Dale as tough as a man as he was didn't have the nerve to look Clint straight in the face.

The next few hours passed so slowly; it seemed like the hands on the clock were going backwards. He noticed subtle things like Roy Dale's big hand always finding a place on Angelina's knee. It nearly took up her whole leg. He looked so strange; his legs stuck out way beyond the couch, and little Angelina's feet didn't quite touch the floor. The girls looked like two play dolls sitting on each side of him. It was weird, a grown man with two dolls, and he was trying to act so nice. It was macabre, with little Angie combing his hair. It was like some strange, bizarre, childish, pedophilia game. One time, he even got up to get them a drink. It was peculiar watching a man his age trying to be coy around children. It was so out of place.

209

Little Angie's throat was so tight; she gulped the water like she was trying to force it down a straw. He could see her little hand shaking from across the room. He could tell by Roy Dale's actions that they had divvied up the booty: he was taking Angie, Tyrone was taking Faith. That might have even been what some of the argument was about outside. He didn't know for sure; he could only suspect the degree of their plot. Clint had also figured rightly that Roy Dale wasn't too happy to be in the position they were in. It all started with the man in Oklahoma, and it didn't matter how it came about or who started what, after that first man was dead, there's just no point in stopping; the spree was on. What's another one? Right? What's three or four or five more? You can only fry in the chair one time; every criminal will tell you that, and so after it gets going, you have but one aim, not to get caught, to get away. And that means leaving no witnesses. None.

Clint looked at his beautiful daughter and wondered with every glance if this was the last time he'd see her. All the years, all the thoughts, all the hugs and kisses ran through his mind. She was growing up to be such a beautiful young lady. She was stunning. Another couple of years and there wouldn't be a beauty pageant in the whole country she couldn't win, though that was never her true ambition. Her dream was to help others; she just hadn't narrowed down her field of choice yet on how she would best accomplish that. It was a veterinarian one day, a nurse the next, a teacher the next. Whatever her choice, her kind soul would bless the world.

It was the same for Angelina, the apple of her father's eye. He had written songs about her, painted portraits of her since she was a baby. Her parents had left her in his care, and Clint felt so bad because he had let them down. He should have thought more, been more cognitive of the circumstances. Another few seconds and the yomen would have drifted right on past, been someone else's problem but not his.

He had time to think of a lot of things sitting in that chair, waiting. If he did live, by some miracle, if they all lived, he knew he would not be the same kind of man. Experiences like this he reasoned either makes one better or they make one worse, but they never leave the person the same. It's impossible. Clint didn't know which way he'd be in the aftermath. He would probably be neither; he would probably be dead. That was the preeminent possibility if he didn't find a way out, and the hours left were few. He concentrated on what he'd do. He ran various scenarios through his mind over and over again. He had to plan, if only it would work.

He wondered that if there was any way he could reach Roy Dale—now was his chance while Tyrone was asleep. He thought perhaps the girls could reach him, perhaps give him a chance to become a hero, at least in his own mind. Maybe, he would let the girls go if they begged him. He thought that maybe Roy Dale and Tyrone could become convinced to take him, and leave the girls tied up at the cabin. They could get a twelve hour head start and then call the sheriff's office. Clint called to him whispering. This was their chance. "Roy Dale. Roy Dale."

As soon as he said the words, the door from the bedroom slammed. Tyrone walked in with his hand down his crotch, obviously taking pleasure with himself. He grunted and shuffled into the room, smacking his lips, "Ummmmm." He stretched his arms out and yawned with his pants sagging down below his bulging boxers. He walked over to the refrigerator rubbing himself and groaning. Clint saw that the girls were looking away from him in disgust. It was obvious he was trying to get their attention. He walked past Clint into the living room and turned around, "You were going to ask Roy Dale something? What is it?"

Tyrone sipped on some water and rubbed his crotch. He had a smirk on his face, the same smirk he got when he slapped him before. Clint didn't know what to say, "I was going to ask if I could pee."

"Yeah, you can pee." He laughed, "Why don't we watch ya. You girls ever see him pee? You ever see ya daddy pee? Why don't you go out there on the porch and whip it out, we'll watch ya. If you think we can see it from here." Tyrone laughed and pulled the pistol out from behind the back of his pants. He pointed outside. "Go on pissant."

"That's okay. I don't need to go now."

"What's da *matter*?" He said it mockingly like he was talking to a baby, "You ashamed?"

"I just don't need to pee."

Tyrone walked over to the couch strutting around like a rooster, "Hey, if you pee in your pants, it ain't my fault. I gave ya a chance." He patted Roy Dale on the shoulder, "Why don't ya get some shut eye. We gonna need it. Gonna be a long night, homey."

Roy Dale patted the girls on the leg and stood up. He stepped across the coffee table, "I'll be back." It was so awkward, like he was on a date, like he expected them to say *'Okay sure, hurry back'*. Still he couldn't look at Clint, and Clint knew why. When he got up from his nap, the show would be over or just starting, depending on how you looked at it. It was five o'clock; by 8:30, it was dark. Sometime after that they would be rolling out. The hours to live weren't long. Tyrone slid in between the girls and then put his arms around them as Roy Dale shut the door to the bedroom. He pulled them tight, "How's my pretty ladies doing?"

"Fine."

"Fine."

"What ch'all wanna watch?" He said it like they were going to have some in depth conversation about what shows they liked best. Clint realized that for a guy who probably spent most of his life in a recreation room at a facility this probably was a big treat, getting to choose what you wanted to see. Even having the remote in your hand was more privilege than what he had been used to. He looked upon the fool with utter disgust. They had just watched about 8 straight hours of Dragnet and Superman, and he's asking if they wanted to watch some more. Tyrone tossed the DVD's down on the table, "Ain't cha got nothing else?"

Faith spoke up, "We don't watch a lot of TV."

"Don't watch TV? Yur daddy don't let ya watch TV?"

"It's a…"

"boring." Clint was surprised Angelina said anything

Tyrone turned off the tube, "Okay, ya'll wanna hear me

sing again?" Obviously, he must have thought that his opprobrious ranting gained their favor.

They all felt nauseous. At least with the TV on, they could all be distracted from the lunatic parading around with his play pretend mic in his hand singing to the imaginary audience, the crowd in his head. Clint hoped he wouldn't indulge in a series of hymnodies; it would be too much. Before they could say anything, he started singing a rendition of an old Johnny Cash tune. It was a strange selection, but fitting. Although he didn't have Cash's legendary voice, he was in tune on the ballad, "Don't Take Your Guns to Town." It was about a boy named Billy Joe whose mama told him not to take his guns to town. Tyrone started clapping to the beat and told the girls to clap along, like they were at his concert. They were alright; they had front row seats to the psychotic insane. Tyrone clapped, and the girls moved their hands together not really making a sound, but it didn't matter. In his mind, there were thousands of worshipers, fans of the great Tyrone. He acted through the song performing the scenes even when Billy Joe finally got shot down. Tyrone was obviously seeing himself as the leading role, as the young man dying on stage. No telling what the maniac was envisioning in his mind, but then suddenly he changed, just like a performer. He got up off the floor and started singing a Hank Williams tune, "I'm So Lonely I Could Die."

Clint gasped when he held out his hand to Faith to dance. Tyrone laid his gun on top of his shoulder, tempting her, and pulled her up off the couch. He held her right hand with his left and put her other hand on his hip. He stood almost a foot taller than her and crooned William's classic tune. Clint watched them as Tyrone's back turned toward him. Her hand was inches from the pistol on his shoulder. Tyrone seemed to be oblivious to the gun; he was in a trance, lost in his sick performance. His head rocked back and forth, and his crazy eye looked all around glancing at his imaginary audience. It may be their only chance. Clint knew that; he thought Faith knew that. She was so scared she couldn't move. She looked out of the sides of her eyes glancing nervously at her Daddy tied up in the chair, and he could see that she was absolutely terrified.

Too scared to move, too scared to do anything, she swayed back and forth as if dancing. She looked like a mannequin in the hands of a killer.

When the song was over, he pulled the gun off his shoulder and popped the cylinder open spinning it. "Oh yeah, I forgot the bullets are in here." He pulled them out of his pocket and reloaded the gun, chuckling with a diabolical grin. He had been testing them all along; it was part of his game. He was seeing if she would have grabbed it. He would have slapped her half way across the room. It would have been his excuse to teach her a lesson, his way.

He wasn't just a maniac; Tyrone was cunning. He liked to tease his prey. It was all a game to him. Like a cat that toys with a mouse, he liked to let his catch run before he swatted it down, trapped it in his paws. Let it go again. That was his thrill.

Clint tried to figure out what conjured his sadistic tendencies. He was a mixture of diverse cultures, been raised on Southern Gospel and outlaw singers like Haggard and Cash. Clint surmised that he didn't pick up on the rap until he did his first stint in jail. He was probably a juvenile. That was when he had to have aligned himself with the all the other young thugs to fit in so he just added that to his repertoire. Clint was willing to bet he strutted around the prison yard telling everybody how he was gonna make it big time when he got out. He was quite a performer on his imaginary stage in front of the blood-stained divan. Tyrone winked at the girls as he sang Hank Williams "I'm So Lonesome I Could Cry."

Clint's heart was racing; he knew the girls were beaten down from all the games. Like mice, they all wondered how long the torture would last, especially Faith. She wanted to vomit or scream, just go berserk, and then suddenly, Tyrone gave her the most peculiar stare. He stopped. "I got something for ya. Sit down on the couch. Don't move; I'll be right back."

He walked out on the deck and then disappeared around the side, but they couldn't tell if he was just right outside listening or if he was further away. Clint looked over his back to see if Roy Dale was up; the door was still closed.

Faith started to cry, "Daddy, I..I..can't take it any longer." Her voice trembled. "What are we going to do?" She and Angelina held each other in their arms, both breathing heavily.

"Remember when I give you the nod what to ask?"

"I remember...we're hungry."

"Okay, just wait till Roy Dale is up, and then just watch me. Go along, don't question. You have to trust me. Do exactly what I say."

Tyrone came back in whistling. He had something behind his back. "Close your eyes," he said speaking to Faith obviously courting her, "Gotcha' a surprise."

Faith closed her eyes, and her father watched him swagger across the room with some wild flowers and weeds behind his back.

"Open up."

Faith opened her eyes, and he handed her the flowers. She was stunned. She managed to imitate a slight smile on her face. He winked, "I know how to treat a lady. Close your eyes again. Put out your hand."

She closed her eyes again and felt something strange placed in her palm. "Open."

Faith looked down. She gasped. Clint saw it too, in her hand. It was the black and silver lure with a treble hook. "That's a magic lure. Thought you might want to have it, every fish you catch you'll think of me. Like it?"

Clint couldn't believe it, nor could Faith or Angelina. They recognized it immediately. He probably had to wash the blood off before he gave it to her. A stolen gift from a man he nearly beat to death, that was his gift, that and some weeds he pulled up outside. What was he thinking? Was he thinking that this would capture the affections of a young lady? Was he serious? Did he really think he could terrorize her, hold her hostage and this would make it all okay?

They all realized the extent of his depravity. "You like it?"

She set it down on the table like it was a body part, like he had handed her the man's finger. It might as well been, that lure cost a man his life. Tyrone was deranged, delusional, and they knew that anything at all could set him off, and he'd go on a sanguinary streak.

"Yes, it's nice." She was getting sick. It was all she could do not to throw up, but she knew she had to play along.

He smiled at Angelina, "Maybe Roy Dale will get you some flowers too. You like flowers?"

Angelina knew to say yes; that's what he wanted to hear. And then he looked at the girls, "I'm getting kind of hungry how 'bout y'all?"

Faith looked at her father. He nodded. "Yes, I'm hungry." That was the cue.

"What ch'all hungry for?"

Clint spoke up, "They like fish."

"Fish? Ya got some?"

"I've got some fresh, caught them"… (he paused trying to keep it together) "yesterday." He wanted to say he had caught them with that lure he pried out of a dying man's hands, but Clint didn't. He managed a smile instead, acting stupid for his captor. "I can bake some rolls and make some batter for fried squash if you like that." Clint knew he would.

Tyrone pointing his gun at the kitchen, "Better be good?"

"He's the best."

"Good. I'll wake up Roy Dale. He loves fried fish."

A few minutes later, they heard the thud of Roy Dale's boots hit the floor. He was not a man you would want to wake on any condition but much less on just two hours sleep. They could hear him grumbling and cussing at Tyrone; the door was closed, and then there was whispering. Roy Dale emerged from the bedroom with about the same disposition as a bear; a scowl crossed his face. He didn't know if it was from not enough sleep or the fact that Tyrone grated on his nerves. Roy Dale walked over to Clint and looked back at his partner, "Should I untie him?"

Tyrone moseyed over to the frig; he didn't bother looking back over, "It'll be alright. He ain't going nowhere."

It was the first time his feet were free in almost twenty four hours. The circulation of blood began to sting his toes as Clint gladly wiggled his ankles. Then he freed his hands, and Clint stood up. He balanced himself and then took a step. A smile actually came across Clint's face, and he glanced over at his daughter. Clint walked around in a circle gaining the feeling back in his legs.

He asked the men if it would be okay if he could eat too since he hadn't eaten all day. Tyrone shrugged, and Roy Dale nodded. Then, Tyrone added a stipulation; he "could eat after they were done." Clint figured rightly that Tyrone was planning to eat everything he could so there wouldn't be a scrap left because he was a sick son of a bitch. Clint hadn't asked to eat because he was hungry, he was; he was starved, but he wanted them to relax. You don't watch a man nearly as closely if he is going to eat the same food as you; you don't really think about it. He didn't want them to think about anything. He wanted them to sit back and relax, wait to be served. Not watch what he was doing. That's exactly what Clint wanted.

The girls were still on the couch sitting exactly where they were told, but he needed them so he asked if they could help. Clint said he needed one to chop up the salad and another to slice the squash while he prepared the batter. Clint then added, "They'll need a knife."

"I'll cut it." Roy Dale pulled out his knife, and Angelina went and handed him the squash. He sat at the table and began slicing. Next, Clint heated the oven and put the rolls on the pan. He read the directions and told Faith to pour the oil into the fryer, to get it ready. She picked up the fryer and started to take it outside, "No, leave it right here on the counter." Clint took it out of her hands and set it back down. Both Angelina and Faith looked at him. He reiterated his point before they could say anything. " I want it right here." He looked over to where Tyrone and Roy Dale were sitting. "I want it near the table."

He then instructed Faith on how to make the batter to dip the squash in while Angelina prepared the salad in a big bowl. All during this time, Tyrone was talking to Roy Dale about Mexico. The more he talked the more Clint realized that they had no plans on leaving the cabin with him alive. This would be his last meal, if there was any at all. It was maybe forty minutes until dusk, maybe less. They were going to eat themselves nice and full. Probably tie him back up, take the girls in the bedroom and rape them, and then probably kill all three. If they didn't do that, they would rape the girls and then tie them up and put them in the truck. They would drag him out in the woods someplace and put a slug in his head. That would buy them some time. If anyone came up to the cabin later, they would just see it empty; think they've gone; suspect nothing.

Clint checked on the rolls in the oven; they were just beginning to rise. He could hear the oil popping in the fryer. It was time. He put the squash in first. Neither one was paying much attention to him. Roy Dale sat on one side of the table with his back to the big window. Tyrone sat directly across from him. The gun was in his right hand. Clint motioned to the girls, "Ya'll get the plates down. We are almost *ready*." He took a deep breath and looked at his daughter. "Faith, you take care of the fryer. Okay?" She nodded. He added, "I am going to clean the table; you stand by the squash and make sure it is ready. We are almost ready to cook the fish." He looked at her, and she looked at him. Angelina looked at them both. She understood too.

Clint grabbed the spray bottle under the counter, the one that had the bleach. He shook it to make sure there was still plenty in it. He picked up the cloth and walked over to the table. Tyrone turned around, "What's that?"

"Going to clean the table before we eat." He showed him the rag and bottle.

"Ah, it's alright. Leave it be."

Clint wasn't deterred, "If you were in a restaurant, you'd demand it clean. It will only take a second." He moved the shakers out of the way and sprayed the table and began wiping it. Tyrone was on his right, and Roy Dale was leaning back in his chair, too far away. Clint didn't know what to do; he was thinking. He looked at his face, at all the wrinkles, and then he said to him, "You better have that checked out."

Roy Dale looked at him confused, "What?"

"May be melanoma? Looks like it could be cancer." Clint stretched over the table, "Let me see." Roy Dale leaned up to him. Clint squinted his eyes and as if trying to see. "Look up." Roy Dale's eyes turned up to the ceiling. Clint's finger was on the bottle. This was it. Now was the time.

Clint squirted a stream of bleach straight into his eyes. Roy Dale let out a scream like a mountain lion! He lunged backwards out of his seat with his hands on his face. Without looking, Clint backhanded Tyrone smashing his nose and spewing blood everywhere knocking him out of his chair and half way across the floor. He dove on top of him wrestling for the gun. He shouted to his daughter.

"NOW, FAITH! THE FRYER. ROY!"

Clint had Tyrone's arm pinned down that held the gun. His other fist was wailing blow after blow striking him in the face. Tyrone was yelling, "Bitch, I'm gonna kill you!" He then twisted his arm free and struck Clint with the pistol grip knocking his head back, but Clint was still on top of him. He grabbed for the gun.

"BOOM!" The deafening sound of the shot rang in his ears as pieces of the fan crashed down around them. As he wrestled with Tyrone in a foray on the floor, he could hear Roy Dale screaming and smashing things all about the room. Tyrone was beating him continuously in the back of his head with his fist. Clint yelled for Faith again. He couldn't see anything; his head was buried in Tyrone's chest, and his legs were tangled up with Tyrone's as they rolled back and forth on the floor.

Then Faith yelled at the top of her lungs, "YOU bastard!"

She hurled the fryer full of boiling hot oil directly into his face. Roy Dale let out a blood curdling scream as the oil sizzled through his flesh. The putrid stench of burning flesh popped like popcorn in a vat of grease. He crashed over the table swinging wildly and stumbled around in the kitchen falling over chairs screaming as his skin literally melted off his bone onto the floor. The girls ran for safety from the horror. He kept swinging his arms like a mad man gone berserk with pain.

Clint wanted to help but couldn't shake the gun loose from Tyrone's fierce grip. Finally, he bit down through his wrist sinking his teeth into the bone and nerves. Tyrone screamed and dropped the gun. Quickly, with one foot, Clint managed to kick it away towards the wall. He yelled for the girls to get it, and right as Clint thought he might have the upper hand; Tyrone caught him square on the jaw with a jarring blow. Tyrone hit him again and again brutally pummeling Clint's face, and then like a cat, Tyrone pounced on top of Clint pinning his shoulders down. Clint was defenseless. Tyrone reeled one blow right after another. His eyes were wild and fierce. His head swung back and forth with each blow and sweat and spit sprayed off his face as Clint lied helpless underneath him. Tyrone was cussing, and he could hear the girls screaming. Roy Dale was crashing from wall to wall knocking everything down. He was blindly trying to get the girls. Clint could smell the horrid odor of fried skin in the air, and then he heard the loud sound of shattering glass. Roy Dale crashed through the big window, and Clint yelled for the girls again to help. Tyrone held Clint's head down with one hand and was punching with another. Then all of a sudden, he stopped.

Clint looked up and saw Tyrone raising his arms slowly in the air. It was Faith.

She held the gun to the back of his head with the barrel jammed right up against Tyrone's skull. She cocked the trigger. He froze right then and there. He didn't move.

Clint pushed Tyrone off and took the gun. He told him to lay face down and spread eagle. The room was a wreck; everything was shattered, blood and skin and oil dripped off everything, the tables and floor. He glanced outside; Roy Dale had smashed through the railing on the deck and was running blindly across the yard still yelling. Clint picked up the rope and drew Tyrone's hands up behind his back and tied his wrist together, tight. Then, he slipped his feet into a knot and pulled it snug. Clint didn't even know where Angelina was; he just told Faith not to look, "to turn away". She thought he was going to shoot Tyrone, but instead he stepped through the broken glass up to the busted out window. Roy Dale was running and screaming and falling down like a man on fire. Clint raised the gun. He aimed. "Boom!"

He missed.

There was a loud ringing in his ears. It was so loud; it was as if there wasn't any other sound. Everything else was blocked out. Clint took a deep breath and wiped the blood and sweat from his eyes. He aimed again. His hand was shaking. He took a deep breath and slowly exhaled. He steadied the sights and squinted his eye looking down the barrel. "Boom!"

Roy Dale grabbed the back of his right leg. He fell to one knee and then got up again limping his way to the woods. Clint looked down at Tyrone looking up at him. The sound of the gun still rushed through his ears like a train. He turned back toward Roy Dale again. He aimed and steadied. He pulled. "Boom!"

Roy Dale went down, this time on both knees. His arms hung lifeless by his side as he sat back on the hunches of his legs teetering. Clint could only see the back of his head, and the long gray hair that draped down across his shoulders. He was facing away from the cabin, and a small blotch of blood appeared as it absorbed the life that was leaving him. His head then dropped to his chest, and he fell face forward to the ground. He didn't get up.

Clint then turned around to Tyrone. "Hey man, it, it, it wasn't my idea. It was all Roy Dale's." Tyrone was lying face down in the broken glass on the floor. Clint didn't say anything. He was amazingly calm. He looked down at him and then pointed the gun at his head. Clint cocked back the hammer. His finger stroked the trigger as he looked at him at the end of the barrel with the sight right on his lazy eye. The sounds of the other shots were still ringing in his head. He couldn't hear anything but the train. He stared at him as if staring at a strange monster, a freak, something you'd see in a sideshow at the carnival in a cage with straw and feces. He wasn't an animal; he was worse. He was filth, refuse…something that needed to be destroyed.

"Pppplease man. Ddddon't."

The girls were crying. He could just begin to hear their voices in the room, but they sounded like they were coming from some faraway place. They were calling him, but Clint didn't move. He looked down at Tyrone through the sight and stroked the trigger. His finger slipped around the curved metal appendage and tapped it just slightly.

"Daad. Please."

Clint stopped. He looked over at his daughter standing with Angie in the kitchen. Her arms reached out to him. Clint wanted to hold her, but he was covered in blood and glass. It was the oddest of feelings; he felt numb. It was a feeling he'd never experienced before, and it wasn't satisfaction, and it wasn't fear. He was just numb. He looked out at Roy Dale lying face down in the yard not moving. As the night was setting in, the long shadow of trees were stretching their limbs across the grass where he lay. Clint looked back down at Tyrone again. Faith turned on the light, and he slowly released the hammer back down to the chamber. Clint then walked over to him rolled him over with his foot and reached down in his pants.

"Man, I tried to tell him..."

"Shut up."

Clint pulled out his phone that was in his pocket. He held the gun in one hand and the phone in the other contemplating what to do. He turned around to his daughter, "Honey, you alright?"

She shook her head, no.

"Maybe y'all need to go in your room. I've got to do something."

"No man, no!" Tyrone pleaded. He started to whimper, "I...I...I never touched her…"

"Shut up." Clint pulled him up to his knees. "Don't move." That was all he said. He walked out on the porch, and Faith saw him dialing. She was too scared to go back in her room. She stood at the hallway by the kitchen where she could keep an eye on Tyrone, and listened.

"Sheriff's office."

"This is Clint Roberts. I have a place off 270. I've got Tom Johnson's killers. Better send an ambulance…"

Chapter Nine

You wonder how people can do it sometime, how they have the nerve. You wonder where they get the strength when reason would suggest that they should be drained. Though he looked like he had survived a tornado with glass and debris all over him, he was as calm as could be like he was reporting a fender bender in a parking lot. Faith listened to her dad on the deck talking to the dispatcher. She couldn't believe it was all over, and then suddenly, she saw a blur to her side. Whack! Whack! Whack!

Angelina had grabbed the baseball bat and smashed Tyrone's head. He fell to the floor again, and blood was spewing out of the side of his mouth and down his ears. His eyes wide with shock. She drew back and whacked him again over the top of the head. It sounded just like a ball being knocked out of the park. He pulled on the ropes and scooting across the floor on his knees trying to dodge the blows. Little Angelina pulled back the bat with a grim look of determination and swung at him again. Tyrone curled up in a semi-fetal position, bracing for another blow. "Help!"

Clint came walking back in and looked down at him in disgust. Angelina then bent down and looked at him in the face. Her lip snarled, "How does it feel? Punk!" She spat on him and then kicked him. Then, she walked away.

Clint took the bat from her hand. He picked up the table and set it right, what was left of it. He told the girls to go and pack their things; the police would be there shortly. Clint then went to the sink and ran some water over his hands and splashed his face. He was completely drained. In a matter of a few minutes, he drank five large glasses of water standing by the sink. He stared out across the fields and then looked back at Tyrone lying there in the glass with cuts all over him, blood now oozing from every part of his body. It even rolled down across his neck, and dripped across the noose. He looked like a mad dog, a pit bull that had lost the fight and was headed back to his cage. Clint set the glass down on the counter and walked over to him. He stood above him. "I've got to pee. Wanna see me pee?"

Tyrone didn't say anything. Clint picked up the chair, the chair he had been tied to for so long and sat down next to Tyrone. Tyrone lay there, tied up at his feet. Clint stared at him as if he was staring at a bug that had been crushed on the floor. It was strange; it was like he was drained of all emotion. He put his foot on Tyrone's face and leaned back in the chair.

Clint gazed off down the road waiting for the police to get there. The girls came out with a suitcase packed. "We're ready." Faith then got a wash cloth and began to wipe the blood off his face while Angelina doctored his hands, and arms. They removed the bandage from his throat and replaced it with a new one. "Looks like its healing."

He nodded not saying a word. She kissed her father on his forehead and hugged him while he sat in silence looking out. Then they heard the sirens coming over the mountain wailing as sirens do through the night. The spinning blue lights flashed through the canopy of trees coming up the drive; there were three, and trailing far behind the rest, they saw a forth. They roared up the switchback road swirling dust in the air and came to a screeching halt. Clint told Angelina to turn on the porch light so they could see. Two officers immediately bounced up to the steps with their guns drawn walking through the shattered glass. They looked through the busted out window at all the scattered mess. "Jesus Christ." Their eyes widened in disbelief. "Are you Clint Roberts? You the one that called?"

He pointed to Tyrone slithering on the floor like a snake. "Put your guns away." He pointed out in the field toward the tree line, "There is another one out there. Think he is dead. He ain't been moving."

They yelled to the other deputies prowling the yard. They "had one", and then they picked up Tyrone and slapped the cuffs on his wrists. Just like that, they dragged him out the door and down the steps and threw him into the back of a squad car. He never said a word. Clint felt somewhat robbed by the experience. He expected the customary last second stare like it happened in Dragnet. One last chance to spit in his face, call him a name, but it didn't happen that way. It was rather anticlimactic, and probably for good reason, the girls were traumatized enough. It was better that he didn't have a chance to leave them haunted by a threat to get even. Another deputy came in. It was Hewitt. He looked about the room at all the mess. His voice was apologetic and humble. "Mr. Roberts, I am so sorry."

Clint didn't say a word, just nodded, and Deputy Hewitt pointed outside, "The Sheriff wants to talk to you. I'll stay with the girls."

Clint stood up from the chair; he was a little wobbly. The girls hadn't left his side. "Will y'all be alright? Faith, are you okay?"

"I'm hungry."

"An ice cream bar?"

Clint opened up the frig and pulled out a box of ice cream sandwiches handing them to the girls. "Here." He brushed the hair back that had fallen down over her face. Her lip quivered. She was fighting back the tears. "We made it, baby. We made it. It's behind us now." Faith gave her father a hug, and he kissed her on the forehead. He gave Angie a hug too before walking outside and down the steps to the cop cars where the Sheriff was leaning against his patrol car.

He was a rather stocky man with a slightly bulging belly that hung over a big brass buckle. He tipped back his hat as Clint approached and smiled, "Sir, are you alright?"

"Yep, I'm fine."

"Then, I've got to ask you a couple of questions if you don't mind."

Clint asked if the Sheriff would turn off the blue lights. They were bothering him, so the Sheriff reached inside his car and flipped a switch and yelled for a nearby deputy to do the same on the other units. In the field, he saw flashing lights inspecting the tall grass where Roy Dale laid. The Sheriff lit a cigarette and offered Clint one. He declined. "Suit yourself." He couldn't help but notice that the lawman also had a chew of tobacco tucked under his lip between his cheek and gum. "Mr. Roberts…"

"Yes."

"You're a damn good shot." He spit to the ground.

"Is he dead?"

The Sheriff reached inside his car window and pulled out the mic, "A flea has got more pulse than he does right now, but somehow some of 'em make it. 'Cuse me." He keyed the mic, "Sara, you got hold of the State Police yet?"

"Not yet."

"It's busy 'round here Hank."

"What's the problem?" He spit again.

"Trouble with some fella's in back."

He looked at Clint and rolled his eyes, "You tell them I'm gonna yank a knot in their ass when I get back. You get hold of the State Police, now. Ya hear."

"Yes sir."

The Sheriff pulled out a notepad off the dash and flipped through the pages while puffing on his cigarette. He leaned against the car, "Like to get as much information from ya as I can, while it's fresh. If you don't mind."

Clint began telling him the story. As he talked, he watched the deputies taking pictures; another one taped the place off. No one ever likes to have yellow "Crime Scene" tape wrapped around their house. One deputy brought out the baseball bat and held the gun in a plastic bag. "This the one they had? It is what you shot him with?"

The Sheriff inspected it and gave it back to the deputy. He put the bat on the hood of his car. "Looks like Tom Johnson's gun. The one that's missing from his truck." Clint went on with his story, and as he was giving details, an ambulance finally drove through the canopy of trees and headed up the switchback. After taking a sundry of pictures of Roy Dale, they loaded him on the gurney. The two ambulance guys had trouble lifting him up; he was so heavy, and so a deputy helped. The Sheriff took notes and stopped momentarily to bark out orders to his men. One deputy got in the back of the ambulance, and then they took off with one squad car in tow.

Clint continued to fill him in on as many details as he could. The Sheriff told him that he was sorry for all that had happen. They had just been unable to break the case. There were no clues whatsoever regarding Tom Johnson, "Leaves don't make very good foot prints, and his truck was wiped clean. We had nothing."

"Well, now you do." Clint leaned back against the Sheriff's car and took a deep long breath. "He's a monster. I want you to promise me one thing. I want to be there when he fries."

Sheriff Hank put out a cigarette and lit another one. He offered one to Clint again, "Me too, but I hate to tell ya Mr. Roberts that may not happen. You're in the newspaper business." He shrugged, "Sure you know by now how the system works."

Clint looked at Tyrone in the back of the deputy's car. He could see him smirking in the window. His wondering eye giving him the look. It was like he wasn't worried about a thing. He had been out, and now he was going back. It was like it didn't even bother him. "But he murdered Tom Johnson, for God sakes, Sheriff. Look at what he's done here. He's got to get the chair."

"I've got to build a rock solid case. That ain't easy, we're over loaded. We call it 'catch and release'. We catch 'em, send 'em to prison, and they release them. They are ordered by the courts to release them, hundreds at a time, and right now, they are releasing them faster than we can catch 'em."

Clint was getting mad. He felt his blood begin to boil. He didn't like hearing what he was hearing. "He better never walk free. Ten minutes ago, I could have ended this once and for all. Don't you tell me, sir, that he ain't going to fry."

"Listen, right now we don't have a solid case on them on Tom Johnson or that Oklahoma man. We got that gun; that's our first break, but that's it. You ought to know this, Mr. Roberts, if you were in the newspaper business. A good defense attorney will have them say they found the gun along the road or in a trash can. If you found a gun, it doesn't make you a murderer. In fact, Mr. Johnson wasn't even shot. He was beat to death. So if they had the gun, why didn't they shoot him?"

Clint was furious, "So you're saying that he won't get tried for Tom Johnson or the other man?"

The Sheriff spit some tobacco out of the side of his mouth. He lowered his voice. "Settle down. Not yet. If the big man lives, we might get one to confess against the other, turn rat. If that happens, they'll have separate trials, and each will portray themselves as a victim, made to go along for fear of their life. If that's the case, they won't get the death penalty, probably won't get life. Maybe get twenty, maybe thirty, could be out in fifteen."

"You're kidding me. So that's what I've got to tell the girls in there." He pointed over to the car Tyrone was in, "I've got to tell them that that animal could be out on the streets again! Is that what you're telling me?"

The Sheriff drew a deep breath. He had heard it over and over again. Each victim in every case, he had to tell the grim reality that their assailant, the person who assaulted them, would more than likely be back on the streets. He took a drag off his cigarette and tossed it to the ground. "I wish I could do something about it, but I can't."

"What about protect and defend, aren't you suppose to do that? Isn't that what your job is?"

"It is what our job use to be. Now, we are more babysitters. Guess who has got to feed him three meals a day until he gets his trial? One thing after today, you walk away. I have to look at his face every time I walk back into my jail. He maybe there a year or longer, waiting for his trial. He'll complain and groan. He won't like the food. He'll want to see his attorney. He'll make threats and piss on the floor when he gets mad. Someone has got to clean up his mess. Punks like him stuff the toilets in my jail till it over flows so they can mock the orderly that has to come in and clean it all up. And if I do one thing wrong, deny him one of his rights, then guess what? That bastard can sue me. That's what I've got to deal with! And when he leaves, there is another one, and another and another one. They just keep coming. That's our system, Mr. Roberts."

"What about everything he's done here, to me, to my girls? He should be behind bars for life. He should be executed for this. That bastard shouldn't be allowed one more day for what he has done!"

The Sheriff shook his head. He couldn't even look Clint in the face. He looked down to the ground and sighed, "This happens every day, somewhere in our country. Ain't no place safe anymore. It don't ever make the front page hardly. Other things are too important. Ain't nothing more than a small little article on the back of the paper. People might read about an assault or attempted rape, but they don't know what it means till it happens to them. Now you know, because it happened to you, and eventually, it will happen to everyone because that is what we've become. And I hate to tell you this because you ain't going to like it, but we ain't got much."

"WHAT!"

"Calm down, Mr. Roberts. You've got to understand, see what we go through. First of all, they didn't touch the girls. You said that. They didn't even threaten them. They never mentioned rape or of hurting them, right?"

Sarcastically, "What about kidnapping? Isn't that supposed to be punishable by death? The Lindbergh thing?"

"They weren't tied up; they weren't locked in a closet with a gag. They weren't transported anywhere against their will. The door was right there. They weren't even told they couldn't leave I don't think. See the problem?"

"No way! What about me, Sheriff? They broke in here, beat me unconscious, stuck a knife in my throat. What in the hell is that?"

"They'll admit they broke in, most likely say to get out of the weather. They'll probably say they didn't know anybody was there; that's what they always say when they break in. They'll say *you* attacked *them*. They will probably say you stuck your own self with your own knife. It was an accident, you see.

I've heard it all before, in every trial. They had no choice but to defend themselves and had no choice but to tie you up. You are the violent one; that's what they'll say, and when they finally thought they could trust you, they untied you and you went berserk. You beat one of them half to death, and when the other was running for his life, you shot him in the back in cold blood. I'm sorry but don't expect these guys to get the chair; they are a long ways from it, and they know it. That one in the back knows the system far better than you or I ever will."

"Something is wrong, bad wrong".

He spit and wiped his chin, "You don't think I don't know that? We've got criminals now suing the people whose home they broke in to. They have all been mistreated. They sue us all the time. If he goes to my jail and needs medical attention, doesn't matter if he's started a fight and is injured, if I don't get him to a doctor quick, he can sue me for every dime I've made my entire life. They've done it! That's how bad it's gotten. That's our criminal justice system in America."

The Sheriff lit another cigarette and pulled up his belt. He was sweating in the muggy night. Clint could see the perspiration beading on his forehead in the light. He was trying hard not to get mad at the Sheriff because he knew it was true. Everything he said was true. The Sheriff took a deep puff and blew the smoke out of the side of his mouth. His hands rested on his hips next to the gun strapped to his side. "I hate to tell you this Clint, but it ain't gonna get any safer. Our criminal justice system is like a factory. It produces one Tyrone right after another. Look around; there are millions just like him out there. They come in every color and every creed. There ain't nothing inside of 'em, not even a soul. They never feel guilt or shame. Ain't one drop of remorse in any of 'em. They are like moral amputees."

Clint was in shock. He looked up at the moon just now coming over the mountain. It was a perfectly clear night. The katydids were chirping, the frogs croaking in the pond. The Sheriff got on the mic again. Clint felt numb. Sweat started to bead up on his brow and lip. He felt violated all over again and realized that his nightmare was far from over. It was just beginning. There were to be years of reliving the agony. Trial after trial. He would have to go back through it all over again, and for what? The girls were the ones that would really suffer because they would know that the monster would someday be back out on the street. It would never be over, not for them.

The Sheriff looked at his watch. "I'm gonna hafta' get more of a statement from you tomorrow. Let's get you and the girls someplace safe." He picked up the mic and wiped off the sweat that was rolling down his face. "Sara, gonna need a room for a couple of nights down at the Shangri-La, check and see if one is available."

"Already got it. They are waiting."

He put his arm on Clint's shoulder. "Now, you get what you need. I'll send a deputy as an escort. Don't want you to leave town for a couple of days. There is a chance he may confess if the big guy lives. We may need some more statements." The Sheriff pointed to the cabin, "I can have somebody out tomorrow to fix that window if you like. I can get some people over for clean up too, but not until the State Police is out." Clint nodded appreciatively. "Let's go get your girls and get cha outta' here."

As they were walking up the steps, Clint stopped, "Oh, I've got something you may want to take a look at. It's in my truck. I'll bring it to you inside."

"Sure, fine." Sheriff Turner went on up the steps and was telling one of the deputies to make sure they took pictures with the instamatic as well as the digital, "Don't want to take chances that the digital gets erased again."

He asked the girls if they were alright and told them they were going to stay someplace safe and nice that night which seemed to please them. As they were talking, one of the deputies yelled. He pointed outside to Clint. "Oh. my God! Look, Hank!"

They could see Clint between two cars with the bat in his hand coming down hard with a tremendous force. Tyrone yelled, but it was too late. Clint opened the door and before Tyrone knew what was happening he pulled him out on to the ground. Tyrone might not have even seen the bat in his hand,

and by the time he did, it was too late. Four or five swings and it was just about all over. His head was smashed against the back tire of the cruiser; split wide open and gushing. The officers all ran down to the scene where parts of his skull were lying about the grass and dirt. His blood dripped down the side of the car where the County logo was painted, "Protect and Serve."

"Oh, my God." A pinkish jelly-like substance was clearly visible on the top of his scalp. He laid there twitching spasmodically as his body convulsed from shock.

"Man, what have you done?" Sheriff Turner grabbed the bat from Clint's hand.

Clint's face was dripping in sweat and blood, but he appeared oddly relaxed, even calm you might say. He took a deep breath and looked at Hank and Hewitt. "There's you a justice system." He wiped the blood off his face with his sleeve, "Case closed."

He was right. All it took was twelve seconds, no more. No long trials, no briefs and lawyers, no years behind bars, no wardens and guards. Twelve seconds, and it was over.

Tyrone twitched on the ground with the rope around his throat dripping in blood just like he would be if he were hung from a tree. Unbelievably, his good eye looked up toward them. He was still breathing. Matted blood dripped down from his brow and rolled across his cheek and splattered on the ground.

"Why?"

Clint held out his hands as if to be handcuffed, "To protect them."

The girls were still up at the cabin; one deputy had stayed with them. Hank looked down the road. No one else had come up yet; the press hadn't got there, no State Police. He looked around at all the carnage and then back up to the cabin once again to where the girls were. Hank spit on the ground looking at Tyrone. The monster slowly began to pull his knee up off the ground. He wasn't dead yet. His hand pointed to Clint and fell back into his lap. He was trying to talk but nothing but blood was coming out of his mouth. "Ah, shit," the

Sheriff mumbled as he reached inside for the mic, "Sara, did you send that second ambulance? Where is it?"

"Yes, Hank, it's coming all the way from Hot Springs."

Turner looked at Tyrone on the ground with his ivory white skin and streams of red blood glistening in the moon light. He was trying to figure out what to do.

The dispatcher came back on, "Sheriff, you need me to send you another?"

He pulled out a cigarette and lit it. His hands were trembling as he scratched his head and looked at Clint. Turner keyed the mic again, "Hold on, Sara." The Sheriff took a puff and surveyed all the carnage as a refreshing cool breeze swept through the trees. The tall pines swayed around the cabin, and Clint's shirt fluttered in the wind; his face looked up to the stars. Tyrone was trying to inch his way up the wheel with his shoulders. His eyes fidgeted back and forth reminding Hank of a snake when its head has been cut off. It lays there with his tongue slithering and looks at you wanting to get one last bite. It looks around for the rest of his body. It's gone. He knows what you've done.

The Sheriff keyed the mic, "Call them back. Tell them not to hurry. Tell 'em, *he* didn't make it." Hank picked back up the bat and told Clint to hurry, to get in his truck with his girls.

"What are you going to do?" Clint asked.

He looked down at Tyrone with that crazy eye staring at the two of them. The edge of his lip curled up, twisted slightly into a grin.

"We'll take care of things here." He squeezed his fingers around the handle, "It ain't the first time." He looked at his patrol car with the blood, "Have you got a hose?"

"Yeah, around the side of the house."

He yelled at one of his deputies to go down to the end of the road and block it off, not let anyone else in, no press, no cops, nobody unless he was radioed first.

Clint ran up the steps to the cabin and got the girls. They jumped in his truck without ever seeing Tyrone. Deputy Hewitt drove down through the trees behind them; his orders were to follow them all the way to the motel and let no one talk to them about what happened. They left with one squad car in front and one in back without blue lights or sirens. Under the glimmering full moon light, they drove across the low water bridge before turning onto the highway.

The river wasn't green anymore, but silvery blue, a shining brilliant blue reflecting off the cascading waters. Clint looked at Angelina in the back seat and asked if she was alright. She said she was fine, just hungry. She asked if she could get some peanut butter pie at the Shangri-La. Clint marveled at her resiliency, how someone so timid and frail could become so strong. Clint following behind officer Hewitt all the way into town. The road was surprisingly empty, deserted. There were no cars anywhere. Faith leaned across the console and put her head on her daddy's shoulder. She held up her little finger in the air. Clint wrapped his finger in hers. They made it.

Faith then drew his hand to her, and she kissed his bruised knuckles. Tears began to drip across his fingers. It was then he realized that though they survived, things would never be the same, not for her. He made a promise. He would keep it. He vowed to protect her no matter what the cost; that didn't matter. He loved her too much not to. The Tyrones of the world were taking over. That's the world she'd have to face. The reality was exactly like what the Sheriff said; there were many more Tyrones out there. They were multiplying in mass quantities coming out of prison just like it was an assembly line. Something had to change.

It was ironic; all those years, all those columns and commentaries and editorials changed nothing. Twelve seconds and a baseball bat did. All those talk shows, TV, all the government research and grants, conferences and law, all of it was meaningless. It was all just words, vanity. Clint realized something that night as he drove along back to town with her tears dripping across his hand; the world has never been changed by just words. Never. It has always been changed by action. Without it, the rest is meaningless. That is why things only got worse.

Clint knew deep down inside it wasn't his daughter's job to protect herself; it was his. It was his regardless of whether the *system* worked or not. To do nothing would make him guilty of negligence. He thought back to his grandfather who had been to war. He fought evil for his children's sake. Did it matter if it was abroad or in our midst? Does it matter the color or the shade? Evil is evil, is it not? One either fights it or condones it. There is no middle ground to rest our souls.

He knew then, that moment what he had to do. They crossed over the mountain and into town. They passed by the jail where there were more Tyrones sitting inside, waiting to get out. Maybe they were pissing on the floors, writing on the walls, beating each other up, counting the days until their lawyer got them released. He looked at Angelina in the backseat as they drove by the square. She stared quietly out the window; the lights of the town passed over her face. His finger rubbed softly Faith's dainty hand. There wasn't much hope for their world unless somebody did something to make it all change.

And change did begin to happen.

After that night, lots of things were different. For one thing, they needed a fresh start. Clint decided it was best to move. Within a couple of weeks after getting back, Clint found a job in another town. Where? I'd rather not say. But it was a town that was made safe, at least for the citizens. The criminals weren't that lucky. From all accounts in the papers, they had met their match. Street gangs reported a mysterious stranger who would appear out of nowhere, and who often seemed to know their names. He showed up in alleys and parking lots, and though it is hard to discern what might be true and what might be tale, one thing is for certain, the streets were safer after awhile. The gangs, it seemed, were the ones that were afraid to go out, especially at night, to meet the demise of their homeys. Same could be said for the pedophiles. They began showing up in dumpsters. It didn't take long, and the city became known as a town where serious offenders did not want to be released. And of those charged for heinous crimes, most preferred jail than being released on bond. It was safer.

Crime plummeted. The newspapers were stumped. For the first time in decades, they had plenty of vacancies in the correctional facilities. People could take a stroll at night and not be afraid of a mugger. The playgrounds were once again full of children without anxiety-ridden parents in fear of every stranger passing by.

And Faith? I guess that is the most important part of the story. She met knew friends and loved her school. Children are after all resilient, if given a chance. The memories of that summer will never leave her, but the environment she was in was safer. She did what teenagers do. She went to the movies and sometimes the mall. She knew her dad would always be close by; that's a promise he made her, and kept.

The press, of course, was completely baffled. They had no idea what to call the phenomenon; they had no name for the stranger. Perhaps, it was just a coincidence. I couldn't say for sure. There was talk that maybe it was a spirit, maybe it was. Who knows? But I also know that such occurrences have happened before. They happened long ago when marauders terrorized the land, and bandits ravaged a defenseless people in small rural towns. I remember stories of hearing of such and something my great grandmother had told me about. She said that there are two forces at war in the Universe; though sometimes they go by the same name. One is good, and one is evil. One destroys, and one saves. And long ago, one came to her town when she was just a child. The marauders soon disappeared, and the outlaws vanished.

She called it, simply, the Yomen.

THE END

Afterword to The Yomen

Shocking facts concerning the criminal justice system, i.e., the criminal industrial complex.

- According to the U.S. Bureau of Justice Statistics, **2,292,133** adults were incarcerated in U.S. federal and state prisons, and county jails at year-end 2009----about **1%** of adults in the U.S. resident population. Additionally, **4,933,667** adults at year-end 2009 were on probation or parole. In total, **7,225,800** adults were under correctional supervision (probation, parole, jail, or prison) in 2009 ----about **3.1%** of adults in the U.S. resident population.

- The U.S. has the highest incarceration rate in the world. **743** adults are incarcerated per **100,000** populations.

- There were **86,000** juveniles in detention centers in 2007.

- In 2008, approximately **one in every 31 adults** (7.3 million) in the United States was behind bars, or being monitored (probation and parole). In 2008, the breakdown for adults under correctional control was as follows: **one out of 18 men**, **one out of 89 women**, one in 11 African-American (9.2 percent), one in 27 Latinos (3.7), and one in 45 whites (2.2 percent).

- The prison population has **quadrupled** since 1980.

- The number of incarcerated drug offenders has increased **twelvefold** since 1980. 22 percent of those in federal and state prisons were convicted of drug charges.

- In comparison to other countries, Japan has 49 people in prison per 100,000. England and Wales have 154 people per 100,000. Norway has 71 people per 100,000 and Australia has 133 per 100,000.

$ COST $

- In 2005, it cost an average of **$23,876** dollars per state prisoner. State prison spending varied widely, from **$45,000** a year in Rhode Island to **$13,000** in Louisiana. In 2009, the average annual cost to incarcerate an inmate in California was **$47,102** a year. It increased about $19,500 from 2001 to 2009.

- It costs nearly **$1,000,000** for a person to serve a 20 year sentence in California today. Here are the breakdowns in yearly expenses.

- Security ($19,666); Inmate Health Care ($12,442); Medical ($8,769); Psychiatric Services ($1,922); Pharmaceuticals ($999); Dental ($747); Operations ($7,214); Administration ($3,493); Inmate Support ($2,562); Food ($1,470); Inmate Activities ($430); Inmate Employment and Canteen ($400); Clothing ($170); Religious Activities (70); Rehabilitation

Programs ($1,612); Miscellancous ($116); Total ($47,102)

*Note: This does not include attorney fees or court cost of appeals.

RECIDIVISM

*Estimations are as follows: 67.5% of state inmates return to prison in 3 years. Released prisoners with the highest re-arrest rates were robbers (70.2), burglars (74.0%). Those in prison for weapons charges returned to prison 70.2% within three years.

THE COST OF CRIME IN HUMAN TERMS

- According to the Bureau of Justice Statistics in 2009, there were **10,639, 369** total crimes committed in the United States. **9,320,971** of these were crimes not considered violent (property crimes, embezzlement etc.); whereas **1,318,308** crimes were violent. Here is the breakdown.

Robbery (408,217); Aggravated assault (806,843); Forcible Rape (89,000); Murder (15,241)

- From 2000-2011 there were over **1,000,000** rapes committed in the United States.

- There is a rape committed every 6 minutes in America.

- From 2000-2009, there were **169,910** murders in the United States. In comparison, in an eleven year period of the Vietnam War from 1963-1973, **56,000** American troops lost their lives.

- Three times as many people were murdered in the United States this last decade as were killed during the bloodiest years of the Vietnam War.

- As in comparison to a more current war. In the nine years since the "War on Terror" began in Afghanistan and Iraq, **6,000** servicemen and women have lost their lives. During that same period, we lost over **150,000** lives here at home due to murder. The casualties on our own soil are **twenty-five times** greater than the casualties in war.

- This next statistic is almost unbelievable. Youth in our country committed **8,400** murders last year! In one year alone, our children killed more people than we lost in nine years of combat overseas.

Finally, if you took all the women that were raped in this country between 2000-2011, you could fill up **16 NFL football stadiums**. (Soldiers Field in Chicago holds 60,000 fans). If you think that is appalling, actually more women were raped in the decade before.

Until You

I keep wanting to call you,
but
but, I don't have your number.
It is Friday night again
without you.
Tuesday wasn't great either.
Your smile is missing
in all the picture frames.
Shouldn't you be there?
So are all the cards
on birthdays and holidays
You weren't there
We've never met, so it is insane
to think about you, right?
Was it just minutes we missed
each other?
What's the closest we've ever been?
Were we in the same state?
Same stadium? Same parking lot?
Same class?
A section in a plane? Same aisle in a store?
Same elevator, perhaps? Same floor?
I feel your spirit
I can hear your voice, but there is no phone
I go on walks and think of you
then I go home
I wonder if we had the same professor
but in different times or classes
Were we ever in the same line
you in front, me in back?
Were we ever at the same wedding
or same funeral

Did we go to the same restaurants
with different dates
live different lives with different mates?
Was that you across the room
I could not take my eyes off of?
Did our eyes meet?
Yours and mine?
Were you wearing a ring?
Or was that you in the choir
or you in a show
I may never know anything more than
you are out there....somewhere.
It is Friday night again, it's late
tis goodnight my mate...
Maybe we will still meet
maybe it will be in a nursing home
play canasta, bingo
I'll slip into your room
maybe we'll escape
better late than never
in love.
And should you see me drool
or slump over in my chair
turn away for when I was a younger man
I would have chased after you
and never let you go
And should I pass on into this next life
I will wait for you there
just as I have waited for you here
for love is believing it is never
    too late
    to live.

A Perfect Stranger

Pardon me, but haven't I loved you
Was it a dream or was it déjà vu
Was it a wish from a falling star
Was it fate that now here we are
Why is it that I know you
Could you have slipped into my dreams
How could I know the things
That you yearn for inside
I have heard your laugh
Felt the passion of your moan
You've shared with me your deepest
Thoughts when we have been alone
I've seen the tears drip from your eyes
I've felt your breath when you've sighed
Could it be that we've never met
Or perhaps in another life
You tried harder to forget
Could it have been in another time
Another century…another place
But never has there been for me
  (a memory as lovely as your face)
Pardon me, but haven't I made love to you
Look into my eyes, tell me the truth
Am I a perfect stranger, or
        your perfect lover?
Tell me now that we don't know each other
Yes, I have made love to you
But now you tell me
Was it a dream or déjà vu?

The Trap

If you build a box, then cut a hole
   and slip a banana into the side
   you've built a trap for a monkey
   when the monkey comes swinging by.

He'll slip his hand into the box
   and no matter what he won't let go
   he will try in every way
   to pull the banana through the hole.

Monkeys have been known to die
   when they could have easily just let go
   the trap is never the box, or the banana
      or even the hole,
   the trap, (I think), is in the mind.

And a grip on life I once thought I had
   when it was my grip that had a hold on me
   all the time I thought I was in control
   but would not let myself get free.

The Vagrants and the Wolves

SOMEWHERE in time…

I heard someone say
as the line stood still
something about the soup
as the wind blew chill
and through the puddles
of Depression
I searched for shelter
in the cold December rain
but amongst the vagrants
I searched in vain,
they had pockets full
of despair
and faces full of sorrow,
but amongst the wolves
I learned to kill
my pain until….

Tomorrow.

LINE 21

"Line twenty-one, Line twenty-one move forward, Line twenty-one", a terse female voice barked over the loud speaker system.

I shuffled my feet in the slow moving line grasping the official papers in my right hand. Every step was a painful reminder of the force that was used when I was apprehended, but I knew better than to complain or to gawk. I kept my head facing forward and looked around only by glancing with my eyes. I noticed that nearly everyone else held their identification cards in their hands; some even had them fastened on cheap aluminum chains around their neck. They were accustomed to the process and had been in the system far longer than I. Their dreary faces were embellished on the front of their picture ID's, and each had a "Registered Address" imprinted across the top of their cards, and of course their "Citizen Identification Number". I had none of that for I had been out there, traveling.

Way above us on the exterior wall, spanning perhaps 120 feet across, was a huge jumbo tron towering directly above the entrance to Unit #36, or otherwise known as the "Temporary Housing Authority Resident's Building". The jumbo tron was enormous and certainly as big as any I had seen in a football stadium, that is, when they still had football. The tron continuously projected messages and images for the "detainees" to see. That's what we were officially called during the move from our homes or places where we had lived. None of us wanted to be there, but too much had happened in too short a time. We each were assigned our position and could do nothing more now than just stand in our lines and wait to be processed.

I never thought I would end up here. I had been out

there living on the road. I liked the wide open skies, and living under the stars. So what if I started a little campfire and played my guitar, I never considered myself a danger to anyone or anything. But I must have been wrong or at least that's what the authorities determined when I was arrested. And now I was being processed into the system and standing there in line I watched, as did all the other detainees, the tron and its message of compassion and caring. There was a picture of a lone wolf howling; his silhouette was cast from a ridge outlined by the moon. In bold letters, the message appeared across the screen, "ANY THREAT TO THE PLANET IS A THREAT TO MANKIND."

I thought to myself, 'Who could argue with that, huh?' and looked at the drab faces of others standing in line. I wondered, 'Were they threats? Or were they just people?'

"Line twenty-one, advance," the voice barked over the loud speaker system. It was a warning; I understood that. My line had a lot of old people. Some struggled with their walkers, and most were tired and weary. We had been there almost three hours and had not been able to sit down. The children, age eleven and under, had already been separated and were deported (transferred) to the "Youth Unit." I had not seen it personally, but the government reports credited it as having fine facilities and an excellent educational program. Their parents could be thankful that our government cared so much, but we were not so fortunate. We were going to he housed in the "GP (General Population) Unit" which was designed to house "Citizens of Civil Disobedience"; that was us. We had violated the codes or procedures. Perhaps, it was a minor infraction or a more serious violation, but one way or another we were deemed a risk, a "threat" as the message on the jumbo tron stated. We had to be reassigned housing to meet the AEIC, Acceptable Environmental Living Standards as dictated by the convention rules. There, we would be given a chance to reform.

"Line nine, advance!"

The exterior wall of the encampment (Temporary Housing Resident Building) was approximately 500 yards long, maybe longer. There were guard towers on each corner and a look out post between each tower. Cameras, electronic detection devices, were placed everywhere scanning automatically from robotic arms. Total observation, that was their goal. The Environmental Convention determined that the right of privacy was not as significant in importance as our global environment; so it of course became an early sacrifice. None of us knew that it would be taken to such an extreme, but none of us, or few of us anyway, knew that we were the ones that would be determined a threat. We didn't know that would be the outcome when our leaders signed the treaty. But we were wrong.

Glancing up at the towers, I watched the guards. They walked around each tower with their machine guns, and I wondered, 'why would the guards need machine guns?' Shouldn't they have high powered rifles with scopes? If someone was going to try to escape, or if they were a threat, a high power rifle should be used. It was precise; it made a direct hit. I was very careful not to let them see me observing them and kept my head down low and just gave them passing glances, studying the type of weaponry they were using. They weren't American made; I knew that. They had Chinese assault rifles, not that accurate but good for crowd control. And once inside, I would figure who could escape. The wall was at least twenty feet high and had rolls of Constantine wire on top. It would be humanly impossible to scale the wall, and I seriously doubted that anyone but a raving lunatic would try. But what bothered me was that if there was any trouble inside; lots of people would be hurt, innocent people.

The line was at a standstill, and I was getting a little hungry. My eyes were drawn to the huge jumbo tron. It seemed like it had an almost magnetic pull to it. There were thousands of people standing in line, and nearly all of them stood there with their eyes just glued to the huge screen. It showed images of smoke stacks bellowing out a gray smoke across a city. I had seen the image before and knew it was from the 1960's. The cars in the foreground dated the images, and the people probably didn't know they were from fifty years ago. I watched the screen as fish were shown flopping on the bank of some contaminated river. Then, there were pictures of congested freeway traffic and smog, probably LA. We had all seen them before, many times, many, many times. We watched film footage of men clubbing sea lions and dolphins pulled from fishermen nets. We had all seen it over and over and over again. I cast my eyes around, and everyone was still watching. Next, the screen displayed a killer whale leaping into the air and then splashing into the sea. A voice over blurted from the speakers, "This is my home. How would you like it if someone took your home?"

The next line over I heard someone say, "They did." I was afraid to turn around to see who it was. I didn't want to get them in trouble, but it was how I felt, or at least it is how I use to feel. I wasn't so sure now. Perhaps, I had been wrong; maybe, I was taking their home. Seeing those images shown over and over sometimes made me feel guilty and left me confused. I had not thought of myself as a threat to the environment, but maybe I was wrong. Maybe I had been selfish. I had just considered myself a traveler; I didn't think I was hurting anyone. I hadn't even had a home for years, not since the wars started.

A recorded message came across the speakers; it was the same message that played every few minutes. "Have your documentation ready. You will be processed quickly to your new home." The jumbo tron flashed images of children planting flowers and a doe grazing on grass in an open meadow. It was a beautiful sight indeed. It showed an eagle feeding its young, a mother bear and her cubs, and then the owl, the woodpecker and the buffalo. A soft strumming guitar playing in the background made me want to tap my feet except that they hurt, especially my throbbing ankle. Then, the tron showed the new homes that would be built for us; they would be energy efficient and smaller. They were apartments really and according to the artist rendition appeared to be about ten stories high. Each apartment would have a patio to plant and enjoy our own small garden. The apartment buildings surrounded an urban living space of a few acres with pathways for joggers. It showed a small pond with a fountain in the middle and park benches where people could sit and read or toss crumbs to the pigeons (if that was permissible). I couldn't help but be impressed with the architectural design for our living space in the future, and to think, it would all happen in just a few short years. A lot of work had gone into the planning of it all as the voice on the tron said, "We should all be grateful that our government is working so hard for us." Then, it quoted the handsome John F. Kennedy, "Ask not what your country can do for you, but what you can do for your country." A few in the crowd affirmatively nodded their heads, and I said to myself 'That does make sense; doesn't it?'

The lines were moving along orderly. They were all perfectly straight. Every head was positioned foreword obeying the commands to "Look straight. Pay attention." With each step we moved, the wall kept getting higher, and the screen was now uncomfortably overhead so that I had to look nearly straight up to see it. I wanted to turn around and look back at the city, but we weren't allowed to look back. But still, I could smell it; it was burning.

There had been too many homes, too much urban sprawl. That's what they said, and who could argue with that? We had wasted too much fuel, been selfish and self-indulgent. That too, I surmised was true as well. But, we were also told that we posed an imminent threat to the environment; we were a threat to the world. But not me, that's what I couldn't understand. I was a traveler. I lived under the stars and pitched my tent. The thoughts kept racing back and forth through my head; had I been wrong? Was I causing harm taking a few fish from a stream or picking blackberries and muscodine? Was I really depriving other animals? I once had asked, but no one would tell me how I posed a threat, and if I was an animal, like they said, didn't I at least have equal rights to these things?

A big brute of a man stood up at the processor table and yelled out over the crowd, "Have your identification cards ready, or you'll be sent to the back of the line." I wondered to myself, 'what was he thinking?' That's all we had, that and the clothes on our back. No one was allowed to have anything else. It had all been taken from us, put in storage until we could be released from the Temporary Housing Authority. That's what we had been told anyway, and that's what most believed.

As the line moved closer, I could now see into the great building. There was a long corridor stretching down the middle like what I'd seen in an airport except that it wasn't as nice or as colorful. It was really void of color, just very well lit and bright. I could see the guards and the divider in the middle which I had already been told about separating the men's living quarters from the women's. A big M banner hung down from the ceiling on the left and a big W banner was on the right. I have to admit, it did look very sterile and clean. Unit #36 was the newest unit to open in the country and from what I had heard was better than all the others.

"Advance Line twenty-two." They had lots of old people in twenty-two, and many others were seriously overweight. No wheelchairs were permitted; only walkers and canes were acceptable. Those that could not stand in line to be processed had to be assigned to another unit, another temporary housing unit. No one wanted to go there; we had all heard the stories, or rumors about the other unit. At least in Unit #36, we would all be treated equally. Everybody was rationed the same amount of food each day, and every meal was vitamin enriched with the government recommended doses of fiber, protein and minerals.

Unit #36 was also touted for it medical services division, although I wondered how it could achieve its high ranking for excellence if it had never been opened. We knew not to question the information that was given us because that was a sign of insubordination and noncompliance which was a "threat to the environment." All I know is that I didn't want the Universal Health Care services. I didn't want their shots nor did anyone else that I knew. I wasn't sure what they would be injecting me with. Years ago, I heard about the side effects of their vaccinations, and they caused more problems than they cured, but it was mandated now. We had no choice. To refuse was civil disobedience.

As I stood there in line, I couldn't help but notice a woman in Line twenty. She was in front of me, but I couldn't see her face except that occasionally she turned her head to the side. She wore a simple brown dress that came down to her knees; her hair was brown and her skin a light tan. She wore loafers which might have been her only offense since leather had been outlawed for personal use. I kept wanting to see her face but couldn't. It sounds strange, but I just wanted to see her eyes. I stood there in line wanting to look into them. I wanted so badly for her to look into mine.

As her line moved up, I marveled at her shape. She was beautiful and poised with grace. I would have given anything that I possessed for just a moment to see her face, for our eyes to meet because once we were processed I would never see her again. They would lead her down the hall and shave her head. She would be showered and sprayed with a lice decontaminate and then given a uniform. There would be no contact between the genders; our quarters were separate; our recreational areas were separate, even the cafeterias. This is the last I would see of her until the new urban living spaces were built, and so I took photographs of her in my mind and put them away. That's why I wanted so desperately for her to turn so that I could see her face and take a picture of it. It would be the last thing I would have for years to hold on to. I started saying in my mind over and over again, 'Look around, look at me.' Then suddenly, I thought, 'Don't.' I didn't want to get her in trouble or to be sent to another unit, and so I began saying 'Don't turn around. Look straight ahead.'

I couldn't believe myself for all the thoughts in my head that I was beginning to think. It was strange, so very strange, but I was beginning to be scared of what I would think, like I had to whisper to myself in my own brain. I was becoming paranoid like maybe they could hear me. Everything was so advanced; maybe they could monitor the thoughts within my own head, but then I thought, 'that's insane!' They can't do that. It may be the last thing I've got, but I have got my mind; I can still think. 'To hell with them,' is what I thought. I said it again. It felt good. I screamed it, 'TO HELL WITH YOU!'

A smile broke across my face. I tried to tuck it away, to hide it, but couldn't; so I bent my head down and let my face smile. I couldn't believe how strange it felt, smiling that is. It was as if my face was unaccustomed to using those muscles because I hadn't smiled in so long. No one had. I laughed inside, and kept saying 'To hell with you.' I looked up at the processor and then the guards and said it inside. The smile was inside now, but if they looked in my eyes, they could see it. I looked around to the other people, glancing out of the corners of my eyes. They couldn't tell what I was thinking, no one could, and there was a sigh of relief inside. I might be standing in line, be assigned a cell, but I was not a prisoner. They could not reach my mind.

Line twenty moved up again, and my eyes followed the beautiful lady. I memorized her moves, how she stood. My eyes followed down her arms, and how she held them. I looked carefully at her hands; she had long dainty fingers with clear polished nails. I imagined she might have played piano or maybe a violin. Her hair came just below her shoulders and curled at the ends. It was clean and shiny, and I for some reason imagined my fingers wrapping themselves in her curls. This would be the thought I would remember. It would be the thought I'd have when they locked me up, when I would lay on my bunk at night. It would be the thought I would hold onto, just that small thought to keep me sane.

Just then, a green "Peace Guard" walked up beside me. She took the paperwork from my hand and studied it with a condescending eye. Her hair was tucked underneath a green military hat, and she was short and stout. Hardly any expression showed on her face at all. She flipped through my papers and handed them back. I knew not to say anything. Peace Guards were feared. They didn't carry guns just pepper spray, but some did have tasers. Any refusal to comply warranted use of the spray, and many of us had to be restrained at one time or another. I had been sprayed on several occasions already, and it felt like acid had been thrown in my face. I was nauseous and vomited, and without water, the spray burns for hours. She walked on down the line, and I was relieved. Any act that she construed as being disobedient could not only warrant being sprayed but also being taken away and placed in the Criminal Unit. No one wanted to go there.

As bad as Unit #36 was, we weren't tortured like they were in the Criminal Unit. We were just provided temporary housing until the Urban Living Units could be built. It wasn't that bad, an inconvenience, a sacrifice maybe, but we weren't subject to daily torture. I rationalized in my mind that I just had to pay a small price to put the world back in balance. We all had to do our part to keep us within the SRA, the Sustainable Resource Allocation, as dictated by the world government. A few years, and I thought, 'it will all be over.'

My line moved up and I with it. I could see even better now the long corridor in the middle. It did indeed look efficient. We had been informed by the Tron that the resident temperature would be between 55 degrees and 85 degrees, the acceptable temperature range for a comfortable living environment. Animals after all "had to endure much more temperature extremes". Huge fans that were in the ceiling sucked the hot air out like an attic fan. We could all hear them, and they were noisy for sure but very efficient. I had heard the Houston, Texas Housing Authority used sprinklers in the ceiling to dispense a fine mist in the air to keep the temperature down, but Unit #36 was more advanced.

Unit #36 was also in the middle of the country, and I was glad we wouldn't suffer through the extremely cold winters like they did in Milwaukee and Chicago. They had antiquated oil furnaces in the Units up there, and they worked (supposedly), but last year, there was a shortage of heating oil, and the oil reserves had to be used at other government installations. That wouldn't be a problem this winter; we were assured. As I stood there in line and listened to the tron, it was all good news. Due to the conservation efforts, the global temperature appeared to be dropping. "Keep up the good work!" A few citizens were seen nodding their heads. The man behind me nudged my back, "See, I told ya."

In a few years, the DSI, the desired global temperature, would be attainable, and then we could reach a safe level again for renewed industrial output. The tron played an excerpt from a televised talk show that aired that day; both sides seemed to agree that the Temporary Housing Authority was having a positive impact on the global habitat. It was just further proof that the Environment Conference Plan of the World Body was working. I nodded my head too because that was acceptable and looked down my line to the processors with a very faint smile and thought, 'Go to hell.'

Glancing around at the sea of people out of the corners of my eyes, I thought to myself, 'What are they thinking? Do they believe this?' They all stood almost lifeless like looking at the tron sign. Every few minutes, they would take a step forward. It was as if they weren't even aware that the black cloud that crossed the sky was from their homes. Entire sections of the city were being burned, but maybe they were aware but just couldn't cope. Maybe, they wanted to believe that it was all for the better. Perhaps, they were holding on to the images of the Urban Living Units and the artist renditions of the urban parks.

The tron played a short piece on the government's "Global Reclamation Project." That's what they called it, reclaiming the lands for the animals. Subdivisions and malls and many environmentally unfit businesses were being reclaimed for forest and wildlife reserves. They did not use the terms bulldozed and burned, but that's what reclamation was. I had seen it with my own eyes, miles after miles, city after city. Destruction on a massive scale. That's why I became a traveler; I knew it would happen. I saw it coming and left behind all that I knew would one day be destroyed.

From town to town, I saw the same thing, and it's why there was an outbreak of civil disobedience. The home owners (environmental terrorists) fought against the greens, but lost. Their arms were futile against bulldozers and tanks. The United Nations' police forces surrounded the cities allowing no escape, and the citizens of disobedience were rounded up. They were hungry and tired and homeless, but the government had a plan, and this was it. The Temporary Housing Authority would provide us all a home until they could build the new Urban Living Units, and it would be so much better.

I surmised that most the people were still in shock, but they still believed there might be hope, and this was it. This was their only hope for tomorrow; they had lost everything else. It is why they stood in line; they had nowhere else to go. But I wondered as I looked at them, 'How do they think they'll make a living when they get out?' The remaining homes, most of the nicest homes in fact, were occupied by the greens and the "designated appointed workers." I questioned, 'Even if they were to live in the Urban Living Units, how would they survive? What job would they perform?'

The short Peace Guard officer jabbed me with her nightstick, "Advance!" I looked up and realized the line had moved up; I had been daydreaming.

"I'm sorry".

"No talking. Advance!"

I nodded my head and shuffled my feet. I was getting closer now to the front. Like the rest, I was getting weary; my legs were beginning to tire. I was actually looking forward to being assigned my living quarters. The tron said there were 45 to each "block", fifteen triple bunks. I rationalized that the top bunk would be preferable in the winter and the bottom would be preferable in the summer. I wondered if we would get to choose or were we assigned that too.

My stomach growled, but it did not bother me that much, not like it did others. I had conditioned myself to go without. I lived off the land and ate relatively little in my travels, and that's why I couldn't figure out why I was detained and assigned to Unit #36. I didn't think I posed a threat to the environment, none at all.

I looked to the front of the line; there were maybe only twelve or thirteen people ahead of me now. Still, I knew it would be hours before we ate. We would have to be shaved and showered and then issued new clothes. Somewhere along the line, we'd be inspected and given shots, and reality sunk in that there probably wouldn't even be time enough for a meal, not today. The sun, what I could see of it, was in the western sky hidden behind black plumes of smoke, and the awful smell of soot filtered through the air. I wanted to turn around and look, but I feared I'd be sprayed. I'd seen cities burn for weeks. I heard that Phoenix burned for over a month. Standing there, I was ashamed because I shouldn't want to look; it was all so horrible, but there was some sort of morbid curiosity that made me want to watch it, and I didn't understand why. I feared I might have become desensitized, for I had seen a lot. But I knew I wasn't. It was just like watching hell; it was not something you see every day, but it was not something you forget either. And for some reason, I didn't want to forget it. I wanted to burn the picture in my brain. I memorized the features of the woman ahead of me because I wanted to remember the beautiful, but for some reason, I didn't want to forget the horror either. I didn't want to ever forget the tragedy of our own ignorance and complacency. That's why the cities burned. We did nothing; we gave in.

The tron was too high for me to see, but I listened as "New data" was released. The WFS, World Food Supply, was dangerously low. "Experts were suggesting a mandatory 23.7 decrease in DHI" (Daily Human Intake), for the next two years. 'That's pretty much self-explanatory,' I thought. The only question I had was whether they were going to cut back each meal or skip every forth meal. I thought about it and hoped they would cut back every fourth meal; otherwise, the people would feel hungry all the time, but what was I thinking; those decisions were too important for us to make. We weren't experts or scientists; we were just people. I listened as the story ended with its usual inspiring theme, "Don't worry, the world government is looking out for you."

"Line twenty-one, advance".

I stepped right up without delay. I had my information ready in my hand. I was ready to be processed. In a few short years, we'd be released again, and maybe I'd be allowed to travel again. Perhaps, the world would indeed be a better place. Maybe, they were right after all. I wondered if I could still fish where I use to. Would they allow me to hike some of the same trails or would they all be closed. I wondered quietly if I would be able to finally reach my dream and make it down to the Gulf of Mexico and lay on the beach. That's where I was going when they detained me. The beach had been closed. I didn't know that; I had violated a restricted order. I was unaware that it was off limits to humans; heck, I never listened to the radio or watched TV. I had just wanted to lie out under the stars and feel the sand in my feet. It had been my dream to run down across the beach and dive into the waves, especially at sunrise or sunset. I didn't know we couldn't do that anymore; no one told me.

"psst".

I looked to the left, and there was a little lady about the age of my mother in the line next to me. She was frail and used a walker. I nervously glanced at her out of the corner of my eye, and she whispered to me, "It won't be long now."

I didn't say anything. I didn't know exactly what she meant and thought she must have been talking about being processed. The beautiful woman was two people ahead of her, and I wondered (hoped) she might look around if she heard the woman too. But she didn't look back. She put her hands behind her, and she looked like she was giving some sort of signal, but I couldn't make it out, and then I realized she was signaling to be quiet, meaning that if she could hear the woman the guards could too.

"Psst. Did you hear me?" she softly whispered, "It won't be long now."

I hesitated, then whispered back out of the corner of my mouth, "for what?"

"Freedom."

I thought that was odd, "Freedom?" My eyes glanced at her curiously.

She pointed her finger towards the sky, "Heaven."

I hadn't heard that word since I was a child; I almost forgot it existed. It sounded so beautiful. It was the most lovely word I had heard in a long time. There would be no worries there, no concern about the global warming or housing, or food shortages.

Looking at her, I slightly nodded my head.

"It won't be long now," she whispered.

Her line, Line Twenty moved forward. The beautiful woman was the next one to be processed. I could still see her hands behind her, and she gave a signal. It was "Okay." That was the signal she gave me, and then she rotated her hand and pointed her index finger towards the sky. She had heard too; she knew the message.

"Next."

She showed them her identification, and they looked up her data on the computer screen. I could hear them offer her the two choices, "The injection or not." She shook her head no, and then they asked her to step aside. A green Peace Guard came up and took her by her arm, and just then she turned and looked back at me. She was beautiful with soft brown caramel eyes and a very faint teasing smile. It might have been three seconds, no longer, that I was able to capture her face before they took her away. Such peace, that's the only way I could describe it, such tranquility. But I did get my wish, and our eyes met. I had seen eyes that said good-bye and eyes that said hello. Her eyes said both. They were hello, and good bye.

"Next." They processed the man in front of me and injected something into his hand. I knew we'd never be released; the majority of us would never get out unless there was a "labor shortage." I had heard all the reports about "over population" and the "diminishing food supply." I knew what the term "expendability" meant. If the world population was going to have to be reduced, why not the "anti-environmentalist" and "citizens of civil disobedience?" Decreasing the world's population solved so many problems, and it might actually reduce global warming, preserve the food supply and natural resources. It was as fundamental as supply and demand; reduce the demand, and you decrease the cost of supply. It was simple economics really, and who could argue with that?

The little woman in Line twenty was processed, and I knew she would refuse the injection before they asked her. Voluntarily, she walked over with her walker to the green Peace Guard, and as calmly as anyone I had ever seen, she simply said, "I'm ready."

I knew then I would never travel again. I'd never get to go back to that beach and race across the sand. I'd never watch another sunset from the top of a mountain or pull a rainbow out of a stream, but I was okay with all that. I would be a traveler again, though not as I was. I would see new sights, a new land. I'd see places in the universe they would never see or ever know. The world they were creating was far from perfect; the world where I was going was the epitome of perfection. I smelled the burning city behind me and could see Utopia just up head. The little woman was right, "It would not be long now." It surely would not be long.

"Next."

I handed them my papers and shook my head "no" when they asked me if I would take the "Identification injection." I really didn't want to live in one of their little blocks or for that matter in one of their Urban Living Units. I didn't want to live under their laws and rules anymore, or listen to their reports and findings. I didn't want to live by their temperature or eat their rations, or wear their clothes. I didn't want to be part of their inhumane barbaric world.

They stamped my papers one by one, "CIVIL DISOBEDIENT." I was fine with that; I didn't want to have any part of them or their world anymore. I knew the punishment for my offense, and that was the great irony, for it wasn't really a punishment at all. Not where I was going. Housing would not be a problem, nor food, or health or pain. And what amazed me is that I didn't hate them, the woman who angrily stamped my papers, or the guards with guns, the people that made the decisions or even our leaders that betrayed us. I hated none of them; in fact, at that moment, I felt sorry for them because they were all left behind. They created their own hell, and now they had to live in it.

When she finished stamping my papers, I walked over to the guard. I was ready to go on, ready to check into a better place. I understood the pretty woman's smile now. I felt what she felt, an awesome tranquility and peace. I glanced back at the crowd and their sad demoralized faces. I saw the city burning and looked at the guard and smiled.

"I'm ready."

THE END

And Then Came the Rains

And then came the rains...
Liquid droplets falling pitter patter
Rat-tat-tat on awnings, rooftops
The liquid beads of water splat!
A lovely day (is it not?) for it to rain?
And then came the rains...
Cracks of lightning! Booms of thunder!
Dark clouds split their belly down under
Stumbling away into the distance
They fell gushing from their side
And then came the rains...
The streets began to swell
The rivers began to rise
The deluge dropped from the sky
The waters rose in tides
Families watched from their porches
Cars washing down the drive
Into streams like morning traffic
Bumper to bumper they floated by
From the rivers, streams and lakes
The water began to wash the earth away
And the yards where children had played
Swarmed a body of snakes
Two story homes became one story soon
And one story homes were underwater too
And looking across the neighborhood
One could see where every family stood
Like scattered rafts tossed to sea
For help every family would plea.
And then came the rains...
Help had always come, or had it not?
Hadn't there always been helicopters
And rescue boats they thought?
Hadn't they always seen on T.V.
Daring rescue and evacuation teams?

Wade Rivers

Hadn't the floods always stopped?
I guess not.
For in these days streams become rivers
Rivers become lakes
And then every dam and dike will break
Everything that was on solid ground
Everything that was at stake
Everything they owned, everything they made
Everything they stored, everything they saved
Everything they loved and even everything they hate
In the end was washed away
And then came the rains…
There are rising waters and rising tides
But it is rising debts that will take more lives
More than wars and more than plagues
More than all our other mistakes
And this poem ends where it started from
And then came the rains…

(1991)

The Riverboats Churn

On a cold and gray
  misty morning
  rising along the riverbanks shore
  crept the dawning
  of a new day born.
And up through the canyons
  and into the town
  echoed a fog horn
  and the riverboats sound.
Sittin' in moss
  under a cypress tree
  a blind man sat
  unable to see.
But with his talents
  and the will to learn
  even a blind man can vision
  the riverboats churn.

Age 16

The Long Ride through a Midnight Storm

Running from someplace cold to someplace warm
 taking a long ride through a midnight storm
 in a runaway car through rundown towns
 sleeping from sunup to sundown,
Making all the trucks stops and cheesy motels
 whether companions or strangers
 no one could tell.

Masters of illusions, creatures of chance
 they skipped from town to town
 like they were in a ballroom dance,
Driving through a long midnight storm
 they masked their faces in sunglass frames
 one held the wheel, the other gripped the chain
 they chased tomorrow like it was falling rain.

Somewhere down an old abandoned road
 the car parked quietly, the night turned cold
 was she his prisoner, or along for the ride?
He pressed his gun firmly next to her side,
 bolts of lightning flashed across the sky
 she pulled up the blanket to cover her eyes
 and the damsel sobbed through the midnight storm
 crying, "Hold me tighter, love me more."

Songbird

"Songbird, songbird
why don't you sing?"
I opened my mouth
but could only scream.
Darkness overtook me
it fell like the night
alone and frightened
I longed for light,
And the voice would say
"Songbird, songbird
why don't you sing?"
Still I opened my mouth
but could only scream!
From under the cover of darkness
a hand reached in with feed
"Oh, songbird, songbird
do you long for me?"
Then daily, from Him, I began to eat
A kind voice beckoned me
"Oh, songbird, songbird
why won't you sing?"
Then, I felt His hand beneath my feet
and gained my voice and began to tweet.
Then one day my master said to me
"I am going to set my songbird free"
The darkness lifted, the veil removed
He opened the door for me to leave
"I made the world for you to see
But it is only in darkness
Do songbirds learn to sing
Go now my sweet songbird
And spread your wings."
So when it was time for me to leave
I did not tweet nor did I scream
But from my heart sang…a symphony.

About the Author

Wade Rivers was born in Oklahoma City but has resided in Arkansas most of his adult life. As a young man, he lived in Europe and travelled extensively before returning to the states where he attended the University of Arkansas and then the University of Oregon.

Out of college, he became the Director of a consumer affairs group where he was very involved in lobbying on legislation and travelled frequently between Washington D.C. and Little Rock. Afterwards, he became an investment banker (stockbroker) for ten years and specialized primarily in trading for banks across the country. In the 1990's, Rivers retired from a lifestyle that was very destructive and nearly killed him. He became sober and left the investment business preferring a less stressful and more serene life. He became a painter and eventually a realtor where he bought the farm on the Ouachita River where he now lives with his doting wife and daughter.

Though he is still somewhat involved indirectly in government affairs, Rivers' primary ambition is just to write. It is his love. He also covets his time with God and nature. A naturalist, (in the truest sense), he and his family live on a farm surrounded by a river in a virtual wilderness. When he is not tending to his orchards and "chores", he is on the river with his dogs, fishing and kayaking.

Currently, Rivers is working on his fourth book, another thriller, and is deeply immersed in his lifelong interest, the pursuit and discovery of mass alternative energy sources. For more information on Mr. Rivers, go to www.waderivers.com.

17262669R00145

Made in the USA
Charleston, SC
03 February 2013